A DANCE TO THE MUSIC OF TIME

✳ ✳ ✳ ✳ ✳ ✳

THE KINDLY ONES

Books by Anthony Powell

NOVELS

Afternoon Men
Venusberg
From a View to a Death
Agents and Patients
What's Become of Waring

A DANCE TO THE MUSIC OF TIME

A Question of Upbringing
A Buyer's Market
The Acceptance World
At Lady Molly's
Casanova's Chinese Restaurant
The Kindly Ones
The Valley of Bones
The Soldier's Art
The Military Philosophers
Books Do Furnish a Room
Temporary Kings

GENERAL

John Aubrey and his Friends
Brief Lives: and other Selected Writings
of John Aubrey

PLAYS

Two Plays: The Garden God;
The Rest I'll Whistle

ANTHONY POWELL

The Kindly Ones

A Novel

FONTANA BOOKS
IN AGREEMENT WITH
HEINEMANN

First published by William Heinemann Ltd 1962
First issued in Fontana Books 1971
Second Impression December 1973
Third Impression September 1975

Made and printed in Great Britain by
William Collins Sons & Co Ltd Glasgow

FOR R. W. K. C.

ONE

Albert, fleshy, sallow, blue chinned, breathing hard, sweating a little, fitted an iron bar into sockets on either side of the wooden shutters he had just closed across the final window of the stable-block. Rolled shirt-sleeves, green baize apron, conferred a misleadingly businesslike appearance, instantly dispelled by carpet-slippers of untold shabbiness which encased his large, chronically tender feet. All work except cooking abhorrent to him, he went through the required movements with an air of weariness, almost of despair. In those days he must have been in his middle to late thirties. We were on good terms, although he possessed no special liking for children. Indeed, I was supposedly helping him lock up these outbuildings for the night, a task in principle all but completely accomplished, for some unknown reason, in late afternoon. Up to that moment, it is true, I had done no more than examine a coloured picture, fastened to the wall by four rusting drawing-pins, of Mr Lloyd George, fancifully conceived as extending from his mouth an enormous scarlet tongue, on the liquescent surface of which a female domestic servant in cap and apron, laughing heartily as if she much enjoyed the contact, was portrayed vigorously moistening the gum of a Health Insurance stamp. I was still contemplating this lively image of state-aided social service—which appeared in some manner to hint at behaviour unseemly, even downright improper—when night, as if arbitrarily induced at that too early hour by Albert's lethargic exertions, fell abruptly in the shuttered room, blurring all at once the outlines of the anonymous artist's political allegory. Albert withdrew ponderously from the dusk now surrounding us. I followed him into the broad daylight of the yard, where tall pine trees respired on the summer air a resinous, somehow alien odour, gently disinfectant like the gardens of a sanatorium in another country than England.

'Don't want any of them Virgin Marys busting in and burning the place down,' Albert said.

Aware of a faint sense of horror at the prospect of so monstrous a contingency—enigmatic, no less than unhallowed, in its heretical insistence on plurality—I asked explanation.

'Suffragettes.'

'But they won't come here?'

'Never know.'

'Do you think they will?'

'Can't tell what those hussies will do next.'

I felt in agreement with Albert that the precariousness of life was infinite. I pondered his earlier phrase. It was disconcerting. Why had he called suffragettes 'Virgin Marys'? Then I remembered a fact that might throw light on obscurity. At lessons that morning—the subject classical mythology—Miss Orchard had spoken of the manner in which the Greeks, because they so greatly feared the Furies, had named them the Eumenides—the Kindly Ones—flattery intended to appease their terrible wrath. Albert's figure of speech was no doubt employed with a similar end in view towards suffragettes. He was by nature an apprehensive man; fond, too, of speaking in riddles. I recalled Miss Orchard's account of the Furies. They inflicted the vengeance of the gods by bringing in their train war, pestilence, dissension on earth; torturing, too, by the stings of conscience. That last characteristic alone, I could plainly see, made them sufficiently unwelcome guests. So feared were they, Miss Orchard said, that no man mentioned their

6

names, nor fixed his eyes upon their temples. In that respect, at least, the Furies differed from the suffragettes, whose malevolence was perpetually discussed by persons like Edith and Mrs Gullick, the former of whom had even seen suffragette processions on the march under their mauve-and-green banners. At the same time, the nature of suffragette aggression seemed to bear, in other respects, worthy comparison with that of the Furies, feminine, too, so far as could be judged, equally the precursors of fire and destruction. Thought of them turned my mind to other no less awe-inspiring, in some ways even more fascinating, local terrors with which we might have to contend during the hours of darkness.

'Has Billson seen the ghost again?'

Albert shook his head, giving the impression that the subject of spectres, generally speaking, appealed to him less than to myself. He occupied one of the two or three small rooms beyond the loose-boxes, where he slept far away from the rest of the household. The occasional intrusion of Bracey into another of the stable rooms offered small support where ghosts were concerned. Bracey's presence was intermittent, and, in any case, there was not sufficient fellow-feeling between the two of them to create a solid resistance to such visitations. It was, therefore, reasonable enough, since he inhabited such lonely quarters, for Albert to prefer no undue emphasis to be laid on the possibilities of supernatural appearance even in the house itself. To tell the truth, there was always something a little frightening about the stable-block in daytime too. The wooden bareness of its interior enjoyably reconstructed—in my own unrestricted imagination—a log cabin or palisade, loop-holed and bullet-scarred, to be defended against Zulus or Red Indians. In such a place, after nightfall, the bravest might give way to nameless dread of the occult world; more to be feared, indeed, than any crude physical onslaught from

7

suffragettes, whose most far-fetched manifestations of spite and perversity would scarcely extend to an incendiary attack on the Stonehurst stables.

The 'ghosts' of Stonehurst, on the other hand, were a recognised feature of the place, almost an amenity in my own eyes, something far more real than suffragettes. Billson, the parlourmaid, had waked at an early hour only a week or two before to find a white shape of immense height standing beside her bed, disappearing immediately before she had time to come fully to her senses. That, in itself, might have been dismissed as a wholly imaginary experience, something calling for banter rather than sympathy or interest. Bilson, however, confessed she had also on an earlier occasion found herself confronted with this or another very similar apparition, a spectre unfortunately reported in much the same terms by Billson's immediate predecessor. In short, it looked very much as if the house was undeniably 'haunted'. Maids were, in any case, disinclined to stay in so out-of-the-way a place as Stonehurst. Ghosts were likely to be no encouragement. Perhaps it was a coincidence that two unusually 'highly strung' persons had followed each other in that particular maid's bedroom. Neither Albert himself, nor Mercy, the housemaid, had at present been subjected to such an ordeal. On the other hand, my nurse, Edith (herself, before my own day, a housemaid), had from time to time heard mysterious rappings in the night-nursery, noises which could not—as first supposed—be attributed to myself. What was more, my mother admitted to a recurrent sense, sometimes even in the day, of an uncomfortable presence in her bedroom. At night, there, she had waked once or twice overwhelmed with an inexplicable feeling of doom and horror. I record these things merely as a then accepted situation. Such circumstances might have been disregarded in a more rationalistic family; in one less metaphysically flexible, they could

8

have caused agitation. In my own, they were received without scepticism, at the same time without undue trepidation. Any discussion on the subject took place usually behind closed doors, simply in order that the house should not acquire a reputation which might dry up entirely the sources of domestic staff. No effort was made to keep such talk from my own ears. My mother—together with her sisters in their unmarried days—had always indulged a taste for investigation of the Unseen World, which even the threatened inconveniences of the Stonehurst 'ghosts' could not entirely quench. My father, not equally on terms with such hidden forces, was at the same time no less imbued with belief. In short, the 'ghosts' were an integral, an essential part of the house; indeed, its salient feature.

All the same, hauntings were scarcely to be expected in this red-tiled bungalow, which was almost capacious, or so it seemed in those days, on account of its extreme, unnatural elongation. It had been built only thirteen or fourteen years before—about 1900, in fact—by some retired soldier, anxious to preserve in his final seclusion tangible reminder of service in India, at the same time requiring nothing of architecture likely to hint too disturbingly of the exotic splendours of Eastern fable. Stonehurst, it was true, might be thought a trifle menacing in appearance, even ill-omened, but not in the least exotic. Its configuration suggested a long, low Noah's Ark, come uncomfortably to rest on a heather-grown, coniferous spur of Mount Ararat; a Noah's Ark, the opened lid of which would reveal myself, my parents, Edith, Albert, Billson, Mercy, several dogs and cats, and, at certain seasons, Bracey and Mrs Gullick.

'Tell her to give over,' said Albert, adverting to the subject of Billson and her 'ghost'. 'Too much cold pork and pickles. That's all the matter. Got into trouble with the indigestion merchants, or off her nut, one or the other.

She'll find herself locked up with the loonies if she takes on so.'

'Billson said she'd give notice if it happened again.'

'Give notice, I don't think.'

'Won't she, then?'

'Not while I'm here she won't give notice. Don't you believe it.'

Albert shook off one of his ancient bedroom slippers, adjusting the thick black woollen sock at the apex of the foot, where, not over clean, the nail of a big toe protruded from a hole at the end. Albert was an oddity, an exceptional member of the household, not only in himself and his office, but in relation to the whole character of my parents' establishment. He had started life as hall-boy—later promoted footman—in my mother's home before her marriage. After my grandmother's death—the dissolution, as it always seemed in Albert's reminiscence, of an epoch—he had drifted about from place to place, for the most part unhappily. Sometimes he quarrelled with the butler; sometimes his employers made too heavy demands on his time; sometimes, worst of all, the cook, or one of the maids, fell in love with him. Love, of course, in such cases, meant marriage. Albert was not, I think, at all interested in love affairs of an irregular kind; nor, for that matter, did he in the least wish to take a wife. On that subject, he felt himself chronically persecuted by women, especially by the most determined of his tormentors (given to writing him long, threatening letters), whom he used to call 'the girl from Bristol'. This preoccupation with the molestations of the opposite sex probably explained his fears that evening of suffragette attack.

In the end, after moving from London to the country, from the country back to London, up to Cumberland, down to Cardigan, Albert had written to my mother—habitually in touch with almost everyone who had ever worked for her—suggesting that, as she was soon to lose a cook, he himself should exchange to that profession, which had always appealed to him, the art of cooking running in his blood through both parents. He was, indeed, known, even in his days as footman, for proficiency in cooking, which had come to him almost by the light of nature. His offer was, therefore, at once accepted, though not without a few privately expressed reservations as to the possibility of Albert's turning out a 'handful'. 'Handful' to some extent he was. Certainly his cooking was no disappointment. That was soon clear. The question why he should prefer employment with a family who lived on so unpretentious a scale, when he might have found little or no difficulty in obtaining a situation as chef in much grander circumstances, with more money and greater prestige, is not easily resolved. Lack of enterprise, physical indolence, liking for the routine of a small domestic community, all no doubt played a part; as also, perhaps, did the residue from a long-forgotten past, some feudal secretion, dormant, yet never entirely defunct within his bones, which predisposed him towards a family with whom he had been associated in his early days of service. That might have been. At the same time, such sentiments, even if they existed, were certainly not to be romantically exaggerated. Albert had few, if any, illusions. For example, he was not at all keen on Stonehurst as a place of residence. The house was little to his taste. He often said so. In this opinion there was no violent dissent from other quarters. Indeed, all concerned agreed in thinking it just as well we should not have to live at Stonehurst for ever, the bungalow being rented 'furnished' on a short renewable lease, while my father's battalion was stationed in the Aldershot Command.

The property stood in country partaking in general feature of the surroundings of that uniquely detestable town, although wilder, more deserted, than its own immediate outskirts. The house, built at the summit of a steep hill, was reached by a stony road—the uneven, treacherous surface of pebbles probably accounting for the name—which turned at a right-angle halfway up the slope, running between a waste of gorse and bracken, from out of which emerged an occasional ivy-strangled holly tree or withered fir: landscape of seemingly purposeful irresponsibility, intentional rejection of all scenic design. In winter, torrents of water gushed over the pebbles and down the ruts of this slippery route (perilous to those who, like General Conyers, attempted the journey in the cars of those days) which continued for two or three hundred yards at the top of the hill, passing the Stonehurst gate. The road then bifurcated, aiming in one direction towards a few barely visible roofs, clustered together on the distant horizon; in the other, entering a small plantation of pine trees, where Gullick, the Stonehurst gardener (fascinatingly described once by Edith in my unobserved presence as 'born out of wedlock'), lived in his cottage with Mrs Gullick. Here, the way dwindled to a track, then became a mere footpath, leading across a vast expanse of heather, its greyish, pinkish tones stained all the year round with great gamboge patches of broom: country taking fire easily in hot summers.

The final limits of the Stonehurst estate, an extensive wired-in tract of desert given over to the devastations of a vast brood of much interbred chickens, bordered the heath, which stretched away into the dim distance, the heather rippling in waves like an inland sea overgrown with weed. Between the chickens and the house lay about ten acres of garden, flower beds, woodland, a couple of tennis courts. The bungalow itself was set away from the road among tall pines. Behind it, below a bank of laurel and Irish yews, espaliered roses sloped towards a kitchen-garden, where Gullick, as if gloomily contemplating the accident of his birth, was usually to be found pottering among the vegetables, foretelling a bad season for whichever crop he stood among. Beyond the white-currant bushes, wild country began again, separated from Stonehurst civilisation by only a low embankment of turf. This was the frontier of a region more than a little captivating—like the stables—on account of its promise of adventure. Dark, brooding plantations of trees; steep, sandy slopes; soft, velvet expanses of green moss, across which rabbits and weasels incessantly hurried on their urgent business: a terrain created for the eternal campaign of warring armies, whose unceasing operations justified recognition of Albert's sleeping-quarters as the outworks of a barbican, or stockade, to be kept in a permanent state of defence. Here, among these woods and clearings, sand and fern, silence and the smell of pine brought a kind of release to the heart, together with a deep-down wish for something, something more than battles, perhaps not battles at all; something realised, even then, as nebulous, blissful, all but unattainable: a feeling of uneasiness, profound and oppressive, yet oddly pleasurable at times, at other times so painful as to be almost impossible to bear.

'General and Mrs Conyers are coming next week,' I said.

'It was me told you that,' said Albert.

'Will you cook something special for them?'

'You bet.'

'Something *very* special?'

'A mousse, I 'spect.'

'Will they like it?'

'Course they will.'

'What did Mrs Conyers's father do to you?'

'I told you.'

'Tell me again.'

'All years ago, when I was with the Alfords.'

'When you helped him on with his overcoat——'

'Put a mouse down the sleeve.'

'A real one?'

'Course not—clockwork.'

'What did you do?'

'Let out a yell.'

'Did they all laugh?'

'Not half, they did.'

'Why did he do it?'

'Used to tell me, joking like, "I've got a grudge against you, Albert, you don't treat me right, always telling me her Ladyship's not at home when I want most to see her. I'm going to pay you out"—so that's what he did one day.'

'Perhaps General Conyers will play a trick on Bracey.'

'Not him.'

'Why not?'

'Wasn't General Conyers put the mouse down the sleeve, it were Lord Vowchurch. No one's going to do a thing like that to Bracey—let alone General Conyers.'

'When does Bracey come back from leave?'

'Day-after-tomorrow.'

'Where did he go?'

'Luton.'

'What did he do there?'

'Stay with his sister-in-law.'

'Bracey said he was glad to get back after his last leave.'

'Won't be this time if the Captain has something to say to him about that second-best full-dress tunic put away in the wrong place.'

Bracey was the soldier-servant, a man unparalleled in smartness of turn-out. His appearance suggested a fox-terrier, a clockwork fox-terrier perhaps (like Lord Vow-church's clockwork mouse), since there was much of the automaton about him, especially when he arrived on a bicycle. Sometimes, as I have said, he was quartered in the stables with Albert. Bracey and Albert were not on the best of terms. That was only to be expected. Indeed, it was a 'miracle'—so I had heard my parents agree—that the two of them collaborated even so well as they did, 'which wasn't saying much'. Antagonism between soldier-servant and other males of the establishment was, of course, traditional. In the case of female members of the staff, association might, still worse, become amorous. Indeed, this last situation existed to some extent at Stonehurst, where the endemic difficulties of a remote location were increased by the burden of Bracey's temperament, moody as Albert's, though in an utterly different manner.

Looking back, I take Bracey to have been younger than Albert, although, at Stonehurst, a large moustache and face shiny with frenzied scrubbing and shaving made Bracey seem the more time-worn. Unmarried, he was one of those old-fashioned regular soldiers with little or no education—scarcely able to read or write, and on that account debarred from promotion—whose years of spotless turn-out and absolute reliability in minor matters had won him a certain status, indeed, wide indulgence where his own idiosyncrasies were concerned. These idiosyncrasies could be fairly troublesome at times. Bracey was the victim of melancholia. No one seemed to know the precise origin of this affliction: some early emotional mishap; heredity; self-love allowed to get out of hand—any of these could have caused his condition. He came of a large family, greatly dispersed, most of them earning a respectable living; although I once heard Edith and Billson muttering together about a sister of Bracey's said to have been found drowned in the Thames estuary. One brother was a bricklayer in Cardiff; another, a cabman in Liverpool. Bracey liked neither of these brothers. He told me that himself. He greatly preferred the sister-in-law at Luton, who was, I think, a widow. That was why he spent his leave there.

Bracey's periodic vexation of spirit took the form of his 'funny days'. Sometimes he would have a 'funny day' when on duty in the house. These always caused dismay. A 'funny day' in barracks, however trying to his comrades, could not have been equally provoking in that less intimate, more spacious accommodation. Perhaps Bracey had decided to become an officer's servant in order that his 'funny days' should enjoy their full force. On one of these occasions at Stonehurst, he would sit on a kitchen chair, facing the wall, speaking to no one, motionless as a man fallen into a state of catalepsy. This would take place, of course, only after he had completed all work deputed to him, since he was by nature unyieldingly industrious. The burden of his melancholy was visited on his colleagues, rather than my parents, who had to put up with no more than a general air of incurable glumness diffused about the house, concentrated only whenever Bracey himself was addressed by one or other of them. My father would sometimes rebel against this aggressive, even contagious, depression—to which he was himself no stranger—and then there would be a row. That was rare. In the kitchen, on the other hand, they had to bear with Bracey. On such occasions, when mealtimes approached, Bracey would be asked, usually by Billson, if he wanted anything to eat. There would be silence. Bracey would not turn his head.

'Albert has made an Irish stew,' Billson—as reported by Edith—might say. 'It's a nice stew. Won't you have a taste, Private Bracey?'

At first Bracey would not answer. Billson might then repeat the question, together with an inquiry as to whether Bracey would accept a helping of the stew, or whatever other dish was available, from her own hand. This ritual might continue for several minutes, Billson giggling, though with increased nervousness, because of the personal element involved in Bracey's sadness. This was the fact that he was known to be 'sweet on' Billson herself, who refused to accept him as a suitor. Flattered by Bracey's attentions, she was probably alarmed at the same time by his melancholic fits, especially since her own temperament was a nervous one. In any case, she was always very self-conscious about 'men'.

'I'll have it, if it is my right,' Bracey would at last answer in a voice not much above a whisper.

'Shall I help you to a plate then, Private Bracey?'

'If it's my right, I'll have a plate.'

'Then I'll give you some stew?'

'If it's my right.'

'Shall I?'

'Only if it's my right.'

So long as the 'funny day' lasted, Bracey would commit himself to no more gracious acknowledgment than those words, spoken as if reiterating some charm or magical formula. No wonder the kitchen was disturbed. Behaviour of this sort was very different from Albert's sardonic, worldly dissatisfaction with life, his chronic complaint of persecution at the hands of women.

'I haven't had one of my funny days for a long time,' Bracey, pondering his own condition, would sometimes remark.

There was usually another 'funny day' pretty soon after self-examination had revealed that fact. Indeed, the observation in itself could be regarded as a very positive warning that a 'funny day' was on the way. He was a great favourite with my father, who may have recognised in Bracey some of his own uncalm, incurious nature. From time to time, as I have said, there was an explosion : dire occasions when Bracey would be ordered back to the regiment at twenty-four hours' notice, usually after a succession of 'funny days' had made kitchen society so unendurable that life in the world at large had also become seriously contaminated with nervous strain. In the end, he was always forgiven. After-wards, for several weeks, every object upon which a lustre

17

could possible be imposed that fell into Bracey's hands would be burnished brighter than ever before, reduced almost to nothingness by energetic scouring.

'Good old Bracey,' my father would say. 'He has his faults, of course, but he does know the meaning of elbow-grease. I've never met a man who could make top-boots shine like Bracey. They positively glitter.'

'I'm sure he would do anything for *you*,' my mother would say.

She held her own, never voiced, less enthusiastic, views on Bracey.

'He worships you,' she would add.

'Oh, nonsense.'

'He does.'

'Of course not.'

'I say he does.'

'Don't be silly.'

This apparently contrary opinion of my father's—the sequence of the sentences never varied—conveyed no strong sense of disagreement with the opinion my mother had expressed. Indeed, she probably put the case pretty justly. Bracey certainly had a high regard for my father. Verbal description of everything, however, must remain infinitely distant from the thing itself, overstatement and understatement sometimes hitting off the truth better than a flat assertion of bare fact. Bearing in mind, therefore, the all but hopeless task of attempting to express accurately the devious involutions of human character and emotions, you might equally have said with some authenticity that Billson was loved by Bracey, while Billson herself loved Albert. Albert, for his part, possessed that touch of narcissism to be found in some artists whatever their medium—for Albert was certainly an artist in cooking—and apparently loved no one but himself. To make these clumsy statements about an immensely tenuous complex of relationships without hedging them in with every kind of limitation of meaning would be to give a very wrong impression of the kitchen at Stonehurst. At the same time, the situation must basically have resolved itself to something very like these uncompromising terms: a triangular connexion which, by its own awful, eternal infelicity, could almost be regarded by those most concerned as absolutely in the nature of things. Its implications confirmed, so to speak, their worst fears, the individual inner repinings of those three, Billson, Bracey and Albert: Albert believing, with some excuse, that 'the women were after him again'; Bracey, in his own unrequited affections, finding excuse for additional 'funny days'; Billson, in Albert's indifference and Bracey's aspirations, establishing corroboration of her burning, her undying, contempt for men and their lamentable goings-on.

'Just like a man,' Billson used to say, in her simile for human behaviour at its lowest, most despicable.

In spite of her rapid accumulation of experience, both emotional and supernatural, while living at Stonehurst, Billson had not been with us long, two or three months perhaps. Like Albert, she must have been in her late thirties, though my mother used to say Billson looked 'very young for her age'. Like Bracey, Billson, too, came of a large family, to whom, unlike Bracey, she was devoted. She talked without end about her relations, who lived, most of them, in Suffolk. Billson was fond of telling Edith that her people 'thought a lot of themselves'. Fair, not bad-looking, there was something ageless about Billson. Even as a child, I was aware of that. She had been employed at a number of 'good' houses in London: the only reason, so Albert used to imply, why he was himself so indulgent of her vagaries. A 'disappointment'—said to have been a butler—was known to have upset her in early life, made her 'nervy', too much inclined to worry about her health. One of the many doctors consulted at one time or another had advised a 'situation' in the country, where, so the physician told her, she would be less subject to periodical attacks of nausea, feelings of faintness. London air, Billson often used to complain, did not suit her. This condition of poorish health, especially her 'nerves', explained Billson's presence at Stonehurst, where maids of her experience were hard to acquire.

Behind her back (with reference to the supposed poverty of intellectual resource to be found in the county of her origin), Albert used to call Billson 'Silly Suffolk', and complain of her clumsiness, which was certainly notable. To her face, he was more respectful, not, I think, from chivalrous feelings, but because he feared too much badinage on his own part might be turned against himself, offering Billson indirect means of increasing their intimacy. Billson, in spite—perhaps because—of her often expressed disdain for men (even with Albert her love took a distinctly derisive shape), rated high her own capacity for raising desire in them. She would never, for example, mount a step-ladder (for some such purpose as to re-hang the drawing-room curtains) if my father, Albert or Bracey happened to be in the room. She always took care to explain afterwards that modesty—risk of exposing to a male eye even a minute area of female leg—was her reason for avoiding this physical elevation. I never learnt the precise form taken by her 'chasing after' Albert, about which even Edith—on the whole pretty discreet—was at times prepared to joke, nor, for that matter, the method—equally accepted by Edith—by which Bracey courted Billson. Bracey, it is true, would sometimes offer to clean the silver for her, a job he certainly performed better than she did. It was also true that Billson would sometimes tease Albert by subjecting him to her invariable, her all-embracing pessimism. She could also, of course, show pessimism about Bracey's affairs, but in a far less interested tone.

'Pity it's going to rain now your afternoon off's come

round, Albert,' she would say. 'Not that you can want to go into Aldershot much after losing the money on that horse. Why, you must be stony broke. If you're not quick you'll miss the carrier again.'

To Bracey she would be more formal.

'I expect you'll have to go on one of those route-marches, Private Bracey, now the hot weather's come on.'

Billson would upset Albert fairly regularly every few weeks by her fearful forebodings of ill. Once, when she saw the local constable plodding up the drive, she had rushed into the kitchen in a state of uncontrolled agitation.

'Albert!' she had cried, 'what have you done? There's a policeman coming to the door.'

Albert, as I have said, was easily frightened himself. On this occasion, so Edith reported, he 'went as white as a sheet'. It was a relief to everyone when the subject of inquiry turned out to be nothing worse than a dog-licence. I did not, of course, know all these things at the time, certainly not the relative strength of the emotions imprisoned under the surface of passing events at Stonehurst. Even now, much remains conjectural. Edith and I, naturally, enjoyed a rather separate existence, segregated within the confines of night- and day-nursery. There was also, to take up one's time, Miss Orchard, who—teaching all children of the neighbourhood—visited the house regularly. Edith, reasonably enough, felt the boundaries of her own domain were not to be too far exceeded by intrusion on my part into kitchen routine; while Miss Orchard's 'lessons' occupied important expanses of the day. All the same, I did not propose to allow myself to be excluded utterly from a society in which life was lived with such intensity. Edith used to suffer from terrible 'sick headaches' every three or four weeks (not unlike Billson's bouts of nausea), and from what she herself called 'small aches and pains few people die of', so that, with Edith laid low in this manner, my parents away from home, Miss Orchard teaching elsewhere, the veil would be lifted for a short space from many things usually hidden. As a child you are in some ways more acutely aware of what people feel about one another than you are when childhood has come to an end.

For that reason, I always suspected that Billson would—to use her favourite phrase—'get her own back' on Albert for calling her 'Silly Suffolk', even though I was at the same time unaware, of course, that her aggressiveness had its roots in love. Indeed, so far was I from guessing the true situation that, with some idea of arranging the world, as then known to me, in a neat pattern, I once suggested to Billson that she should marry Bracey. She laughed so heartily (like the maid damping the Insurance stamp on Mr Lloyd George's tongue) at this certainly very presumptuous suggestion, while assuring me with such absolute candour of her own determination to remain for ever single, that—not for the last time within similar terms of reference—I was completely taken in.

'Anyway,' said Billson, 'I wouldn't have a soldier. None of my family would ever look at a *soldier*. Why, they'd disown me.'

This absolute disallowance of the profession of arms as the calling of a potential husband could not have been more explicitly expressed. Indeed, Billson's words on that occasion gave substantial grounds for the defiant shape taken by Bracey's bouts of gloom. There was good reason to feel depression if this was what women felt about his situation. A parallel prejudice against even military companionship, much less marriage, was shared by Edith.

'Nice girls don't walk out with soldiers,' she said.

'Why not?'

'They don't.'

'Who says not?'

'Everybody says not.'

'But why not?'

'Ask anybody.'

'Not even the Life Guards?'

'No.'

'Nor the Blues?'

'Tommies are all the same.'

That seemed to settle matters finally so far as Bracey was concerned. There appeared to be no hope. There was Mercy, the housemaid, but even my own reckless projects for adjusting everyone else's personal affairs according to my whim did not include such a fate for Bracey. I could see that was not a rational proposition. In fact, it was out of the question. There were several reasons. In the first place, Mercy herself played little or no part in the complex of personalities who inhabited the Stonehurst kitchen—no emotional part, at least. Certainly Mercy herself had no desire to do so. She was a quite young girl from one of the villages in the neighbourhood, found for my mother by Mrs Gullick. Together with her parents, Mercy belonged to a local religious sect, so small that it embraced only about twenty individuals, all related to one another.

'They don't believe anyone else is going to Heaven,' Edith said of this communion.

'No one at all?'

'Not a single soul.'

'Why not?'

'They say they're the only ones saved.'

'Why?'

'Call themselves the Elect.'

'They aren't the only people going to Heaven.'

'I should just about think not.'

'They are silly to say that.'

'Silly, no error.'

Billson went still further than Edith on the same theological issue.

'That girl won't be saved herself,' she said. 'Not if she goes about repeating such things of her neighbours. God won't want her.'

The positivist character of Mercy's religious beliefs, more especially in relation to the categorical damnation of the rest of mankind, was expressed outwardly in a taciturn demeanour, defined by Edith as 'downright disobliging', her creed no doubt discouraging frivolous graces of manner. In personal appearance, she was equally severe, almost deliberately unprepossessing.

'*Her* face will never be her fortune,' Albert once remarked, when Mercy had left the kitchen in a huff after some difference about washing up.

Even Bracey, with all his unvoiced disapproval of Albert, was forced to laugh at the wit, the aptness of this observation. Bracey was, in any case, cheerful enough between his 'funny days'. If his spirits, at the lowest, were very low indeed, they also rose, at other moments, to heights never attained by Albert's. On such occasions, when he felt all comparatively well with the world, Bracey would softly hum under his breath:

> 'Monday, Tuesday, Wednesday, Thursday,
> May be merry and bright.
> But I'm going to be married on Sunday;
> Oh, I wish it was Sunday night.'

Earlier in the year, during one of these bursts of cheerfulness, Bracey had offered to take me to see a football match. This was an unexpected, a highly acceptable invitation. It always seemed to me a matter of complaint that, although my father was a soldier, we saw at Stonehurst, in practice, little or nothing of the army, that is to say, the army as such. We lived on this distant hilltop, miles away from the daily activities of troops, who were to be sighted only very occasionally on some local exercise to which summer manœuvres had fortunately brought them. Even so much as the solitary outline of a Military Policeman was rare, jogging his horse across the heather, a heavy brush-stroke of dark blue, surmounted by a tiny blob of crimson, moving in the sun through a Vuillard landscape of pinkish greys streaked with yellow and silver. I had mentioned to Bracey the sight of one of these lonely riders. He showed no warmth.

'Them Redcaps ain't loved all that.'

'Aren't they?'

'Not likely.'

'What do they do?'

'Run a bloke in soon as look at him.'

'What for?'

'They'll find somethink.'

'What happens to him?'

'Does a spell of clink.'

'What's that?'

'Put behind bars.'

'But they let him out sometime?'

'Twenty-eight days, might be, if he's lucky.'

'In prison?'

'Some blokes want to get even when they comes out.'

'How?'

'Waits behind a hedge on a dark night.'

'And then——'

'Takes the Redcap unawares like. Makes an ambush like. Give him a hiding.'

I accepted this picture of relaxed discipline in the spirit offered by Bracey, that is to say, without expression of praise or blame. Clearly he had described one of those aspects of army life kept, generally speaking, in the background, a world of violent action from which Stonehurst seemed for ever excluded.

Nor was our separation from the army only geographical. Military contacts were further lessened by my mother's distaste—her morbid horror, almost—of officers' wives who were 'regimental'—ladies who speculated on the Battalion's chances of winning the Cup, or discussed with too exact knowledge the domestic crises in the life of Mrs Colour-Sergeant Jones. My mother did not, in fact, enjoy any form of 'going out', military or civilian. Before marriage, she had been keen enough on parties and balls, but, my father having little or no taste for such amusements, she forgot about them herself, then developed greater dislike than his own. Even in those distant days my parents had begun to live a life entirely enclosed by their own domestic interests. There was a certain amount of routine 'calling', of course; subalterns came to tennis-parties; children to nursery-tea.

Bracey's invitation to the football match was therefore welcome, not so much because I was greatly interested in football but more on account of the closer contact the jaunt offered with army life. Permission was asked for the projected excursion. It was accorded by authority. Bracey and I set off together in a dog-cart, Bracey wearing blue walking-out dress, with slight screws of wax at each end of his moustache, a small vanity affected by him on important occasions. I had hoped he would be armed with a bayonet, but was disappointed. It seemed just worthwhile asking if he had merely forgotten it.

'Only sergeants carries sidearms, walking out.'

'Why?'

'Regulation.'

'Don't you ever?'

'On parade.'

'Never else?'

'Reckon we will when the Germans comes.'

The humorous possibilities of a German invasion I had often heard adumbrated. Sometimes my father—in spite

of my mother's extreme dislike of the subject, even in jest
—would refer to this ludicrous, if at the same time rather
sinister—certainly grossly insulting—incursion as something
inevitable in the future, like a visit to the dentist or ultimately going to school.

'You'll carry a bayonet always if the Germans come?'

'You bet.'

'You'll need it.'

'Bayonet's a man's best friend in time of war,' said
Bracey.

'And a rifle?'

'And a rifle,' Bracey conceded. 'Rifle and bayonet's a
man's best friend when he goes to battle.'

I thought a lot about that remark afterwards. Clearly its
implications raised important moral issues, if not, indeed,
conflicting judgments. I used to ponder, for example, what
appeared to be its basic scepticism, so different from the
supreme confidence in the claims of heroic companionship
put forward in all the adventure stories one read. (Thirty
years later, Sunny Farebrother—in contrast with Bracey—
told me that, even though he cared little for most books, he
sometimes re-read *For Name and Fame; or Through
Khyber Passes*, simply because Henty's narrative recalled to
him so vividly the comradeship he had himself always
enjoyed under arms.) Bracey shared none of the uplifting
sentiments of the adventure stories. That was plain. Even
within my own then strictly limited experience, I could see,
unwillingly, that there might be something to be said for
Bracey's point of view. All the same, I knew Bracey had
himself seen no active service. His opinion on such subjects
must be purely theoretical. In short, the door was not
irretrievably closed on the romantic approach. I felt glad of
that. During the rest of our journey to the Barracks,
however, Bracey did not enlarge further upon the theme
of weapons *versus* friendship.

We had a brief conversation at the gate with the Orderly Corporal, stabled the pony, set off across the parade-ground. The asphalt square was deserted except for three figures pacing its far side, moving briskly and close together, as if attempting to keep warm in the sharp weather of early spring. This trio marched up and down continually, always turning about at the same point in their beat. The two out-side soldiers wore equipment; the central file was beltless, his right hand done up in a white bandage.

'Who are they?'

'Prisoner and escort.'

'What are they doing?'

'Exercise a bloke under arrest.'

'What's he done?'

'Chopped off his trigger finger.'

'By accident?'

'Course not.'

'How, then?'

'With a bill.'

'On purpose?'

'You bet.'

'Whatever for?'

'Saw his name in Orders on the draft for India.'

'Why didn't he like that?'

'Thought the climate wouldn't suit him, I reckon.'

'But he won't have any finger.'

'Won't have to go to India neither.'

'Were you surprised?'

'Not particular.'

'Why not?'

'Nothing those young blokes won't do.'

Once again Bracey expressed no judgment on the subject of this violent action, but I was aware on this occasion of a sense of disapproval stronger than any he had allowed to take shape in relation to assaulting Military Policemen.

Here, certainly, was another story to make one ponder. I saw that the private soldier under arrest must have felt a very active dislike for the thought of army life in the East to have taken so extreme a step to avoid service there: a contrast with the builder of Stonehurst, deliberately reminding himself by the contents and architecture of his house of former Indian days. Like Bracey's picture of ambushed Redcaps, the three khaki figures, sharply advancing and retiring across the far side of the square, demonstrated a seamy, menacing side of army life, one which perhaps explained to some extent the reprobation in which Edith and Billson held soldiers as husbands. These haphazard—indeed, decidedly disreputable—aspects of the military career by no means entirely repelled me; on the contrary, they provided an additional touch of uneasy excitement. At the same time I saw that such episodes must have encouraged Bracey to form his own strong views as to the ultimate unreliability of human nature, his reliance on bayonets rather than comrades. In fact his unspoken attitude towards this painful, infinitely disagreeable, occurrence fitted perfectly with that philosophy. What use, Bracey seemed by implication to argue, would this bandaged soldier be as a companion in arms, if he preferred the loss of a forefinger to the completion of his military engagements when their circumstances threatened to be uncongenial to himself? That was Bracey's manner of looking at things, his inner world, perhaps to some extent the cause of his 'funny days'. A bugle, shrill, yet desperately sad, sounded far away down the lines.

'What is he blowing?'

'Defaulters.'

We passed through hutted cantonments towards the football field.

'Albert cut his finger the other day,' I said. 'There was a lot of blood.'

'Lot of fuss too,' said Bracey.

That was true. Albert's world of feeling was a very different one from Bracey's. A nervous man, he disliked violence, blood, suffragettes, anything of that kind. He was always for keeping the peace in the kitchen, even when his own scathing comments had started the trouble.

'I should not wish to cross the Captain in any of his appetites,' he had once remarked to my mother, when discussing with her what the savoury was to be on the menu for dinner that night.

Accordingly, Albert had been dreadfully alarmed when my father, on a day taken from duty to follow the local hounds, a rare occurrence (heaven knows what fox-hunting must have been like in that neighbourhood), having cut himself shaving that morning, managed in the course of breakfast, the wound reopening, to get blood all over his white breeches. Certainly the to-do made during the next half-hour justified perturbation on a cosmic scale. For my father all tragedies were major tragedies, this being especially his conviction if he were himself in any way concerned. On this occasion, he was beside himself. Bracey, on the other hand, showed calmness in the face of the appalling dooms fate seemed to have decreed on the bungalow and all its inhabitants. While my mother, distressed as ever by the absolutely unredeemed state of misery and rage that misfortune always provoked in my father's spirit, attempted to prepare infinitesimal morsels of cotton-wool to stem the equally small, no less obstinate, flux of blood, Bracey found another pair of riding-breeches, assembled the equipment for extracting my father from his boots, fitted the new breeches, slid him into his boots again. Finally, all this in a quite remarkably short space of time for the completion of so formidable, so complicated, so ultimately thankless a series of operations, Bracey gave my father a leg into the saddle. The worst was over; too much time had not been lost. Later, when horse and rider had disappeared from sight on the way to the meet, the nervous strain he had been through caused Bracey to remain standing at attention, on and off, for several minutes together before he retired to the kitchen. I think the day turned out, in any case, no great success: rain fell; hounds streamed in full cry through a tangle of wire; my father was thrown, retaining his eyeglass in his eye, but hurting his back and ruining his hat for ever. In short, evil influences—possibly the demons of Stonehurst or even the Furies themselves—seemed malignantly at work. However, that was no fault of Bracey's.

'Why did you think it wrong of Billson to give the little boy a slice of cake?' I asked.

We were still looking at the match, which, to tell the truth, did not entirely hold my attention, since I have never had any taste for watching games.

'Not hers to give,' said Bracey, very sternly.

I can see now, looking back, that the question was hopelessly, criminally, lacking in tact on my own part. I knew perfectly well that Bracey and Albert did not get on well together, that they differed never more absolutely than on this particular issue. I had often, as I have said, heard my parents speak of the delicacy of the Albert-Bracey mutual relationship. There was really no excuse for asking something so stupid, a question to which, in any case, I had frequently heard the answer from other sources. All the same, the incident to which my inquiry referred had for some reason caught my imagination. In fact everything to do with 'Dr Trelawney's place', as it was called locally, always gave me an excited, uneasy feeling, almost comparable to that brought into play by the story of the bandaged soldier. Sometimes, when out for a walk with Edith or my mother, we would pass Dr Trelawney's house, a pebble-dashed, gabled, red-tiled residence, a mile or two away, somewhere beyond the roofs on the horizon faced by the Stonehurst gate.

Dr Trelawney conducted a centre for his own peculiar religious, philosophical—same said magical—tenets, a cult of which he was high priest, if not actually messiah. This establishment was one of those fairly common strongholds of unsorted ideas that played such a part in the decade ended by the war. Simple-lifers, utopian socialists, spiritualists, occultists, theosophists, quietists, pacifists, futurists, cubists, zealots of all sorts in their approach to life and art, later to be relentlessly classified into their respective religious, political, aesthetic or psychological categories, were then thought of by the unenlightened as scarcely distinguishable one from another: a collection of visionaries who hoped to build a New Heaven and a New Earth through the agency of their particular crackpot activities, sinister or comic, according to the way you looked at such things. Dr Trelawney was a case in point. In the judgment of his neighbours there remained an unbridgable margin of doubt as to whether he was a holy man—at least a very simple and virtuous one—whose unconventional behaviour was to be tolerated, even applauded, or a charlatan—perhaps a dangerous rogue—to be discouraged by all right thinking people.

When out with his disciples, running through the heather in a short white robe or tunic, his long silky beard and equally long hair caught by the breeze, Dr Trelawney had an uncomfortably biblical air. His speed was always well maintained for a man approaching middle years. The disciples were of both sexes, most of them young. They, too, wore their hair long, and were dressed in 'artistic' clothes of rough material in pastel shades. They would trot breathlessly by, Dr Trelawney leading with long, loping strides, apparently making for nowhere in particular. I used to play with the idea that something awful had happened to me—my parents had died suddenly, for example—and ill chance forced me to become a member of Dr Trelawney's juvenile community. Casual mention of his name in conversation would even cause me an uneasy thrill. Once, we saw Dr Trelawney and his flock roaming through the scrub at the same moment as the Military Policeman on his patrol was riding back from the opposite direction. The sun was setting. This meeting and merging of two elements—two ways of life—made a striking contrast in physical appearance, moral ideas and visual tone-values.

My mother had once dropped in to the post office and general shop of a neighbouring village to buy stamps (perhaps the Health Insurance stamps commemorated in Albert's picture of Mr Lloyd George) and found Dr Trelawney already at the counter. The shop, kept by a deaf old woman, sold groceries, sweets, papers, almost everything, in fact, only a small corner behind a kind of iron hutch being devoted to postal business. Dr Trelawney was negotiating the registration of a parcel, a package no doubt too valuable—too sacred perhaps—to be entrusted to the hand of a neophyte. My mother had to wait while this laborious matter was contrived.

'He looked as if he was wearing his nightshirt,' she said afterwards, 'and a very short one at that.'

When the complicated process of registration had at last been completed, Dr Trelawney made a slight pass with his right hand, as if to convey benediction on the old woman who had served him.

'The Essence of the All is the Godhead of the True,' he said in a low, but clear and resonant vooice.

Then he left the shop, making a great clatter—my mother said—with his sandals. We heard later that these words were his invariable greeting, first and last, to all with whom he came in contact.

'Horrid fellow,' said my mother. 'He gave me a creepy feeling. I am sure Mr Deacon would know him. To tell the truth, when we used to visit Mr Deacon in Brighton, he used to give me just the same creepy feeling too.'

In saying this, my mother was certainly expressing her true sentiments, although perhaps not all of them. As I have said before, she had herself rather a taste for the occult (she loved delving into the obscurities of biblical history and prophecy), so that, however much Dr Trelawney may have repelled her, there can be no doubt that she also felt some curiosity, even if concealed, about his goings-on. She was right in supposing Mr Deacon would know about him. When I myself ran across Mr Deacon in later life and questioned him on the subject, he at once admitted that he had known Dr Trelawney slightly at some early point in their careers.

'Not a person with whom I ever wanted my name to be too closely associated,' said Mr Deacon, giving one of his deep, sceptical laughs. 'Too much abracadabra about Trelawney. He started with interests of a genuinely scientific and humane kind—full of idealism, you know—then gradually involved himself with all sorts of mystical nonsense, transcendental magic, goodness knows what rubbish. Made quite a good thing out of it, I believe. Contributions from the Faithful, women especially. Human beings are sad dupes, I fear. The priesthood would have a thin time of it were that not so. Now, I don't expect Trelawney has read a line of economics—probably never heard of Marx. "The Essence of the All is the Godhead of the True," forsooth. Then you were expected to answer: "The Vision of Visions heals the Blindness of Sight." I was too free a spirit for Trelawney in spite of his denial of the World. Still, some of his early views on diet were on the right track.'

More than that, Mr Deacon would not say. He had given

himself to many enthusiasms at one time or another, too many, he sometimes owned. By the time I met him, when Pacifism and Communism occupied most of the time he could spare from his antique shop, he was inclined to deride his earlier, now cast-down altars. All the same, he never wholly lost interest in Vegetarianism and Hygienic Clothing, even after he had come to look upon such cases as largely frivolous adjuncts to World Revolution.

As it happened, the Trelawney teaching on diet brought the Trelawney establishment more particularly to Stonehurst notice. These nutritional views played a part in local legend, simply because the younger disciples, several of whom were mere children, would from time to time call at the door of some house in the neighbourhood and ask for a glass of milk or a snack. Probably the fare at Dr Trelawney's, carefully thought out, was also unsubstantial, especially when it came to long, energetic rambles over the countryside, which stimulated hunger. In my own fantasies of being forced to become one of their number, semi-starvation played a macabre part. On one such occasion—it was a first visit by one of Dr Trelawney's flock to Stonehurst—Billson, answering the door, had, on request, dispensed a slice of rather stale seed-cake. She had done this unwillingly, only after much discussion with Albert. It was a moment when Bracey was having one of his 'funny days', therefore, by definition, unable to take part in any consultation regarding this benefaction. When the 'funny day' was over, however, and Bracey was, as it were, officially notified of the incident, he expressed the gravest disapproval. The cake, Bracey said, should never have been given. Billson asserted that she had Albert's support in making the donation. Always inclined to hysteria, she was thoroughly upset by Bracey's strictures, no doubt all the more severe on account of his own warm feelings for her. Albert, at first lukewarm on the subject, was driven into more energetic support of

Billson by Bracey's now opening the attack on two fronts. In the end, the slice of seed-cake became a matter of bitter controversy in the kitchen. Bracey upholding the view that the dispensation of all charity should be referred to my parents; Billson sometimes defending, sometimes excusing her action; Albert of the opinion that the cake did not fall within the sphere of charity, because Dr Trelawney, whatever his eccentricities, was a neighbour, to whom, with his household, such small acts of hospitality were appropriate. No doubt Albert's experience of a wider world gave him a certain breadth and generosity of view, not in the least sentimental, but founded on a fundamental belief in a traditional civilisation. Whether or not that was at the root of his conclusions, the argument became so heated that at last Billson, in tears, appealed to my mother. That was before the 'ghost' appeared to Billson. Indeed, it was the first serious indication of her highly strung nerves. She explained how much it upset her to be forced to make decisions, repeated over and over again how she had never wanted to deal with the 'young person from Dr Trelawney's.' My mother, unwilling to be drawn into the controversy, gave judgment that dispensation of cake was 'all right, if it did not happen too often'. There the matter rested. Even so, Billson had to retire to bed for a day. She felt distraught. In the same way, my mother's ruling made no difference whatever to Bracey's view of the matter; nor was Bracey to be moved by Albert's emphasis on the undeniable staleness of the cake. It did not matter that Edith and Mrs Gullick supported my mother, or that Mercy did not care, since in her eyes donor and beneficiary were equally marked out for damnation. Bracey maintained his position. From this conflict, I lived to some extent apart, observing mainly through the eyes of Edith, a medium which left certain facts obscure. Getting Bracey alone was therefore an opportunity to learn more, even if an opportunity better disregarded. The fact was, I wanted to hear Bracey's opinion from his own lips.

'She didn't ought to have done it,' Bracey said.

'But Albert thought it was all right.'

'Course he thought it was all right. What's it matter to him?'

'Billson said the little boy was very grateful.'

Bracey did not even bother to comment on this last aspect of the transaction. He only sniffed, one of his habits when displeased. Billson's statement must have struck him as beneath discussion. In fact that foolish question of mine came near to ruining the afternoon. The match ended. There was some ragged cheering. We passed once more across the barrack-square, from which prisoner and escort had withdrawn to some other sphere of penal activity. Bracey was silent all the way home. I knew instinctively that a 'funny day'—almost certainly provoked by myself— could not be far off. This presentiment proved correct. Total spleen was delayed, though stormily, until the following Friday, when a sequence of 'funny days' of the most gruel- ling kind took immediate shape. Those endured for the best part of a week, causing much provocation to Albert, who used to complain that Bracey's 'funny days' affected his own culinary powers, for example, in the mixing of mayonnaise, which—making mayonnaise being a tricky business—could well have been true.

Billson's tactics to entrap Albert matrimonially no doubt took place to some considerable extent in his own imagina- tion, but, as I have said, even Edith accepted the fact that there was a substratum of truth in his firm belief that 'she had her eye on him', hoped to make him 'hang up his hat'. Billson may have refused to admit even to herself the strength of her passion, which certainly showed itself finally in an extreme, decidedly inconvenient form. Anxiety about her own health no doubt amplified a tendency in her to abandon all self-control when difficult situations arose: the loneliness of Stonehurst, its 'ghosts', also working adversely on her nerves. For the occasion of her breakdown Billson could not, in some ways, have picked a worse day; in others, she could not have found a better one. It was the Sunday when General and Mrs Conyers came to luncheon.

Visitors were rare at Stonehurst. No one but a relation or very, very old friend would ever have been invited to spend the night under its roof, any such bivouac (sudden descent of Uncle Giles, for example) being regarded as both exceptional and burdensome. This was in part due to the limited accommodation there, which naturally forbade large-scale entertaining. It was also the consequence of the isolated life my parents elected to live. Neither of them was lacking in a spirit of hospitality as such, my father especially, when in the right mood, liking to 'do well' anyone allowed past the barrier of his threshold. Even so, guests were not often brought in to meals. That was one of Albert's grievances. If he cooked, he liked to cook on as grand a scale as possible. There was little opportunity at Stonehurst. Indeed, Albert's art was in general largely wasted on my parents: my mother's taste for food being simple, verging on the ascetic; my father—again in certain moods—liking sometimes to dwell on the delights of the gourmet, more often crotchety about what was set before him, dyspeptic in its assimilation.

General Conyers, however, was regarded as 'different', not only as a remote cousin of my mother's—although very much, as my brother-in-law, Chips Lovell, would have said, a cousin *à la mode de Bretagne*—but also for his countless years as an old, if never particularly close, friend of the family. Even at the date of which I speak, Aylmer Conyers was long retired from the army (in the rank of brigadier-general), having brought to a close, soon after he married, a career that might have turned out a brilliant one. Mrs Conyers, quite twenty years younger than her husband, was also on good terms with my mother—they would usually exchange letters if more than a year passed without meeting —although, again, their friendship could never have been called intimate. Bertha Conyers, rather sad and apologetic in appearance, had acquired, so people said, a persecuted manner in girlhood from her father's delight in practical jokes (like the clockwork mouse he had launched on Albert), and also from his harrying of his daughters for failing to be born boys. In spite of this air of having spent a lifetime being bullied, Mrs Conyers was believed to exercise a firm influence over her husband, to some extent keeping his eccentricities in check.

'Aylmer Conyers used to have rather a roving eye,' my father would say. 'That's all changed since his marriage. Wouldn't look at another woman.'

'He's devoted to Bertha, certainly,' my mother would agree, perhaps unwilling to commit her opinion in that respect too definitely.

For my father, the Conyers visit presented, like so many other elements of life, a sharp diffusion of sentiment. By introducing my father a short time earlier in the guise, so to speak, of a fox-hunter wearing an eyeglass, I risk the conveyance of a false impression, indeed, a totally erroneous one. The eyeglass was on account of extreme short sight, for, although he had his own brand of dandyism, that dandyism was not at all of the eyeglass variety. Nor was hunting his favourite pastime. He rode fairly well ('blooded' at the age of nine out with the Belvoir, his own father being an unappeasable fox-hunter), but he took little pleasure in horses, or any outdoor occupation. It is true that he liked to speak of hunting in a tone of expertise, just as he liked to talk of wine without greatly caring to drink it. He had little natural aptitude for sport of any sort and his health was not

39

good. What did he like? That is less easy to say. Consecrated, in one sense, to his profession, he possessed at the same time none of that absolute indifference to his own surroundings essential to the ambitious soldier. He was saddled with the equally serious military—indeed, also civilian—handicap of chronic inability to be obsequious to superiors in rank, particularly when he found them uncongenial. He was attracted by the Law, like his brother Martin; allured by the stock-market, like his brother Giles. One of the least 'intellectual' of men, he took intermittent pleasure in pictures and books, especially in such aspects of 'collecting' as rare 'states' of prints, which took his fancy, or 'first editions' of comparatively esoteric authors: items to be safely classified in their own market, without excessive reference, critically speaking, to their standing as works of art or literature. In these fields, although by no means a reactionary in aesthetic taste, he would recognise no later changes of fashion after coming to his own decision on any picture or school of painting. After a bout of buying things, he would almost immediately forget about them, often, a year or two later purchasing another copy (sometimes several copies) of the same volume or engraving; so that when, from time to time, our possessions were taken out of store, duplicates of most of his favourite works always came to light. He used to read in the evenings, never with much enjoyment or concentration.

'I like to rest my mind after work,' he would say. 'I don't like books that make me think.'

That was perfectly true. In due course, as he grew older, my father became increasingly committed to this exclusion of what made him think, so that finally he disliked not only books, but also people—even places—that threatened to induce this disturbing mental effect. Perhaps that attitude of mind—one could almost say process of decay—is among many persons more general than might be supposed. In my father's case, this dislike for thought seemed to stem from a basic conviction that his childhood had been an unhappy one. His melancholy was comparable, even though less eccentrically expressed, with Bracey's, no doubt contributing to their mutual understanding. Much the youngest of his family, his claim to have been neglected was probably true. Happy marriage did not cure him. Painfully sensitive to criticism, he was never (though he might not show this) greatly at ease with other men; in that last characteristic resembling not a few of those soldiers, who, paradoxically, reach high rank, positively assisted by their capacity for avoiding friendship, too close personal ties which can handicap freedom of ascent.

'These senior officers are like a lot of ballerinas,' said my friend Pennistone, when, years later, we were in the army together.

Certainly the tense nerves of men of action—less notorious than those of imaginative men—are not to be minimised. This was true of my father, who, like many persons who believe primarily in the will—although his own will was in no way remarkable—hid in his heart a hatred of constituted authority. He did his best to conceal this antipathy, because the one thing he hated, more than constituted authority itself, was to hear constituted authority questioned by anyone but himself. This is perhaps an endemic trait in all who love power, and my father had an absolute passion for power, although he was never in a position to wield it on a notable scale. In his own house, only he himself was allowed to criticise—to use a favourite phrase of his—'the powers that be'. In private, he would, for example, curse the Army Council (then only recently come into existence); in the presence of others, even those 'in the Service' with whom he was on the best of terms, he would defend to the last ditch official policy of which in his heart he disapproved.

These contradictory veins of feeling placed my father in

41

a complex position *vis-à-vis* General Conyers, whom Uncle Giles, on the other hand, made no secret of finding 'a bit too pleased with himself'. As a much older man, universally recognised as a first-rate soldier, the General presented a figure to whom deference on my father's part was obviously due. At the same time, the General held revolutionary views on army reform, which he spared no opportunity of voicing in terms utterly uncomplimentary to 'the powers that be', military or civil. My father, of course, possessed his own especial likes and dislikes throughout the hierarchy of the army, both individual and general, but deplored too plain speaking even when he was to some considerable extent in agreement.

'Aylmer Conyers is fond of putting everyone right,' he used to complain. 'If he'd stayed in the Services a few years longer, instead of devoting his life to training poodles as gun-dogs, and scraping away at that 'cello of his, he might have discovered that the army has changed a little since the Esher Report.'

Uncle Giles would immediately have been reproved for making so open a criticism of a senior officer, but my father must have felt that to criticise General Conyers was the only method of avoiding apparent collusion in an attack on the whole Army Council. In any case, Uncle Giles's unsatisfactory mode of life, not to mention his dubious political opinions, radical to the point of anarchism, put him out of court in most family discussions. He was at this period employed in a concern fascinatingly designated a 'bucket-shop'. My father had, in truth, never forgiven his brother for transferring himself, years before—after some tiff with his commanding officer—to the Army Service Corps.

'It's not just snobbishness on my part,' my father used to say, long after Uncle Giles had left that, and every other, branch of the army. 'I know they win a lot of riding events at gymkhanas, but I can't stick 'em. They're such an unco-operative lot of beggars when you have to deal with 'em about stores. I date all Giles's troubles from leaving his regiment.'

However, I mention Uncle Giles at this point only to emphasise the manner in which the Conyers visit was regarded for a number of reasons with mixed feelings by my parents. There were good aspects; there were less good ones. Albert, for instance, would be put into an excellent humour for several weeks by this rare opportunity for displaying his talents. He would make his mousse. He would recall Lord Vowchurch's famous practical joke with the clockwork mouse, one of the great adventures of Albert's life, not only exciting but refreshingly free from the artifices of women—although Mrs Conyers herself was allowed some reflected glory from her father's act.

Mrs Conyers was one of the few people with whom my mother liked to chat of 'old times': the days before she set out on the nomadic existence of a soldier's wife. Mrs Conyers's gossip, well informed, gently expressed, was perfectly adapted to recital at length. This mild manner of telling sometimes hair-raising stories was very much to the taste of my mother, never at ease with people she thought to be 'worldly', at the same time not unwilling to enjoy an occasional glimpse of 'the world', viewed through the window briefly opened by Mrs Conyers. The General had become a Gentleman-at-Arms after leaving the army, so that her stories included, with a touch of racing at its most respectable, some glimpse of the outskirts of Court life.

'Bertha Conyers has such an amusing way of putting things,' my mother would say. 'But I really don't believe all her stories, especially the one about Mrs Asquith and the man who asked her if she danced the tango.'

The fact that General Conyers was occasionally on duty at palaces rather irked my father, not so much because the General took this side of his life too seriously—to which my father would have been quite capable of objecting—but because he apparently did not take his court duties seriously enough.

'If I were the King and I heard Aylmer Conyers talking like that, I'd sack him,' he once said in a moment of irritation.

The General and his wife were coming to Stonehurst after staying with one of Mrs Conyers's sisters, whose husband commanded a Lancer regiment in the area. Rather adventurously for that period, they were undertaking the journey by motor-car, a vehicle recently acquired by the General, which he drove himself. Indeed, the object of the visit was largely to display this machine, to compare it with the car my father had himself bought only a few months before. There was a good deal of excitement at the prospect of seeing a friend's 'motor', although I think my father a little resented the fact that a man so much older than himself should be equally prepared to face such grave risks, physical and financial. As a matter of fact, General Conyers, who always prided himself on being up-to-date, was even rumoured to have been 'up' in a flying machine. This story was dismissed by my parents as being unworthy of serious credence.

'Aylmer Conyers will never get to the top of that damned hill,' said my father more than once during the week before their arrival.

'Did you tell him about it?' said my mother.

'I warned him in my letter. He is a man who never takes advice. I'm told he was just the same at Pretoria. Just a bit of luck that things turned out as well as they did for him—due mostly to Boer stupidity, I believe. Obstinate as a mule. Was up before Bobs himself once for disobeying an order. Talked himself out of it, even got promotion a short time after. Wonderful fellow. Well, so much the worse for him if he gets stuck—slip backwards more likely. That may be a lesson to him. Bad luck on Bertha Conyers if there's an accident. It's her I feel sorry for. I've worried a lot about it. He's a selfish fellow in some ways, is old Aylmer.'

'Do you think I ought to write to Bertha again myself?' asked my mother, anxious to avoid the awful mishaps envisaged by my father.

'No, no.'

'But I will if you think I should.'

'No, no. Let him stew in his own juice.'

The day of the Conyers' luncheon came. I woke up that morning with a feeling of foreboding, a sensation to which I was much subject as a child. It was Sunday. Presentiments of ill were soon shown to have good foundation. For one thing, Billson turned out to have seen the 'ghost' again on the previous night; to be precise, in the early hours of that morning. The phantom had taken its accustomed shape of an elongated white figure reaching almost to the ceiling of the room. It disappeared, as usual, before she could rub her eyes. Soon after breakfast, I heard Billson delivering a first-hand account of this psychical experience to Mrs Gullick, who used to lend a hand in the kitchen, a small, elderly, red-faced woman, said to 'give Gullick a time', because she considered she had married beneath her. Mrs Gullick, although a staunch friend of Billson's, was not prepared to accept psychic phenomena at any price.

'Don't go saying such ignorant things, dear,' was her comment. 'You need a tonic. You're run down like. I thought you was pale when you was drinking your cup of tea yesterday. See the doctor. That's what you want to do. Don't worry about that ghost stuff. I never heard such a thing in all my days. You're sickly, that's what you are.'

Billson seemed partially disposed to accept this display of incredulity, either because it must have been reassuring to think she had been mistaken about the 'ghost', or because any appeal to her own poor state of health was always sympathetic to her. At that early stage of the day, she was in any case less agitated than might have been expected in the light of the supernatural appearance she claimed to have witnessed. She was excited, not more than that. It was true she muttered something about 'giving notice', but the phrase was spoken without force, obviously making no impression whatever on Mrs Gullick. For me, it was painful to find people existed who did not 'believe' in the Stonehurst ghosts, whose uneasy shades provided an exciting element of local life with which I did not at all wish to dispense. My opinion of Mrs Gullick fell immediately, even though she was said by Edith to be the only person in the house who could 'get any work out of' Mercy. I found her scepticism insipid. However, a much more disturbing incident took place a little later in the morning. My mother had just announced that she was about to put on her hat for church, when Albert appeared at the door. He looked very upset. In his hand was a letter.

'May I have a word with you, Madam?'

I was sent off to get ready for church. When I returned, my mother and Albert were still talking. I was told to wait outside. After a minute or two, Albert came out. My mother followed him to the door.

'I do quite understand, Albert,' she said. 'Of course we shall all be very, very sorry.'

Albert nodded heavily several times. He was too moved to speak.

'Very sorry, indeed. It has been a long time . . .'

'I thought I'd better tell you first, ma'am,' said Albert, 'so you could explain to the Captain. Didn't want it to come to him as a shock. He takes on so. I've had this letter since yesterday. Couldn't bring myself to show you at first. Haven't slept for thinking of it.'

'Yes, Albert.'

My father was out that morning, as it happened. He had

to look in at the Orderly Room that Sunday, for some reason, and was not expected home until midday. Albert swallowed several times. He looked quite haggard. The flesh of his face was pouched. I could see the situation was upsetting my mother too. Albert's voice shook when he spoke at last.

'Madam,' he said, 'I've been goaded to this.'

He shuffled off to the kitchen. There were tears in his eyes. I was aware that I had witnessed a painful scene, although, as so often happens in childhood, I could not analyse the circumstances. I felt unhappy myself. I knew now why I had foreseen something would go wrong as soon as I had woken that morning.

'Come along,' said my mother, turning quickly and giving her own eyes a dab, 'we shall be late for church. Is Edith ready?'

'What did Albert want?'

'Promise to keep a secret, if I tell you?'

'I promise.'

'Albert is going to get married.'

'To Billson?'

My mother laughed aloud.

'No,' she said, 'to someone he knows who lives at Bristol.'

'Will he go away?'

'I'm afraid he will.'

'Soon?'

'Not for a month or two, he says. But you really must not say anything about it. I ought not to have told you, I suppose. Run along at once for Edith. We are going to be dreadfully late.'

My mother was greatly given to stating matters openly. In this particular case, she was probably well aware that Albert himself would not be slow to reveal his future plans to the rest of the household. No very grave risk was therefore run in telling me the secret. At the same time, such news would never have been disclosed by my father, a confirmed maker of mysteries, who disliked imparting information of any but a didactic kind. If forced to offer an exposé of any given situation, he was always in favour of presenting the substance of what he had to say in terms more or less oracular. Nothing in life—such was his view—must ever be thought of as easy of access. There is something to be said for that approach. Certainly few enough things in life are easy. On the other hand, human affairs can become even additionally clouded with obscurity if the most complicated forms of definition are always deliberately sought. My father really hated clarity. This was a habit of mind that sometimes led him into trouble with others, when, unable to appreciate his delight in complicated metaphor and ironic allusion, they had not the faintest idea what he was talking about. It was, therefore, by the merest chance that I was immediately put in possession of the information that Albert was leaving. I should never have learnt that so early if my father had been at home. We went off to church, my mother, Edith and I. The morning service took about an hour. We arrived home just as my father drove up in the car on his return from barracks. Edith disappeared towards the day-nursery.

'It's happened,' said my mother.

'What?'

My father's face immediately became very grave.

'Albert.'

'Going?'

'Getting married at last.'

'Oh, lord.'

'We thought it was coming, didn't we?'

'Oh, lord, how awful.'

'We'll get someone else.'

'Never another cook like Albert.'

'We may find someone quite good.'

'They won't live up here.'

'Don't worry. I'll find somebody. I'll start on Monday.'

'I knew this was going to happen.'

'We both did.'

'That doesn't help.'

'Never mind.'

'But today, of all days, oh, lord.'

Their reception of the news showed my parents were already to some extent prepared for this blow to fall, anyway accepted, more or less philosophically, that Albert's withdrawal into married life was bound to come sooner or later. Nevertheless, it was a disturbing state of affairs: the termination of a long and close relationship. No more was said at that moment because—a very rare occurrence—the telegraph-boy pedalled up on his bicycle. My parents were still standing on the doorstep.

'Name of Jenkins?'

My father took the telegram with an air of authority. His face had lightened a little now that he was resigned to Albert's departure, but the features became overcast again as he tore open the envelope, as if the news it brought must inevitably be bad.

'Who can it be?' said my mother, no less disturbed.

My father studied the message. He went suddenly red with annoyance.

'Wait a moment,' he said to the boy, in a voice of command.

My mother followed him into the hall. I hung about in the background.

'For goodness' sake say what's happened,' begged my mother, in an agony of fearing the worst.

My father read aloud the words, his voice shaking with irritation:

'Can you house me Sunday night talk business arrive teatime Giles.'

He held the telegram away from him as if fear of some awful taint threatened him by its contact. There was a long pause. Disturbing situations were certainly arising.

'Really too bad of him,' said my mother at last.

'Damn Giles.'

'Inconsiderate, too, to leave it so late.'

'He can't come.'

'We must think it over.'

'There is no time. I won't have him.'

'Where is he?'

'It's sent from Aldershot.'

'Quite close then.'

'What *the devil* is Giles doing in Aldershot?'

My parents looked at each other without speaking. Things could not be worse. Uncle Giles was not much more than a dozen miles away.

'We heard there was some trouble, didn't we?'

'Of course there is trouble,' said my father. 'Was there ever a moment when Giles was not in trouble? Don't be silly.'

There was another long pause.

'The telegram was reply-paid,' said my mother at last, not able to bear the thought that the boy might be bored or inconvenienced by this delay in drafting an answer. 'The boy is still waiting.'

'Damn the boy.'

My father was in despair. As I have said, all tragedies for him were major tragedies, and here was one following close on the heels of another.

'With the Conyerses coming too.'

'Can't we put Giles off?'

'He may really need help.'

'Of course he needs help. He always needs help.'

'Difficult to say he can't come.'

'Just *like* Giles to choose this day of all days.'

50

'Besides, I never think Giles and Aylmer Conyers get on very well together.'

'Get on well together,' said my father. 'They can't stand each other.'

The thought of this deep mutual antipathy existing between his brother and General Conyers cheered my father a little. He even laughed.

'I suppose Giles will have to come,' he admitted.

'No way out.'

'The Conyerses will leave before he arrives.'

'They won't stay late if they are motoring home.'

'Shall I tell Giles he can come?'

'We must, I think.'

'It may be just as well to know what he is up to. I hope it is not a serious mess this time. I wouldn't trust that fellow an inch who got him the bucket-shop job.'

Uncle Giles did not at all mind annoying his relations. That was all part of his policy of making war on society. In fact, up to a point, the more he annoyed his relations, the better he was pleased. At the same time, his interests were to some extent bound up with remaining on reasonably good terms with my father. Since he had quarrelled irretrievably with his other brother, my father—also on poorish terms with Uncle Martin, whom we never saw—represented one of the few stable elements in the vicissitudes of Uncle Giles's life. He and my father irritated, without actually disliking, each other. Uncle Giles, the older; my father, the more firmly established; the honours were fairly even, when it came to conflict. For example, my father disapproved, probably rightly, of the form taken by his brother's 'outside broking', although I do not know how much the firm for which Uncle Giles worked deserved the imputation of sharp practice. Certainly my father questioned its bona fides and was never tired of declaring that he would advise no friend of his to do business there. At the same time, his own interest in the stock market prevented him from refraining entirely from all financial discussion with Uncle Giles, with whom he was in any case indissolubly linked, financially speaking, by the terms of a will. Their argument would often become acrimonious, but I suspect my father sometimes took Uncle Giles's advice about investments, especially if a 'bit of a gamble' was in the air.

'Shall I say *Expect you teatime today*?'

'How is Giles going to get here?'

'I won't fetch him. It can't be done. The Conyerses may not leave in time.'

My mother looked uncertain.

'Do you think I should?'

'You can't. Not with other guests coming.'

'Giles will find his way.'

'We can be sure of that.'

My mother was right in supposing Uncle Giles perfectly capable of finding his way to any place recommended by his own interests. She was also right in thinking that Albert, after confiding his marriage plans to herself, would immediately reveal them in the kitchen. Edith described the scene later. She was having a cup of tea before church when Albert made the official announcement of his engagement. Billson had at once burst into tears. Bracey was having a 'funny day'—though a mild one—brought on either by regret at the necessity of resuming his duties, or, more probably, as a consequence of nervous strain after a spell in the house of his Luton sister-in-law. Accordingly, he showed no interest in the prospect of being left, as it were, in possession of the field so far as Billson was concerned. After issuing his pronouncement, Albert turned his attention to the mousse, the cooking of which always caused him great anxiety. Billson moved silently from kitchen to dining-room, and back again, laying the table miserably, red-eyed, white-faced, looking as much like a ghost as any she had described. She had taken

52

badly Albert's surrender to the 'girl from Bristol'. The house had an uneasy air. I retired to my own places of resort in the garden.

The Conyers party was scheduled to arrive about one o'clock, but the notorious uncertainty of motor-cars had given rise to much head-shaking on the probability of their lateness. However, I was loitering about the outskirts of the house, not long after the telegraph-boy had disappeared on his bicycle over the horizon, when a car began painfully to climb the lower slopes of the hill. It could only contain General and Mrs Conyers. This was an unexpected excitement. I watched their slow ascent, which was jerky, like the upward movement of a funicular, but, contrary to my father's gloomy forecast, the steep incline was negotiated without undue difficulty. I was even able to open the Stonehurst gate to admit the vehicle. There could be no doubt now of the identity of driver and passenger. By that period, of course, motorists no longer wore the peaked cap and goggles of their pioneering days, but, all the same, the General's long check ulster and deerstalker seemed assumed to some extent ritualistically.

'It is always cold motoring,' my mother used to say.

The car drew up by the front door. The General, leaping from it with boundless energy, came to meet me, leaving his wife to extract herself as best she could from a pile of wraps and rugs, sufficient in number to perform a version of the Dance of the Seven Veils. Tall, distinguished, with grey moustache and flashing eyes, he held out his hand.

'How do you do, Nicholas?'

He spoke gravely, in a tone no different from that to be used with a contemporary. There was about him a kind of fierceness, combined with a deep sense of understanding.

'We are a little earlier than I expected,' he said. 'I hope your father and mother will not mind. I drove rather fast, as your mother said you lived at the back of be-

53

yond, and I am always uncertain of my own map-reading. I see now what she meant. How are they educating you up here? Do you go to school?'

'Not yet. I have lessons with Miss Orchard.'

'Oh, yes. Miss Orchard is the governess who teaches all the children round here. I know her well by name. What children are they?'

'The Fenwicks, Mary Barber, Richard Vaughan, the Westmacott twins.'

'Fenwick in the Gloucesters?'

'Yes, I think so—the regiment that wears a badge at the back of their cap.'

'And Mary Barber's father?'

'He's in the Queen's. Richard Vaughan's is in the "Twenty-Fourth"—the South Wales Borderers.'

'What about the father of the Westmacott twins?'

'A Gunner.'

'What sort of a Gunner?'

'Field, but Thomas and Henry Westmacott say their father is going to get his "jacket" soon, so he may be Royal Horse Artillery by now.'

'An exceedingly well-informed report,' said the General. 'You have given yourself the trouble to go into matters thoroughly, I see. That is one of the secrets of success in life. Now take us to your parents.'

This early arrival resulted in my seeing rather more of General and Mrs Conyers than I should have done had they turned up at their appointed hour. First of all there was a brief examination of the Conyers car, a decidedly grander affair than that owned by my father, a fact which possibly curtailed the period spent over it. Since there was still time to kill before luncheon, the guests were shown round the garden. Permitted to accompany the party, I walked beside my mother and Mrs Conyers, the General and my father strolling behind.

'Has your ghost appeared again?' asked Mrs Conyers. 'Aylmer was fascinated when I told him your parlourmaid had seen one. He is very keen on haunted houses.'

Her husband was famous for the variety of his interests. In this particular connection—the occult one—there was some story, probably mythical, about General Conyers having taken advantage of his appointment to the Body Guard to investigate on the spot some allegedly ghostly visitation at Windsor or another of the royal palaces. This intellectually inquisitive side of the General's character specially irked Uncle Giles, who liked to classify irreparably everyone he knew, hating to be forced to alter the pigeon-hole in which he had himself already placed any given individual.

'Aylmer Conyers may be a good tactician,' he used to say, 'at least that is what he is always telling everyone—never knew such a fellow for blowing his own trumpet—but I can't for the life of me see why he wants to lay down the law about all sorts of other matters that don't concern him in the least. The last thing I heard was that he had taken up "psychical research", whatever that may be.'

My father, although he would never have admitted as much to Uncle Giles, was inclined to agree with his brother in the view that General Conyers would be a more dignified figure if he accepted for himself a less universal scope of interests; so that when the General began to make inquiries about the Stonehurst 'ghost', my father tried to dismiss the subject out of hand.

'A lot of nonsense, General,' he said, 'I assure you.'

General Conyers would have none of that.

'External agency,' he said, 'that's the point. Find it hard to believe in actual entities myself. Ought to be looked into more. One heard some strange stories when one was in India. The East is full of that sort of thing—a lot pure invention, of course.'

'I believe ghosts are thought-forms,' said Mrs Conyers, as

if that settled the whole matter.

'If you are experiencing hallucination,' said her husband, 'then something must cause the hallucination. Telepathic side, too, of course. I've never had the opportunity to cross-question first-hand someone who's seen a ghost. What sort of a girl is this parlourmaid of yours?'

'Oh, please don't cross-question her,' said my mother. 'We have such dreadful difficulties in getting servants here, and we are losing Albert as it is. She is not by any means a girl. You will see her waiting at table. Very hysterical. All the same, the maid we had before used to tell the same story.'

'Indeed? Did she? Did she?'

'I must say I think there is something peculiar about the house myself,' said my mother. 'I shall not be altogether sorry when the time comes to leave it.'

'What about the people who let it to you?'

'The fellow who built the place is dead,' said my father, now determined to change the subject, come what may. 'The lease was arranged through executors. We got it rather cheap on that account. He was in the Indian Army—Madras cavalry, I believe. What do you think about the reorganisations in India, by the way, General? Some people say the latest concentrations of command are not working too well.'

'We want mobility, mobility, and yet more mobility,' said General Conyers, 'in India and everywhere else, more especially since the Baghdad Agreement. If the Germans continue the railway to Basra, that amounts to our recognising the northern area of Mesopotamia as a German sphere of influence.'

'How much does Mesopotamia matter?' enquired my father, unaware that he would soon be wounded there.

'Depends on when and where Germany decides to attack.'

'That will be soon, you think?'

'Between the Scylla of her banking system, and the

56

Charybdis of her Socialist Party, Germany has no alternative.'

My father nodded respectfully, at the same time a trifle ironically. Although, in principle, he certainly agreed that war must come sooner or later—indeed, he was often saying it would come sooner—I am not sure that he truly believed his own words. He did not, indeed, much care for talking politics, national or international, unless in the harmless form of execration of causes disliked by himself. Certainly he had no wish to hear strategic situations expressed in classical metaphor, with which he was not greatly at ease. He had merely spoken of the Indian Army as a preferable alternative to discussing the Stonehurst 'ghosts'. The General, however, showed no sign of wishing to abandon this new subject.

'One of these fine mornings the Germans will arrive over here,' he said, 'or walk into France. Can't blame them if they do. Everyone is asking for it. We shall be squabbling with the Irish, or having a coal strike, or watching cricket. In France, Cabinet Ministers will be calling each other out to duels, while their wives discharge pistols at newspaper editors. And when the Germans come, it will be a big show —Clausewitz's Nation in Arms.'

'Able fellow, Clausewitz,' my father conceded.

'You remember he said that war was in the province of chance?'

'I do, General.'

'We are a great deal too fond of accepting that principle in this country,' said General Conyers. 'All the same, I thank God for the mess we made in South Africa. That brought a few people to their senses. Even the Treasury.'

My father, equally unwilling to admit the Boer War to have been prosecuted without notable brilliance, or that the light of reason or patriotism could penetrate, in however humble a degree, into the treasonable madhouse of the

57

Treasury, did not answer. He gave a kind of half-sneer, half-grunt. I think my mother must have thought there had been enough talk of war for the time being, because she suggested a return to the house. The hour of luncheon was in any case approaching. I departed to the nursery.

'Everyone's in a taking today,' said Edith, herself rather ruffled when I arrived at table. 'I don't know what has come over the house. It's all your Uncle Giles coming to stay without warning, I suppose. Albert says it's just like him. Now, don't begin making a fuss because the gravy is too thick. I haven't given you much of it.'

In the subsequent rather sensational events of the afternoon, I played no direct part. They were told to me later, piecemeal; most of the detail revealed by my mother only many years after. She herself could never repeat the story without her eyes filling with tears, caused partly by laughter, perhaps partly by other memories of that time. All the same, my mother always used to insist that there had been nothing to laugh about at the moment when the incident took place. Then her emotion had been shock, even fear. The disturbing scene in question was enacted while Edith and I were out for our traditional Sunday 'walk', which took its usual form that afternoon of crossing the Common. We were away from home about an hour and a half, perhaps two hours. Meanwhile, my parents and their guests had moved from dining-room to drawing-room, after what was agreed later to rank as one of the best meals Albert had ever cooked.

'Aylmer Conyers does love his food,' my mother used to say.

When announcing that fact, she would speak as if kindly laughter were the only possible manner of passing off lightly so distressing a frailty in friend or relation. Indeed, the General's pride in his own appreciation of the pleasures of the table was regarded by people like my parents, in the fashion of that day, as a tendency to talk rather more than was decent of eating and drinking. On this occasion he had certainly been full of praise for Albert. Possibly his eulogies continued too long entirely to please my father, who grew easily tired of hearing another man, even his own cook, too protractedly commended. Besides, apart from anything he might feel about the General, the impending arrival of Uncle Giles had justifiably set my father's nerves on edge, in fact thoroughly upset him. As a result he was very fretful by the middle of the afternoon. He freely admitted that afterwards; feeling, indeed, always rather proud of being easily irritated. Mrs Conyers and my mother, come to the end of their gossip, had begun to discuss knitting techniques. Conversation between the two men must have dragged, because the General returned to Near Eastern affairs.

'We haven't heard the last of Enver and his Young Turks,' he said.

'Not by a long chalk,' agreed my father.

'You remember Skobeloff's dictum?'

'Quite so, General, quite so.'

My father rarely, if ever, admitted to ignorance. He could, in any case, be pretty certain of the calibre of any such quotation offered in the circumstances. However, the General was determined there should be no misunderstanding.

'The road to Constantinople leads through the Brandenburger Tor.'

My father had visited Munich, never Berlin. He was, therefore, possibly unaware of the precise locality of the monument to which Skobeloff referred. However, he could obviously grasp the gist of such an assertion in the mouth of one he rightly judged to be a Russian general, linking the aphorism immediately in his own mind with the recent Turkish request for a German officer of high rank to reorganise the Ottoman forces.

'If Liman von Sanders——' began my father.

He never finished the sentence. The name of that militarily celebrated, endlessly discussed, internationally disputed, Britannically unacceptable, German General-Inspector of the Turkish Army was caught, held, crystallised in mid-air. Just as the words left my father's lips, the door of the drawing-room opened quietly. Billson stood on the threshold for a split second. Then she entered the room. She was naked.

'It's always easy to be wise after the event.' My mother used invariably to repeat that saying when the incident was related—and it was to be related pretty often in years to come—implying thereby criticism of herself. Her way was habitually to accept responsibilities which she considered by their nature to be her own, her firm belief being that most difficulties in life could be negotiated by tactful handling. In this case, she ever afterwards regarded herself to blame in having failed to notice earlier that morning that things were far from well with Billson. My mother had, it was true, suspected during luncheon that something was amiss, but by then such suspicion was too late. Billson's waiting at table that day had been perceptibly below—a mere parody of—her accustomed standard. Indeed, her shortcomings in that field had even threatened to mar the good impression otherwise produced on the guests by Albert's cooking. Not only had she proffered vegetables to the General in a manner so entirely lacking in style that he had let fall a potato on the carpet, but she had also caused Mrs Conyers to 'jump' painfully—no doubt in unconscious memory of her father's hoaxes—by dropping a large silver ladle on a Sheffield plate dish-cover. Later, when she brought in the coffee, Billson 'banged down' the tray as if it were red-hot, 'scuttling' from the room.

'I made up my mind to speak to her afterwards about it,' my mother said. 'I thought she wasn't looking at all well. I knew she was a great *malade imaginaire*, but after all, she had seen the ghost, and her nerves are not at all good. It really is not fair on servants to expect them to sleep in a haunted room, although I have to myself. Where else could we put her? She can't be more frightened than I am sometimes. Then Aylmer Conyers stared at her so dreadfully with those very bright blue eyes of his. I was not at all surprised that she was nervous. I was terrified myself that he was going to begin asking her about the ghost, especially after she had made him drop the potatoes on the floor.'

In short, Billson's maladroitness had been judged to be no more than a kind of minor derangement to be expected from her for at least twenty-four hours after her 'experience', although, as I have said, listening in the first instance to the story about the 'ghost', my mother had been pleased, surprised even, by the calm with which Billson had spoken of the apparition.

'I really thought familiarity was breeding contempt,' said my mother. 'I certainly hoped so, with parlourmaids so terribly hard to come by.'

Albert's announcement of impending marriage was scarcely taken into account. Probably Billson's passion for him had never been accepted very seriously—as, indeed, few passions are by those not personally suffering from them. Possibly I myself knew more of it, from hints dropped by Edith, than did my mother. On top of everything, the prospective arrival of Uncle Giles had distracted attention from whatever else was happening in the house. However, even if the extent of Billson's distress at Albert's decision to marry had been adequately gauged—added, as it were morally speaking, to the probable effect of seeing a ghost that morning—no one could have foreseen so complete, so deplorable, a breakdown.

'I thought it was the end of the world,' my mother said.

I do not know to what extent she intended this phrase, so far as her own amazement was concerned, to be taken literally. My mother's transcendental beliefs were direct, yet imaginative, practical, though possessing the simplicity of complete acceptance. She may have meant to imply, no more, no less, that for a second of time she herself truly believed the Last Trump (unheard in the drawing-room) had sounded in the kitchen, instantly metamorphosing Billson into one of those figures—risen from the tomb, given up by the sea, swept in from the ends of the earth— depicted in primitive paintings of the Day of Judgment. If, indeed, my mother thought that, she must also have supposed some awful, cataclysmic division from on High just to have taken place, violently separating Sheep from Goats, depriving Billson of her raiment. No doubt my mother used only a figure of speech, but circumstances gave a certain aptness to the metaphor.

'Joking apart,' my mother used to say, 'it was a dreadful moment.'

There can be no doubt whatever that the scene was disturbing, terrifying, saddening, a moment that summarised, in the unclothed figure of Billson, human lack of co-ordination and abandonment of self-control in the face of emotional misery. Was she determined, in the habit of neurotics, to try to make things as bad for others as for herself? In that, she largely succeeded. There seemed no solution for the people in the room, no way out of the problem so violently posed by Billson in the shape of her own nude person. My father always confessed afterwards that he himself had been utterly at a loss. He could throw no light whatever on the reason why such a thing should suddenly have happened in his drawing-room, see no way of cutting short this unspeakable crisis. In telling—and re-telling—the highlights of the story, he contributed only one notable phrase.

'She was stark,' he used to say, '*absolutely stark*.'

This was a relatively small descriptive ornament to the really vast saga that accumulated round the incident; at the same time, it was for some reason not without a certain narrative force.

'I've come to give notice, m'm,' Billson said. 'I don't want to stay if Albert is leaving your service, and besides, m'm, I can't stand the ghosts no longer.'

Stonehurst, as I have said, was a 'furnished' house, the furniture, together with pictures, carpets, curtains, all distinctly on the seedy side, all part of the former home of people not much interested in what the rooms they lived in looked like. However, India, one way and another, provided a recurrent theme that gave a certain cohesion to an otherwise undistinguished, even anarchic style of decoration. In the hall, the brass gong was suspended from the horn or tusk of some animal; in the dining-room hung water-colours of the Ganges at Benares, the Old Fort at Calcutta, the Taj Mahal; in the smoking-room, a small revolving bookcase contained only four books: Marie Corelli's *Sorrows of Satan*, St John Clarke's *Never to the Philistines*, an illustrated volume of light verse called *Lays of Ind*, a volume of coloured pictures of Sepoy uniforms; in the drawing-room, the piano was covered with a Kashmir shawl of some size and fine texture, upon which, in silver frames, photographs of the former owner of Stonehurst (wearing a pith helmet surmounted with a spike) and his family (flanked by Indian servants) had stood before being stowed away in a drawer.

In human life, the individual ultimately dominates every situation, however disordered, sometimes for better, sometimes for worse. On this occasion, as usual, all was not lost. There was a place for action, a display of will. General Conyers took in the situation at a glance. He saw this to be no time to dilate further upon Turkish subjection to German intrigue. He rose—so the story went—quite slowly from his chair, made two steps across the room, picked up the Kashmir shawl from where it lay across the surface of the piano. Then, suddenly changing his tempo and turning quickly towards Billson, he wrapped the shawl protectively round her.

'Where is her room?' he quietly asked.

No one afterwards was ever very well able to describe how he transported her along the passage, partly leading, partly carrying, the shawl always decently draped round Billson like a robe. The point, I repeat, was that action had been taken, will-power brought into play. The spell cast by Billson's nakedness was broken. Life was normal again. Other people crowded round, eventually took charge. Mrs Gullick and Mercy appeared from somewhere. The doctor was summoned. It was probably just as well that Albert was having a nap in his room over at the stables, where Bracey, too, surrounded by saddlery, was prolonging his 'funny day'. By the time these two reappeared, the crisis was long at an end. Having taken the first, the essential step, General Conyers, like a military dictator, who, at the close of a successful *coup d'état*, freely transfers his power to the civil authority, now moved voluntarily into the background. His mission was over, the situation mastered. He could return to private life, no more than the guest who happened to have been fortunate enough to find the opportunity of doing his host and hostess a trifling good turn. That was the line the General took about himself when all was over. He would accept neither praise nor thanks.

'She made no trouble at all,' he said. 'More or less walked beside me—just as if we were going to sit out the next one in the conservatory.'

In fact he dismissed as laughable the notion that any difficulty at all attached to the management of Billson in her 'state'. To what extent this modest assessment of his own agency truly represented his experience at the time is hard to estimate. He may have merely preferred to speak of it in that careless manner from dandyism, an unwillingness to admit that anything is difficult. I have sometimes speculated as to how much the General's so successful dislodgement of Billson was due to an accustomed habit of command over 'personnel', how much to a natural aptitude for handling 'women'. He was, after all, known to possess some little dexterity in the latter sphere before marriage circumscribed him.

'Aylmer Conyers couldn't keep away from the women as a young man,' Uncle Giles once remarked. 'They say some fellow chaffed him about it at a big viceregal bun-fight at Delhi—Henry Wilson or another of those talkative beggars who later became generals—"Aylmer, my boy," this fellow, whoever he was, said, "you're digging your grave in bed with Mrs Roxborough-Brown and the rest of them," he said. Conyers didn't give a dam. Not a dam. Went on just the same.'

Whether or not General Conyers would have done well to have heeded that warning, there can be little doubt that some touch of magic in his hand provided Billson with a particle of what she sought, a small substitute for Albert's love, making her docile when led to her room, calming her later into sleep. Certainly he had shown complete disregard for the risk of making a fool of himself in public. That is a merit women are perhaps quicker to appreciate than men. Not that Billson herself can be supposed to have sat in judgment on such subtleties at that uncomfortable moment; yet even Billson's disturbed spirit must have been in some manner aware of a compelling force that bound her to submit without protest to its arbitration.

'I'll just smoke another cigarette, if I may,' said the General, when everything had been accomplished, 'then Bertha and I really must set off in our motor-car. I've got to think about getting down that hill.'

Edith and I returned from the 'walk' just at the moment when General and Mrs Conyers were leaving. Their car had paused at the gate. My parents had come to the end of the drive to see the guests safely down the hill, my father full of advice about gears and brakes. Naturally enough, there was still a certain air of disturbance about the whole party. Even the General looked flushed. When Edith and I appeared, nothing of course was said, there and then, about what had taken place, but I could tell from my mother's face that something very out of the way had happened. The rather forced laughter, the apologies to be heard, confirmed that. The events of the day were by no means at an end, however. My father opened the gate. The Conyers car began to move slowly forward. As it entered the road over a hump in the ground, making rather a jerk, an unexpected impediment was suddenly put in the General's way. This was caused by a group of persons, unusually dressed, who were approaching from the left. They were running towards us. It was Dr Trelawney, followed by a pack of his disciples. They must suddenly have appeared over the brow of the hill. Without pausing to get breath they were now advancing up the road at a sharp pace, Dr Trelawney as usual leading. General Conyers, accelerating through the Stonehurst gate—an awkward one to negotiate—wheeled left, taking the corner in a wide arc, possibly owing to imperfect control of the steering. He had to apply his brakes sharply to avoid collision. Dr Trelawney leapt nimbly aside. He was not hit. The car came to a standstill in the middle of the road. General Conyers opened the door and jumped out with all his habitual energy of movement. At first it might have been thought that he intended to call Dr Trelawney to order for obstructing the highway in this manner, strike him, kill him even, like a dog. Some tremendous altercation seemed about to take place. In due course, violence was shown to be far from the General's intention, although for a second or two, while he and Dr Trelawney stood facing each other, anything appeared possible. The same vivid contrast might have been expected, graphically speaking, as when the Military Policeman had ridden through Dr Trelawney's flock, like a hornet flying slowly through a swarm of moths. On the contrary, this pair, so far from being brought into vivid physical and moral opposition, had the air of being linked together quite strongly by some element possessed in common. The General's long, light ulster and helmet-like deerstalker, Dr Trelawney's white draperies and sandals, equally suggested temple ceremonial. The two of them might have met on that high place deliberately for public celebration of some rite or sacrifice. At first neither said a word. That seemed an age. At last Dr Trelawney took the initiative. Raising his right arm slightly, he spoke in a low clear voice, almost in the accents of one whose very perfect enunciation indicates that English is not his native tongue.

'The Essence of the All is the Godhead of the True.'

Then a very surprising thing happened. General Conyers gave an almost imperceptible nod, at the same time removing his hands from the pockets of his ulster.

'The Vision of Visions,' he said, 'heals the Blindness of Sight.'

By that time most of Dr Trelawney's disciples had caught up with their master. They now clustered in the background, whispering together and staring at the car. Through its windscreen, Mrs Conyers gazed back at them a little nervously, perhaps again fearing that some elaborate practical joke was being staged for her benefit. From the gate my parents watched the scene without approval.

'Well, Trelawney,' said the General, 'I heard you had come to live in this part of the world, but I never thought we should have the luck to run across each other in this way.'

'If you journey towards the Great Gate, you encounter

the same wayfarers on the road.'

'True enough, Trelawney, true enough.'

'You are approaching the Sublime Threshold.'

'Do you think so?'

'You should make good your promise to spend a rhythmical month under instruction, General. We have a vacancy in the house. There is no time like the present. You should be subjected to none but probationary exercises at first. Disciplines of the Adept would not be expected of you in the early days.'

'Look here, Trelawney,' said General Conyers, 'I'm a busy man at the moment. Besides, I have a strong conviction I should not commit myself too deeply for the rest of the year. Just one of those feelings you have in your bones. I want to be absolutely mobile at the moment.'

'Such instincts should be obeyed. I have heard others say the same recently. The portents are unfavourable. There is no doubt of that.'

'I will write to you one of these days. Nothing I'd like to see more than you and your people at work.'

'At Play, General. Truth is Play.'

'Give me a change of routine. Sort of thing I'm always meaning to do. Got very interested in such things in India. *Bodhisattvas* and such like, *Mahasatipatthana* and all that reflection. However, we shall have to wait. Sure I'm right to wait. Too much business on hand, anyway.'

'Business?' said Dr Trelawney. 'I think you need meditation, General, more than business. You must free the mind from external influences. You must pursue Oneness—the Larger Life.'

'Sure you're right about that too,' said the General. 'Absolutely certain you are right. All the same, something tells me to let Oneness wait for the time being. That doesn't mean I am not going to think Oneness over. Not in the least.'

'Think it over, you must, General. We know we are right. But first you must gain Spiritual Mastery of the Body.'

How long this unusual conversation would have continued in front of the Stonehurst gate, if interruption had not taken place, is hard to say. It was brought to a close by a new arrival, wearing a straw hat and flannel suit, who pushed his way unceremoniously between a group of long-haired boys in short Grecian tunics, who were eyeing the car as if they would very much like to open the bonnet. This person had a small fair moustache. He carried a rolled umbrella and Gladstone bag. The strangeness of Dr Trelawney's disciples clearly made no impression on him. He looked neither to the right nor to the left. The beings round him might just as well have been a herd of cows come to a stop in their amblings along the road. Instead of regarding them, he made straight for my parents, who at once offered signs of recognition. Here was Uncle Giles.

'Hope you did not mind my inviting myself at such short notice,' he said, as soon as he had greeted my mother. 'I wanted to have a word with *him* about the Trust.'

'You know we are always delighted to see you, Giles,' she said, probably even believing that true at the moment of speaking, because she always felt warmly towards hopeless characters like Uncle Giles when they were in difficulties. 'We live so far away from everything and everybody nowadays that it is quite an exception for you to have found Aylmer and Bertha Conyers lunching with us. They were driving away in their motor when——'

She pointed to the road, unable to put into words what was taking place.

'I see Aylmer standing there,' said Uncle Giles, who still found nothing at all unusual in the presence or costume of the Trelawney community. 'I must have a word with him before he leaves. Got a bit of news that might interest him.

He is always very keen on what is happening on the Continent. Interest you, too, I expect. I had quite a good journey here. Was lucky enough to catch the carrier. Took me almost to the foot of the hill. Bit of a climb, but here I am.'

He turned to my father.

'How are you?'

Uncle Giles spoke as if he were surprised not to find my father in hospital, indeed, in his coffin.

'Pretty well, Giles,' said my father, with a certain rasp in his voice, 'pretty well. How has the world been wagging with you, Giles?'

That was a phrase my father tended to use when he was not best pleased; in any case his tone graded low as a welcoming manner.

'I wanted to have a talk about business matters,' said Uncle Giles, not at all put out by this reception. 'Mexican Eagles, among other things. Also the Limpopo Development Scheme. There has been rather a crisis in my own affairs. I'd like to ask your opinion. I value it. By the way, did I mention I heard a serious piece of news in Aldershot?'

'What on earth were you doing in Aldershot?' asked my father, speaking without alleviating the irony of his tone.

He must have seen that he was in for a bad time with his brother.

'Had to meet a fellow there. Soldiered together years ago. Knowledgeable chap. I'll just go across now and have a brief word with Aylmer Conyers.'

Uncle Giles had set down his Gladstone bag by the gate. With characteristic inability to carry through any plan of campaign, he was deflected from reaching the General by the sight of Mrs Conyers sitting in the car. She still looked rather nervous. Uncle Giles stopped and began talking to her. By this time General Conyers himself must have noticed Uncle Giles's arrival. He brought to an end his conversation with Dr Trelawney.

'Well, Trelawney,' he said, 'I mustn't keep you any longer. You will be wanting to lead your people on. Mustn't take up all your day.'

'On the contrary, General, the day—with its antithesis, night—is but an artificial apportionment of what we artlessly call Time.'

'Nevertheless, Trelawney, Time has value, even if artificially apportioned.'

'Then I shall expect to hear from you, General, when you wish to free yourself from bonds of Time and Space.'

'You will, Trelawney, you will. Off you go now—at the double.'

Dr Trelawney drew himself up.

'The Essence of the All is the Godhead of the True.'

The General replied with a jerk of his head.

'The Vision of Visions heals the Blindness of Sight.'

The words were scarcely finished before Dr Trelawney had again begun to hasten along the road, his flock trailing after him. A moment or two later, they were among the trees that concealed Gullick's cottage, where the road became a track. Then the last of them, a very small, pathetic child with a huge head, was finally lost to sight. No doubt they had reached the Common, were pursuing Oneness through the heather. Oneness perhaps also engaged the attention of General Conyers himself, because, deep in thought, he turned towards the car. He stood there for a second or two, staring at the bonnet. Uncle Giles terminated his conversation with Mrs Conyers.

'I was admiring your new motor-car, General,' he said. 'Hope it is not bringing you as much trouble as most of them seem to cause their owners.'

Now that Dr Trelawney was out of the way, my parents moved towards the car themselves, perhaps partly to keep an eye on Uncle Giles in his relations with the General, still lost in reflection.

'Thought I'd better not introduce you,' said General Conyers, straightening himself as they came up to him. 'One never knows how people may feel about a fellow like Trelawney—especially if he lives in the neighbourhood. Not everybody cares for him. You hear some funny stories. I find him interesting myself. Nasty habits, some people say. Can't believe a word he says, of course. We met him years ago with a fellow I used to know in the Buffs who'd taken up yoga.'

The General lifted the starting-handle from the floor of the car.

'Are you an expert in these machines, Giles?' he asked.

He used the tone of one speaking to a child, not at all the manner of an equal in which he had addressed me earlier in the day. Knowing all about Uncle Giles, he was clearly determined not to allow himself to be irritated by him.

'Never driven one in my life,' said Uncle Giles. 'Not too keen on 'em. Always in accidents. Some royalty in a motor-car have been involved in a nasty affair today. Heard the news in Aldershot. Fellow I went to see was told on the telephone. Amazing, isn't it, hearing so soon. They've just assassinated an Austrian archduke down in Bosnia. Did it today. Only happened a few hours ago.'

Uncle Giles muttered, almost whispered these facts, speaking as if he were talking to himself, not at all in the voice of a man announcing to the world in general the close of an epoch; the outbreak of Armageddon; the birth of a new, uneasy age. He did not look in the least like the harbinger of the Furies.

'Franz-Ferdinand?' asked General Conyers sharply.

'And his morganatic wife. Shot 'em both.'

'When did you say this happened?'

'This afternoon.'

'And they're both dead?'

72

'Both of them.'

'There will be trouble about this,' said the General.

He inserted the starting-handle and gave several terrific turns.

'Bad trouble,' he said. 'They'll have to postpone tomorrow night's State Ball. Not a doubt of it. This was a Servian, I suppose.'

'They think so.'

'Was he an anarchist?' asked Mrs Conyers.

'One of those fellows,' said Uncle Giles.

'Mark my words,' said General Conyers, 'this is a disaster. Well, the engine has started. We'd better be off in case it stops again. Good-bye to you both, thank you again enormously. No, no, not another word. I only hope the whole matter settles down all right. Good-bye, Giles. Good-bye, Nicholas. I don't at all like the news.'

They went off down the hill. We all waved. My mother looked worried.

'I don't like the news either,' she said.

'Let me carry your bag, Giles,' said my father. 'You'll find things in a bit of a muddle in the house. One of the maids had an hysterical attack this afternoon.'

'I don't expect it's too easy to get staff up here,' said Uncle Giles. 'Is Bracey still your servant? Albert still cooking for you? You're lucky to have them both. Hope I see something of them. Very difficult to get yourself properly looked after these days. Several things I want to talk about. Rather an awkward situation. I think you may be able to help.'

The whole party was moving towards the house. Edith, who had been standing in the background, now detached me from the grown-ups. We diverged to the nursery. I suppose my father, in the course of the evening, helped to sort out the awkward situation, because Uncle Giles left the following day. No one yet realised that the Mute with the

Bowstring stood at the threshold of the door, that, if they wanted to get anything done in time of peace, they must be quick about it. Already, the sands had almost run out. The doctor, for example, ordered a 'complete holiday' for Billson. Inquiries revealed that she had gone to rest in her room that afternoon, where, contemplating her trouble, she had fallen asleep to awaken later in a 'state', greatly disturbed, but about which she could otherwise remember little or nothing. No doubt one of those nervous shifts of control had taken place within herself, later to be closely studied, then generally regarded as a sudden display of 'dottiness'. It was, of course, agreed that she must go. Billson herself was insistent on that point. That decision on both sides was to be expected. Although the story passed immediately into legend, surprisingly little fuss was made about it at the time. A few days later—while the chancelleries of Europe entered into a ferment of activity— Billson, escorted by Edith, quietly travelled to Suffolk, where her family could take care of her for a time. Left alone with my mother during Edith's absence from home on that occasion, I first heard a fairly full and reliable account of the story, fragments of which had, of course, already reached me in more or less garbled versions, from other sources. A long time passed before all the refinements of the saga were recorded and classified.

I do not know for certain what happened to Billson. Even my mother, with all her instinct for not losing touch with the unfortunate, lost sight of her during the war. More than thirty years later, however, what may have been a clue took shape. When Rosie Manasch—or Rosie Udall, as she had then become—used to hold a kind of salon in her house in Regent's Park, she often told stories of a 'daily' she had employed during or just after the war, a former parlour-maid of the old-fashioned kind, who liked to talk about the people for whom she had worked. By then she was called

'Doreen', and said she was nearly seventy.

'She looked years younger,' Rosie said, 'perhaps in her fifties. A man behaved badly to her. I could never make out if he was a butler or a chef. She also had some rather good ghost-stories when she was on form.'

It was all too complicated to explain to Rosie, but this legendary lost love might well have been Albert incorporated—in the way myths are formed—with Billson's earlier 'disappointment'. Albert himself, as might be expected, was greatly outraged by Billson's behaviour that Sunday afternoon, even though he himself had suffered no inconvenience from the immediate circumstances of her 'breakdown'.

'I told you that girl would go off her crumpet,' he said more than once afterwards.

No doubt a series of 'funny days' would normally have been induced in Bracey, but, as things turned out, neither he nor Albert had much time to brood over Billson's surprising conduct. International events took their swift, their ominous, course, Bracey, characteristically, being swept into a world of action, Albert, firm as ever in his fight for the quiet life, merely changing the locality of his cooking-pots. To my mother, Mrs Conyers wrote:

'. . . I was *so glad* Aylmer did not make you meet that *very rum* friend of his with the beard. He would have been quite capable of introducing you! I do not encourage him to see *too much* of that person. I think between you and me there is something *very odd* about the man. I would rather you did not mention to anyone—unless you know them *very well*—that Aylmer sometimes talks of staying with *him*. Nothing would induce *me* to go! I do not think that Aylmer will ever pay the visit because he feels sure the house will be *very uncomfortable*. No bathroom; What a *dreadful* thing this murder in Austria-Hungary is. Aylmer is very much afraid it may lead to war. . . .'

General Conyers was right. Not many weeks later—by

that time my father and Bracey had been shipped to France with the Expeditionary Force—squads of recruits began to appear on the Common, their evolutions in the heather performed in scarlet or dark blue, for in those early days of the war there were not enough khaki uniforms to go round. Some wore their own cloth caps over full-dress tunics or marched along in column of fours dressed in subfusc civilian suits, so that once more the colour values of the heath were transformed. These exercises of 'Kitchener's Army' greatly perturbed Albert, although his 'feet' precluded any serious suggestion of military service. He used to discuss with Gullick, the gardener, the advisability of offering himself, 'feet' or no 'feet,' in the service of his country.

'If you don't volunteer, they'll come and take you,' he would say, 'they're going to put the blokes who haven't volunteered at the head of the column and march 'em along in their shame without any buttons to their uniforms—just to show they had to be forced to join.'

Gullick, silent, elderly, wizened, himself too old to be called to the colours except in the direst need, nodded grimly, showing no disposition to dissent from the menacing possibilities put forward.

'And I'll soon be a married man too,' said Albert, groaning aloud.

However, like my father, Uncle Giles and General Conyers, Albert survived the war. He spent melancholy years cooking in some large canteen, where there was no alternative to producing food at a level painful to his own standards. When peace came at last, he felt, perhaps justly, that he had suffered as much as many who had performed, at least outwardly, more onerous acts of service and sacrifice. He used to write to my mother every Christmas. The dreaded marriage turned out—as Albert himself put it—'no worse than most'. It appeared, indeed, better than many.

Others were less fortunate. Bracey's 'funny days' came to an end when he was killed in the retreat—or as we should now say, the withdrawal—from Mons. The Fenwicks' father was killed; Mary Barber's father was killed; Richard Vaughan's father was killed; the Westmacott twins' father was killed. Was the Military Policeman who used to jog across the heather killed? Perhaps his duties kept him away from the line. Did the soldier who chopped off his trigger-finger save his own life by doing so? It is an interesting question. Dr Trelawney gave up his house. Edith was told by Mrs Gullick that she had heard as a fact that he had been shot as a spy at the Tower of London. We left Stonehurst and its 'ghosts', inexplicably mysterious bungalow, presaging other inexplicable mysteries of life and death. I never heard whether subsequent occupants were troubled, as Billson and others had been troubled, by tall white spectres, uncomfortable invisible presences. Childhood was brought suddenly, even rather brutally, to a close. Albert's shutters may have kept out the suffragettes: they did not effectively exclude the Furies.

It is odd to think that only fourteen or fifteen years after leaving Stonehurst, essentially a haunt of childhood, I should have been sitting with Moreland in the Hay Loft, essentially, a haunt of maturity: odd, in that such an appalling volume of unavoidable experience had to be packed into the intervening period before that historical necessity could be enacted. Perhaps maturity is not quite the word; anyway, childhood had been left behind. It was early one Sunday morning in the days when Moreland and I first knew each other. We were discussing the roots and aims of action. The Hay Loft—now no more—was an establishment off the Tottenham Court Road, where those kept up late by business or pleasure could enjoy rather especially good bacon-and-eggs at any hour of the night. Rarely full at night-time, the place remained closed, I think, during the day. Certainly I never heard of anyone's eating there except in the small hours. The waiter, white-haired and magisterial, a stage butler more convincing than any to be found in private service, would serve the bacon-and-eggs with a flourish to sulky prostitutes, who, nocturnal liabilities at an end, infiltrated the supper-room towards dawn. Moreland and I had come from some party in the neighbourhood, displeasing, yet for some reason hard to vacate earlier. Moreland had been talking incessantly—by then a trifle incoherently—on the theme that action, stemming from sluggish, invisible sources, moves towards destinations no less indefinable.

'If action is to be one's aim,' he was saying, 'then is it

action to write a symphony satisfactory to oneself, which no one else wants to perform, or a comic song every errand-boy whistles? A bad example—a comic song, obviously. Nothing I should like to do better, if I had the talent. Say some ghastly, pretentious half-baked imitation of Stravinsky that makes a hit and is hailed as genius. We know it's bad art. That is not the point. Is it action? Or *is* that the point? Is art action, an alternative to action, the enemy of action, or nothing whatever to do with action? I have no objection to action. I merely find it impossible to locate.'

'Ask the Surrealists. They are keen on action. Their magazine had a photograph on the cover the other day with the caption: *One of our contributors insulting a priest.*'

'Exactly,' said Moreland. 'Violence—revolt—sweep away the past. Abandon bourgeois values. Don't be a prisoner of outworn dogmas. I'm told on all sides that's how one should behave, that I must live intensely. Besides, the abominable question of musical interpretation eternally bedevils a composer's life. What could make one brood on action more than a lot of other people taking over when it comes to performance, giving the rendering of the work least sympathetic to yourself?'

'You might say that happens in love, too, when the other person takes charge of the performance in a manner unsympathetic to yourself.'

'All right,' said Moreland, 'love, then. Is it better to love somebody and not have them, or have somebody and not love them? I mean from the point of view of action—living intensely. Does action consist in having or loving? In having—naturally—it might first appear. Loving is just emotion, not action at all. But is that correct? I'm not sure.'

'It is a question Barnby would consider absurd.'

'Nevertheless, I put it to you. Can the mere haver be said to live more intensely than the least successful lover? That is, if action *is* to live with intensity. Or is action only when

79

you bring off both—loving and having—leaving your money on, so to speak, like a double-event in racing. Speaking for myself, I get the worst of all worlds, failing to have the people I love, wasting time over the others, whom I equally fail to have.'

'You should commit a *crime passionnel* to liven things up.'

'When I read about *crimes passionnels* in the papers,' said Moreland, scraping his plate from which the last vestige of egg had already been long removed, 'I am struck not by the richness of the emotions, but by their desperate poverty. On the surface, the people concerned may seem to live with intensity. Underneath, is an abject egotism and lack of imagination.'

'Stendhal did not think so. He said he would rather his wife tried to stab him twice a year than greeted him every evening with a sour face.'

'Still, he remained unmarried. I've no doubt my own wife will do both. Beside, Stendhal was equally keen on the glance, the kiss, the squeeze of the hand. He was not really taken in by the tyranny of action.'

'But surely some *crimes passionnels* are fascinating. Suppose one of his girls murdered Sir Magnus Donners in fantastic circumstances—I leave the setting to your own fevered imagination.'

'Now, Sir Magnus Donners,' said Moreland. 'Is he a man of action? In the eyes of the world, certainly. But does he, in fact, live intensely?'

'Like Stendhal, he has never married.'

'Hardly a *sine qua non* of action,' said Moreland, now rubbing the plate with a lump of bread.

'But a testing experience, surely. The baronet's wife's subsequent married life with the gamekeeper opens up more interesting possibilities than any of their adulterous frolics.'

'D. H. Lawrence's ideas about sexual stimulation,' said

Moreland, 'strike me as no less unreal—no less artificial, if you prefer—than any attributed to Sir Magnus Donners. Suburban, narcissistic daydreams, a phallic never-never-land for middle-aged women. However, that is beside the point, which is that I grant, within the sphere of marriage and family life, Sir Magnus has not lived intensely. Setting marriage aside, on the other hand, he has built up a huge fortune, risen to all but the highest peaks in politics, appreciates the arts in a coarse but perfectly genuine manner, always has a succession of pretty girls in tow. Is he to be styled no man of action because he has never married? The proposition is absurd. After all, we are not married ourselves.'

'And, what's more, must cease to live intensely. It's nearly three o'clock.'

'So it is. How time flies.'

'Raining, too.'

'And the buses have stopped.'

'We will return to action on another occasion.'

'Certainly, we will.'

The interest of this conversation, characteristic of Moreland in a discursive mood, lay, of course, in the fact that he subsequently married Matilda Wilson, one of Sir Magnus's 'girls'. The modest account he gave during this discussion at the Hay Loft of his own exploits at that period probably did Moreland less than justice. He was not unattractive to women. At the same time, his own romantic approach to emotional relationships had already caused him to take some hard knocks in that very knockabout sphere. At the moment when we were eating bacon-and-eggs, neither Moreland nor I had yet heard of Matilda. In those days, I think, she had not even come the way of Sir Magnus himself. In fact, that was about the stage in her life when she was married to Carola, the violinist, a marriage undertaken when she was very young, lasting only about eighteen months. However, 'the great industrialist'—as Barnby used to call Sir Magnus—was already by then one of Moreland's patrons, having commissioned him not long before to write the incidental music for a highbrow film which had Donners backing. Barnby, too, was beginning to sell his pictures to Sir Magnus at about that date. Barnby often talked about 'the great industrialist', who was, therefore, a familiar figure to me—at least in song and story—although I had myself only seen Sir Magnus twice: once at a party of Mrs Andriadis, which I had attended quite fortuitously; a second time, spending a week-end with the Walpole-Wilsons, when I had been taken over to Stourwater. Later on, one heard gossip about a *jolie laide* (in contrast with the 'pretty girls' Moreland had adumbrated at the Hay Loft) with whom Sir Magnus used occasionally to appear. She was called Matilda Wilson, said to be an actress. Sir Magnus and Matilda had parted company—at least were no longer seen together in public—by the time Moreland first met her. Afterwards, when Matilda became Moreland's wife, I used sometimes to wonder whether Moreland himself ever recalled that Hay Loft conversation. If so, rather naturally, he never returned to the subject.

I think it would be true to say of Moreland that, up to a point, he did live with intensity. He worked hard at seasons, at others, concentrated whole-heartedly on amusing himself. This was within the limitations of the diffidence that enclosed him in dealings with women. There could be no doubt that Matilda herself had taken the decision that they should marry. Barnby used to say that women always take that decision. In any case, Matilda liked taking decisions. This taste of hers suited them both at the beginning of their married life, because Moreland was wholly without it, except where his own work was concerned.

'The arts derive entirely from taking decisions,' he used

to say. 'That is why they make such unspeakably burden-some demands on all who practise them. Having taken the decision music requires, I want to be free of all others.'

Moreland's childhood—since I have spoken at some length of childhood—had been a very different affair from my own. In the first place, music, rather than military matters, had been regarded as the normal preoccupation of those round him in the house of his aunt who brought him up. I mean music was looked upon there not only as an art, but also as the familiar means of earning a livelihood. In my own home, the arts, to some very considerable extent respected, were not at all regarded in that essentially matter-of-fact, no-nonsense, down-to-earth manner. When my father was attached to a cavalry regiment at Brighton before we moved to Stonehurst, my parents might attend an occasional concert at the Pavilion; meet Mr Deacon there, afterwards visit his flat. They would even be aware that Mr Deacon was a 'bad' painter. At the same time, painting, 'good' or 'bad'—like music, sculpture, writing and, of course, acting—would immutably remain for them an unusual, not wholly desirable, profession for an acquaintance. Indeed, a 'good' painter, certainly a well-known 'modern' painter (even though 'modernism' in the arts was by no means frowned upon by my father), would be considered even more of a freak than Mr Deacon himself, since being 'well-known' was, by its very nature, something of a social aberration. It was in Mr Deacon's Brighton flat that he produced those huge pictures that might have been illustrations to Miss Orchard's lessons about the gods of Olympus. Mr Deacon, in the words of his great hero, Walt Whitman, used to describe them as 'the rhythmic myths of the Greeks, and the strong legends of the Romans'. The Furies were probably never represented by his brush, because Mr Deacon shunned what Dicky Umfraville used always to call 'the female form divine'.

In the household of Moreland's aunt, on the other hand, although there might be no money to spare—keeping solvent in itself rather a struggle—relatively celebrated persons flourished, so to speak, just round the corner. Moreland himself rather reluctantly agreed that some of the musicians who turned up there were 'quite famous', even if the writers and painters 'showed an abysmal lack of talent'. 'Modernism' in the arts, if not much practised, was freely discussed. Life was seedy; it was also conducted on a plane in general more grown-up, certainly more easygoing, than existence at Stonehurst; for that matter at any of the other ever changing residences I had known as a child. For Moreland, the war had been no more than a mysterious, disturbing inconvenience in the background, the disagreeable cause to which indifferent or inadequate food was always attributed. It was not the sudden conversion into action of an idea already to a great extent familiar—even though the stupendous explosion of that idea, rendered into action, had never wholly ceased to ring in one's ears. These were not the only dissimilarities of upbringing. From an early age, Moreland was looked upon by his aunt, and everyone else in their circle, as a boy destined to make a brilliant career in music. Even his childhood had been geared to that assumption. My own more modest ambition—not, as it happened, particularly encouraged by my parents—was to become a soldier. That obviously entailed a divergent manner of regarding oneself. In so far as we ever compared notes about our respective environments in early life, Moreland always maintained that mine sounded the stranger of the two.

'Ours was, after all, a very bourgeois bohemianism,' he used to say. 'Attending the Chelsea Arts Ball in absolutely historically correct Renaissance costume was regarded as the height of dissipation by most of the artists we knew. Your own surroundings were far more bizarre.'

Perhaps he was right. What Moreland and I possessed unexpectedly in common, however, was on the whole more remarkable than these obvious contrasts. With only a month or two between our ages, some accumulation of shared experience was natural enough: the dog following Edward VII's coffin, the Earls Court Exhibition, tents in Hyde Park for George V's coronation—those all found a place. There were, however, in addition to these public spectacles, certain unaccountable products of the *Zeitgeist* belonging to both childhoods, contributing some particle to each personal myth, so abundant in their way that Moreland and I sometimes seemed to have known each other long before meeting for the first time one evening in the saloon bar of the Mortimer.

For example, in the face of energetic protest at the time, neither, on grounds that the theme was too horrific for the eyes of young persons, had been allowed to attend that primitive of cinematographic art, the film version of Dante's *Inferno*. Later, less explicably, both had taken a passionate interest in the American Civil War and the Dreyfus Case, poring over pictures of those two very dissimilar historical events wherever their scenes and characters could be found illustrated. There were also aesthetic prejudices in common: animosity towards R. M. Ballantyne's *The Coral Island*, capricious distaste for framed reproductions of Raphael's *La Madonna della Sedia*.

One of these altogether unwarrantable items in this eccentric scrapbook of faded momentoes that Moreland and I seemed to have pasted up together in the nursery (though Moreland always denied having had a nursery, certainly a nurse) was a precocious awareness of Dr Trelawney, for 'the Doctor'—as Moreland liked to call him—had never, in fact, suffered the fate, attributed to him by Mrs Gullick, of being shot in the Tower. Moreland's Trelawney experiences had been acquired earlier than my own, though still young

85

enough to experience the same uneasy thrill, alarming, yet enjoyable, at the thought of his menacing shadow.

'I used to hear about Trelawney long before I saw him,' Moreland said. 'One of the down-at-heel poets we knew was a friend of his—indeed, the two of them were said to have enjoyed the favours of succubi together out on the Astral Plane. I first set eyes on him when we were living in rooms at Putney. The time is fixed in my mind because of a bit of trouble with the landlady. The fact was my aunt had bought tickets for a concert with money that ought to have gone in paying the rent. Trelawney was pointed out to me that afternoon in the Queen's Hall. He has musical interests, you know—I may add, of the most banal kind. I remember the wonderfully fraudulent look on his face as he sat listening to Strauss' *Death and Transfiguration*, dressed in a black cape, hair down to his shoulders, rather like photographs of Rasputin.'

'He must have changed his style since my day. Then he was a more outdoor type, with classical Greek overtones.'

'Trelawney was always changing his style—even his name, too, I believe, which is, of course, no more Trelawney than my own is. Nor does anyone know why he should be addressed as Doctor. What was more exciting, my aunt knew a girl who—to use her own phrase—fell into his clutches. She was said to be a promising pianist. That must have been before I went to the Royal College, because I remember being more impressed by the idea of a female pianist who was promising, than I should have been after emerging from that famous conservatoire.'

'What happened to the girl?'

'Rather dreadful. She cast herself from a Welsh mountain-top—Trelawney had a kind of temple at that time in a remote farmhouse in North Wales. There was quite a scandal. He was attacked in one of the Sunday papers. It passed off, as such attacks do.'

86

'What had he done to the girl?'

'Oh, the usual things, I suppose—no doubt less usual ones, too, since Trelawney is an unusual man. In any case, possibilities are so limited even for a thaumaturge. The point was her subsequent suicide. There was talk of nameless rites, drugs, disagreeable forms of discipline—the sort of thing that might rather appeal to Sir Magnus Donners.'

'Did you ever meet Trelawney yourself?'

'When I first knew Maclintick, who numbered among his acquaintances some of the most unlikely people, he offered to take me to see the Doctor, then living in Shepherd's Bush. In principle, Maclintick disapproved of persons like that, but he and Trelawney used to talk German philosophy together. They had been educated at the same German university—Bonn, I think—and it was a type of conversation hard to obtain elsewhere.'

'Did you go?'

'Somehow, I never found myself in the mood. I felt it might be embarrassing.

> *Oisive jeunesse*
> *A tout asservie*
> *Par délicatesse*
> *J'ai perdu ma vie.*

That was me in those days.'

'I shouldn't have thought much delicacy was required where Dr Trelawney was concerned.'

'My own occult interests are so sketchy. I've just thumbed over *Dogme et Rituel de la Haute Magie*. Never participated in a Black Mass in my life, or as much as received an invitation to a witches' Sabbath.'

'But I thought Dr Trelawney was more for the Simple Life, with a touch of yoga thrown in. I did not realise he was committed to all this sorcery.'

'After you knew him, he must have moved further to the Left—or would it be to the Right? Extremes of policy have such a tendency to merge.'

'Trelawney must be getting on in age now—Cagliostro in his latter days, though he has avoided incarceration up to date.'

'What will happen to people like him as the world plods on to standardisation? Will they cease to be born, or find jobs in other professions? I suppose there will always be a position for a man with first-class magical qualifications.'

That conversation, too, had taken place long before either of us was married. I recalled it, years later, reading in a weekly paper a letter from Dr Trelawney protesting that some reviewer (Mark Members, as a matter of fact) in noticing a recently published work on prophecy and sortilege in which the author approached the subject in the light of psychiatry and telepathy, had confused the sayings of Paracelsus and Nostradamus. This letter (provoking a lively reply from Members) was composed in Dr Trelawney's most florid manner. I wondered if Moreland would see it. It was a long time since we had met. When we first married, Moreland and Matilda, Isobel and I, used often to see one another. Now those dinners at Foppa's or the Strasbourg took place no longer. They seemed to form an historic period, distinct and definable, even though less remote in time, as the infinitely distant days when Moreland and I had loitered about Soho together.

To explain why you see less of a friend, though there has been no quarrel, no gradual feeling of coldness, is not always easy. In this case, the drawing apart seemed to date from the time when something had been 'on' between Moreland and Isobel's sister, Priscilla. During that period, with Moreland's own marriage in the balance, we had seen little or nothing of him, because the situation was inevitably an awkward one. Now, the Morelands seemed to have settled down again pretty well; Priscilla was married to Chips Lovell. However, married life must always be a little different after an upheaval of that kind. With the Morelands, certain changes were observable from the outside; within, no doubt even more radical adjustments had taken place. Now, as a matter of course, Matilda accepted such parts as she could obtain as an actress. She had made some success in the role of Zenocrate in Marlowe's *Tamburlaine the Great*. She was often away from home for weeks at a time. Moreland himself, moving inexorably into a world exclusively musical in its interests, spent increasing periods working in his room. That was at first the reason why we saw less of him than ever, even after the business with Priscilla had come to an end. By that time, as easily happens, the habit of regular meetings had already passed. We would sometimes talk on the telephone or run across each other casually. Then a further barrier was raised, when, to the surprise of his friends, Moreland announced that he had decided to leave London.

'I'm not going to settle in the country for ever,' he said, 'just retreat for a time from the telephone.'

Moreland, dependent for most of his social life on restaurants and bars, had never been a great hand at entertaining in his own house. Accordingly, after the move, contact ceased almost entirely. That was, in any case, a decidedly eerie period in which to be living. Unlike the Stonehurst epoch, when, whatever jocular references to a German invasion might be made by persons like Bracey, war had come for most people utterly without warning—like being pushed suddenly on a winter's day into a swirling whirlpool of ice-cold water by an acquaintance, unpredictable perhaps, but not actively homicidal—war was now materialising in slow motion. Like one of the Stonehurst 'ghosts' war towered by the bed when you awoke in the morning; unlike those more transient, more accommo-

dating spectres, its tall form, so far from dissolving immediately, remained, on the contrary, a looming, menacing
shape of ever greater height, ever thickening density. The
grey, flickering sequences of the screen showed with increased persistence close-ups of stocky demagogues, fuming,
gesticulating, stamping; oceans of raised forearms; steel-
helmeted men tramping in column; armoured vehicles
rumbling over the *pavé* of broad boulevards. Crisis was
unremitting, cataclysm not long to be delayed.

Such an atmosphere was not at all favourable to writing
novels, the activity which chiefly occupied my own thoughts,
one that may require from time to time some more or
less powerful outside stimulus in the life of a writer, but
needs, in between any such disturbances, long periods of
comparative calm. Besides, the ancillaries of a writer's profession, the odd jobs that make such an existence financially
surmountable, were at that period in by no means a
flourishing condition. I was myself in lowish water and,
what was worse, found it difficult, almost impossible, to
work on a book while waiting for the starting pistol. Even
Chips Lovell, who possessed relatively well-paid employment on a newspaper (contributing to a column of innocuous, almost self-respecting 'gossip'), lived, like others in
Fleet Street, in recurrent fear of being told his services were
redundant.

Since Chips had married Priscilla, he had shown signs of
turning into a model husband. Some people regarded him
as an incurably raffish young man, but now the interest he
had always taken in the affairs of his many relations became
redoubled, growing almost feverish in its intensity. He
attended marriages, christenings, funerals as if his life
depended on it, as, indeed, to some extent it did, since he
would usually introduce later into his column discreet reference to such ceremonies. The trifles Chips offered the public
were on the whole inoffensive enough, sometimes even of

general interest. All the same, not everyone approved of them: Isobel's eldest sister, Frederica Budd, who, since the recent death of the Tollands' stepmother, Lady Warminster, more than ever felt herself custodian of the family's moral and social standards, found Chips's 'paragraphs' particularly vexatious. In any case, Frederica did not much care for Chips, although she, and everyone else, had to admit that his marriage to Priscilla must be reckoned a success. The Lovells had a baby; Priscilla had become quieter, some complained a little sadder, but at the same time her looks had improved, so that now she could almost be called a 'beauty'. Since Moreland had long since removed himself almost entirely from the kind of society in which Chips Lovell liked to move—was to some extent even professionally committed—the two couples never met. Such a meeting would certainly not have embarrassed Chips, who neither minded nor was in a position to mind about such refinements of sensibility where love affairs were concerned. Moreland on the other hand, once things were broken off with Priscilla, certainly preferred to keep out of her and her husband's way.

Then one day, not long after 'Munich', when everyone's nerves were in a thoroughly disordered state, some relieved, some more apprehensive than ever, Isobel ran across Matilda in the hairdresser's. There was a great reunion. The end of it was that a week-end visit was arranged immediately to the Moreland's cottage. Life was humdrum enough at that moment, even though we were living in so unstable, so harassing a period. I mean the events that took place while we were staying with the Morelands formed not only something of a landmark when looked back upon, but were also rather different from the material of which daily life was in general composed.

'Matilda is dying for company,' Isobel said, when she told me of their meeting.

'How is she?'

'Not bad. Out of a job. She says she has decided she is a terrible actress. She is going to give up the stage and take to petit point.'

'Where exactly are they living?'

'A few miles from Stourwater.'

'I had no idea of that. Was it deliberate?'

'Matilda knows the district. She was brought up there. At first I was too delicate to ask how near they were to the castle. Then Matty said Sir Magnus had actually found the cottage for them. Matty rather likes talking of her days with Sir Magnus if one is *tête-à-tête*. They represent, I think, the most restful moment of her life.'

'Life with Hugh can't be very restful.'

'Hugh doesn't seem to mind about being near Stourwater. Matilda said he was delighted to find a cottage so easily.'

I was not sure that I agreed in believing Moreland so indifferent to the proximity of Sir Magnus Donners. It is true that men vary in attitude towards previous husbands and lovers of their wife or mistress. As it happened, that was a favourite theme of Moreland's. Some, at least outwardly, are to all appearance completely unconcerned with what experiences a woman may have had—and with whom—before they took her on; others never become reconciled to their forerunners. I remembered Moreland saying that Matilda's father had kept a chemist's shop in that part of the world. There was a story about her first having met Sir Magnus when she was organising a school play in the precincts of the castle. One side of Moreland was certainly squeamish about the matter of his wife's former connexion with Sir Magnus, the other, tolerant, sceptical, indolent about his own life—even his emotional life—welcomed any easy solution when it came to finding somewhere to live. The cottage might be in the shadow of Stourwater, or anywhere else. It was the characteristic split personality that the arts seem specially to require, even to augment in those who practise them. Matilda, of course, knew very well the easygoing, inactive side of her husband: her grasp of that side of his character was perhaps her chief power over him. She could judge to a hair's breadth just how much to make a convenience of having been Sir Magnus's mistress, while stopping short of seriously upsetting More-land's susceptibilities on that score. Such at least, were the terms in which I myself assessed the situation. That was the background I expected to find when we stayed at the cottage. I thought that half-humorous, half-masochistic shame on Moreland's part at thus allowing his wife to make use of a rich man who had formerly 'kept' her would express itself in banter, partly designed to punish himself for allowing such circumstances to arise.

As it happened, conversation had turned on Sir Magnus Donners a night or two before we were invited to the More-lands'. We were dining (at short notice, because a more 'political' couple had dropped out) with Isobel's sister, Susan, married to Roddy Cutts, a Tory back-bencher. Susan greatly enjoyed giving small political dinner-parties. Roddy, hardly drinking anything himself, saw no reason to encourage the habit in others, so that wine did not exactly flow. Current affairs, however, were unrestrainedly discussed. They inhabited a hideous little mansion flat in Westminster, equipped with a 'division bell' for giving warning when Roddy's vote was required in 'the House'. Said to be rather a 'coming man' in the Conservative Party, he was in some disgrace with its leaders at that moment, having thrown in his lot with Churchill, Eden and the group who had abstained from voting in the 'Munich' division. That evening another MP, Fettiplace-Jones, was present with his wife. Fettiplace-Jones, a sup-porter of the Government's policy, was at the same time too

wary to cut himself off entirely from dissident members of
the party. Like Roddy, his contemporary in age, he represented a northern constituency. Tall, handsome, moon-
faced, with a lock of hair trained across his high forehead for the caricaturist, he seemed to require only side-
whiskers and a high collar to complete the picture of a
distinguished politician of the nineteenth century. His un-
tiring professional geniality rivalled even Roddy's remorse-
less charm of manner. His wife, an eager little woman with
the features of the Red Queen in *Alice in Wonderland*—
possibly advised by her husband not to be controversial about
Czechoslovakia—spoke sagely of public health and housing.
Fettiplace-Jones himself seemed to be exploring avenues
of thought that suggested no basic disagreement between
himself and Roddy; in short, he himself acknowledged that
we must continue to prepare for the worst. When the men
were left alone, Fettiplace-Jones, rightly deciding no cigars
would be available, took one from his pocket and smelled it.

'The sole survivor,' he said apologetically, as he made an
incision. 'Were you in the House when Attlee said that
"armaments were not a policy"?'

'Bobetty was scathing,' said Roddy. 'By the same token, I
was talking to Duff about anti-aircraft shortages the other
night.'

'This continued opposition to conscription is going to do
Labour harm in the long run,' said Fettiplace-Jones, who
no doubt wanted to avoid anything like a head-on clash,
'even if things let up, as I hope they will.'

'I hope you're right,' said Roddy, who was being more
brusque than usual. 'All the same, you'll probably agree we
ought to tackle problems of civil evacuation and food
control.'

'Do you know Magnus Donners?'

'Never met him.'

'I remember being greatly impressed by him as a boy,'

said Fettiplace-Jones. 'I was taken to the House to hear a debate.'

He placed his hand on his forehead, grasping the errant lock, leaning back and smiling to himself, perhaps enjoyably contemplating the young Fettiplace-Jones's first sight of the scene of his own future triumphs.

'Not his delivery,' he said quietly. 'That was nothing. It was the mastery of detail. Now Donners is the sort of man to handle some of those administrative problems.'

'Not too old?'

'He knows the unions and gets on well with them.'

'What does he think about the Czechs?'

'Convinced nothing could be done short of war—at the same time not at all keen on the present situation. More of your view than mine.'

'Is he, indeed?' said Roddy. 'It looked at one moment as if Donners would go to the Lords.'

'I doubt if he ever wanted a peerage,' said Fettiplace-Jones. 'He has no children. My impression is that Donners is gearing his various concerns to the probability of war in spite of the settlement.'

'Is he?' said Roddy.

He had evidently no wish for argument with Fettiplace-Jones at that moment. The subject changed to the more general question of international guarantees.

I knew less of the political and industrial activities of Sir Magnus, than of his steady, if at times capricious, patronage of the arts. Like most rich patrons, his interests leant towards painting and music, rather than literature. Moreland described him as knowing the name of the book to be fashionably discussed at any given moment, being familiar with most of the standard authors. There Sir Magnus's literary appreciation stopped, according to Moreland. He took no pleasure in reading. No doubt that was a wise precaution for a man of action, whose imagination must be rigorously disciplined, if the will is to remain unsapped by daydreams, painting and music being, for some reason, less deleterious than writing in that respect. I listened to Roddy and Fettiplace-Jones talking about Sir Magnus, without supposing for a moment that I should meet him again in the near future. He existed in my mind as one of those figures, dominating, no doubt, in their own remote sphere, but slightly ridiculous when seen casually at close quarters.

We had no car, so reached the Morelands' by train.

'It must be generations since anyone but highbrows lived in this cottage,' said Moreland, when we arrived there. 'I imagine most of the agricultural labourers round here commute from London.'

'Baby Wentworth had it at one moment,' said Matilda, a little maliciously. 'She hated it and moved out almost at once.'

'I've installed a piano in the studio,' said Moreland. 'I get some work done when I'm not feeling too much like hell, which hasn't been often, lately.'

The cottage was a small, redbrick, oak-beamed affair, of some antiquity, though much restored, with a studio-room built out at the back. That was where Moreland had put his piano. He was not looking particularly well. When they were first married, Matilda had cleaned him up considerably. Now, his dark-blue suit—Moreland never made any concession to the sartorial conception of 'country clothes'—looked as if he had spent a restless night wearing it in bed. He had not shaved.

'What's been wrong?'

'That lung of mine has been rather a bore.'

'What are you working on?'

'My ballet.'

'How is it going?'

'Stuck.'

'It's impossible to write with Hitler about.'

'Utterly.'

He was in low spirits. His tangled, uncut hair emphasised the look his face sometimes assumed of belonging to a fractious, disappointed child. Matilda, on the other hand, so far from being depressed, as Isobel had represented her, now seemed lively and restless. She was wearing trousers that revealed each bone of her angular figure. Her greenish eyes, rather too large mouth, for some reason always made one think she would make a more powerful, more talented actress than her stage capabilities in fact justified. These immediately noticeable features, arresting rather than beautiful, also suggested, in some indirect manner, her practical abilities, her gift for organisation. Matilda's present exhilaration might be explained, I thought, by the fact that these abilities were put to more use now than when the Morelands had lived in London. There, except late at night, or when they lay in bed late in the morning, they were rarely to be found in their flat. Here, they must be alone together most of the day, although no doubt much of the time Moreland was shut away in the studio at work. Matilda, when not acting, had sometimes complained in London that time hung on her hands, even though she was—or had formerly been to some extent—a kind of agent for Moreland, arranging much of his professional life, advising as to what jobs he accepted, what interviews he gave, when he must be left in peace. All the same, as I have said, it was chiefly matters outside the musical world that caused him pain and grief. In the business sphere, Matilda no doubt took a burden from him; in his musical life, as such, he may sometimes even have resented too much interference. Since the baby had died, they had had no other child.

'You are eating sausage tonight,' said Matilda, 'and half-a-crown Barbera. As you know, I'm not a great cook. However, you'll have a square meal tomorrow, as we're going over to Stourwater for dinner.'

'Can you bear it?' said Moreland. 'I'm not sure I can.'

'Do cheer up, darling,' said Matilda. 'You know you'll like it when we get there.'

'No so sure.'

'Anyway, it's got to be faced.'

Things had certainly changed. Formerly, Moreland had been the one who liked going to parties, staying up late, drinking a lot; Matilda, bored by people, especially some of Moreland's musical friends, wanted as a rule to go home. Now the situation seemed reversed: Matilda anxious for company, Moreland immersed in work. Matilda's tone, her immediate manner of bringing up the subject of Stourwater, was no doubt intended to show in the plainest terms that she herself felt completely at ease so far as visiting Sir Magnus was concerned. Although she had never attempted to conceal her former association with him —which would certainly not have been easy—she seemed to feel that present circumstances required her specially to emphasise her complete freedom from embarrassment. This demeanour was obviously intended to cover Moreland in that respect, as well as herself. She was announcing their policy as a married couple. Possibly she did not altogether carry Moreland with her. He was rebellious about something, even if not about the visit to Stourwater.

'Have you seen the place before?' he asked. 'You realise we are going to conduct you to a Wagnerian castle, a palace where Ludwig of Bavaria wouldn't have been ashamed to disport himself.'

'I was there about ten years ago. Some people called Walpole-Wilson took me over. They live twenty or thirty miles away.'

'I've heard Donners speak of them,' said Matilda. She always referred to Sir Magnus by his surname.

Isobel and I used to discuss whether Matilda had so addressed him in their moments of closest intimacy.

'After all,' Isobel had said, 'she can only have liked him for his money. To call him "Donners" suggests capital appreciation much more than a pet-name. Beside, "Magnus" —if one could bring oneself to call him that—is almost more formal than "Donners", without the advantage of conjuring up visions of dividends and allotment letters.'

'Do you think Matilda only liked him for his money? She never attempted to get any out of him.'

'It's not a question of *getting* the money. It's the money itself. Money is a charm like any other charm.'

'As a symbol of power?'

'Partly, perhaps. After all, men and women both like power in the opposite sex. Why not take it in the form of money?'

'Do you really think Matilda liked nothing else about poor Sir Magnus?'

'I didn't think him very attractive myself the only time I saw him.'

'Perhaps Matilda was won by his unconventional ways.'

'Perhaps.'

'You don't think so?'

'I don't express an opinion.'

'Still, I must agree, she left him in the end.'

'I think Matilda is quite ambitious,' said Isobel.

'Then why did she leave Sir Magnus? She might have made him marry her.'

'Because she took a fancy to Hugh.'

That was no doubt the answer. I had been struck, at the time she said this, by Isobel's opinion that Matilda was ambitious.

'Who are the Walpole-Wilsons?' asked Moreland.

'Sir Gavin Walpole-Wilson is a retired diplomat. His

daughter, Eleanor, has shared a flat for years with Isobel's sister, Norah. But, of course, you know Norah and Eleanor of old.'

Moreland reddened at the mention of Isobel's sisters. Thought of them must still have called Priscilla uneasily to his mind. The subject of sisters-in-law was obviously one to be avoided. However, Matilda showed some inclination to continue to talk of them. She had rescued her husband from Priscilla, whom she could consider to have suffered a defeat. She may have wanted to emphasise that.

'How are Norah and Eleanor?' she asked.

'Eleanor is trying to make up her mind again whether she will become a Catholic convert,' said Isobel. 'Heather Hopkins became an RC the other day. Hugo says that puts Eleanor in a dilemma. She wants to annoy Norah, but doesn't want to please Hopkins.'

'I practically never go to Stourwater,' Moreland said, determined to change the subject from one that could possibly lead back to Priscilla. 'Matty pops over there once in a way to see some high life. I recognise that Donners has his points—has in the past even been very obliging to me personally. The fact remains that when I did the incidental music for that film of his, I saw enough of him to last a lifetime.'

If Matilda had wanted to make clear her sentiments about Stourwater, Moreland had now been equally explicit about his own. The question of the proximity of Sir Magnus perhaps irked him more than he would admit to himself, certainly more than I expected. On inquiry, it appeared that even Matilda's visits to Stourwater were rare. I thought Moreland was just in a bad mood, exaggerating his own dislike for 'going out'. He was not by any means without a taste for occasional forays into rich life. This taste could hardly have been removed entirely by transferring himself to the country. Even in London, he had suffered periods of acute boredom. As the week-end took shape, it became clear that these fits of ennui were by no means a thing of the past. He would sit for hours without speaking, nursing a large tabby cat called Farinelli.

'Do you think this sell-out is going to prevent a war?' he said, when we were reading the papers on Sunday morning.

'No.'

'You think we ought to have fought this time?'

'I don't know. The one thing everybody agrees about is that we aren't ready for it. There's no point in going to war if we are not going to win it. Losing's not going to help anybody.'

'What are you going to do when it comes?'

'My name is on one of those various army reserves.'

'How did you manage that?'

'Offered myself, and was accepted, before all this last business started.'

'I can only do ladylike things such as playing the piano,' said Moreland gloomily. 'I suppose I shall go on doing that if there's a show-down. One wonders what the hell will happen. How are we getting to this place tonight?'

'Donners rang up and said one of his guests is picking us up in a car,' said Matilda.

'When did he ring up?'

'When you were all at the pub this morning.'

'Why not tell us?'

'I forgot,' said Matilda. 'I told Donners when we were asked he must arrange something. Finding transport is the least the rich can do, if they hope to enjoy one's company. You must shave, sweetie, before we start.'

'All right, all right,' said Moreland, 'I won't let you all down by my tramp-like appearance. Do we know the name of our chauffeur?'

'Somebody called Peter Templer,' said Matilda. 'Anybody ever heard of him?'

'Certainly I've heard of Peter Templer,' I said. 'He's one of my oldest friends. I haven't seen him for years.'

'Who is he? What's he like?'

'A stockbroker. Fast sports car, loud checks, blondes, golf, all that sort of thing. We were at school together.'

'Wasn't he the brother of that girl you used to know?' said Isobel.

She spoke as if finally confirming a fact of which she had always been a little uncertain, at the same time smiling as if she hardly thought the pretence worth keeping up.

'He was.'

'Which girl?' asked Moreland, without interest.

'A woman called Jean Duport, whom I haven't seen for years.'

'Never heard of her,' said Moreland.

I thought what a long time it seemed since I had visited Stourwater on that earlier occasion, when the luncheon party had been given for Prince Theodoric. Prince Theodoric's name, as a pro-British element in a country ominously threatened from without by German political pressure, had been in the papers recently. Stringham, just engaged to Peggy Stepney, had still been one of Sir Magnus's secretaries. Jean Duport, Peter Templer's sister, had been there and I had wondered whether I was not perhaps in love with her. Now, I did not know where she was, was ignorant of the very hemisphere she inhabited. When last seen—parting infinitely painful—she had been on her way to South America, reunited with her awful husband. Baby Wentworth was still—though not long to remain —Sir Magnus's 'girl'. Matilda must have taken on the job soon after that visit of mine. If mere arrival in the neighbourhood had imparted, of itself, a strong sense of having slipped back into the past, that sensation was certainly intensified by the prospect of meeting Peter Templer again. He had passed from my life as completely as his sister.

There was nothing at all surprising about his staying at Stourwater, when I came to examine the question, except his own dislike for houses of that sort. Business affairs might perfectly well have brought him within the orbit of Sir Magnus. One of the odd things about Templer was that, although pretty well equipped for social life of any kind, he found places like Stourwater in general too pretentious for his taste. He preferred circles where there was less competition, where he could safely be tippd as the man most likely to appeal to all the women present, most popular with the men. It was not that Templer was in any way ill-adapted to a large sort of life, so much as the fact that he himself was unwilling to tolerate that larger life's social disciplines, of which the chief was the ever-present danger of finding himself regarded as less important than someone else. That makes him sound intolerable. Templer was, on the contrary, one of the most easygoing, good-natured of men, but he liked being first in the field. He liked, especially, to be first in the field with women. After Mona left him, I imagined he had returned to this former pursuit.

'I have rather suburban tastes in ladies, like everything else,' Templer used to say. 'Golf, bridge, an occasional spot of crumpet, they are all I require to savour my seasonal financial flutter.'

The fact that he could analyse his tastes in this way made Templer a little unusual, considering what those tastes were. I felt pleasure in the thought that I was going to see him again, tempered by that faint uneasiness about meeting a friend who may have changed too much during the interval of absence to make practicable any renewal of former ties.

'We haven't brought any evening clothes,' I said.

'Good God,' said Moreland, 'we're not changing fo Donners.'

It was a warm autumnal evening, so that we were all in

the garden when Templer's car drew up at the gate. The vehicle was of just the kind I had predicted. Templer, too, as he jumped out, seemed scarcely to have changed at all. The car was shaped like a torpedo; Templer's clothes gave the familiar impression—as Stringham used to say —that he was 'about to dance backwards and forwards in front of a chorus of naked ladies'. That outward appearance was the old Templer, just as he had looked at Dicky Umfraville's night-club four or five years before. Now, as he strode up the path with the same swagger, I saw there was a change in him. This was more than the fact that he was distinctly fatter. A coarseness of texture had always coloured his elegance. Now, that coarseness had become more than ever marked. He looked hard, even rather savage, as if he had made up his mind to endure life rather than, as formerly, to enjoy it. From the first impression that he had changed hardly at all, I reversed judgment, deciding he had changed a great deal. When he saw me he stepped back melodramatically.

'Is it really you, Nick?'

'What's left.'

I introduced him to the Morelands and to Isobel.

'I believe you invited me to your wedding, Nick,' said Templer. 'Somehow I never manage to get to weddings —it's an effort even to reach my own.'

'Have you been having many weddings lately, Peter?'

'Oh, well, not for a year or two,' said Templer, suddenly becoming more serious. 'You knew I married again after Mona?'

'I didn't, as a matter of fact.'

'Yes, indeed.'

'How shameful that we should have missed the announcement.'

'I'm not sure that we made one,' Templer said. 'It was all very quiet. Hardly asked a soul. Since then—I don't know—

we've been living in the country. Just see a few neighbours. Betty doesn't like going out much. She has come to Stourwater this week-end, as a matter of fact, but that's rather exceptional. She felt jumpy for some reason about staying at home. She gets these jumpy fits from time to time. Thinks war's going to break out all the time.'

He smiled rather uncomfortably. I felt suddenly certain that Templer's new wife must be responsible for the change that had come over him. At the same time, I tried, quite unsuccessfully, to rationalise in my own mind what exactly this change was. Now that we were face to face and I was talking to him, it was more than ever apparent, almost horrifying. He had slowed up, became more 'serious', at the same time lost that understanding, sympathetic manner formerly characteristic of him, so unexpected in a person of his sort. That was my first thought. Then I wondered whether, in fact, he was even less 'serious'—if that were possible—determined to get as much fun out of living as he could, whatever the obstacles, whatever the cost. These dissections on my own part were rather absurd; yet there was something not far away from Templer that generated a sense of horror.

'What a nice colour your car is,' said Moreland.

I could see he had at once placed Templer in the category of persons he found unsympathetic. That was to be expected. Just as most of the world find it on the whole unusual that anyone should be professionally occupied with the arts, Moreland could never get used to the fact that most people—in this particular case, Templer—lead lives in which the arts play no part whatsoever. That is perhaps an exaggeration of Moreland's attitude. All the same, he always found difficulty in accustoming himself to complete aesthetic indifference. This narrowness of vision sometimes led Moreland, with all his subtlety in some matters, to complete misunderstanding of others, especially to underestimate some of the people who came his way. On Templer's side, the meeting had been equally lacking in fellow feeling. He had no doubt been prepared for the Morelands to look—from his point of view—a pretty extraordinary couple. From Templer's point of view, it had to be admitted, the Morelands did look pretty extraordinary. Matilda was still wearing trousers, bright emerald green in colour, her feet in immensely thick cork-soled sandals, her hair done up on the top of her head, in the fashion of the moment, like a bird's nest. Moreland had shaved, otherwise made no effort to tidy himself, a carelessly knotted tie slipping away from the buttonless collar of his blue shirt. Templer began to laugh, partly, I supposed, at the thought of our having met again after so long, partly, too, I felt sure, at the strange picture the Morelands presented to one unaccustomed to people like them. Templer must also have known of Matilda's former relationship with Sir Magnus. Perhaps that was what made him laugh.

'Come on,' he said, 'all aboard for Stourwater and the picturesque ruins.'

We climbed into the car. The Morelands were rather silent, because there is always something a shade embarrassing about an old friend suddenly encountering another old friend, quite unknown to you. They were perhaps meditating on their own differences of opinion regarding the desirability of accepting the hospitality of Sir Magnus. Templer himself kept up a running fire of questions, as if anxious to delay the moment when he had to speak of his own life.

'It is really too extraordinary our meeting again in this way, Nick,' he said. 'Though it's just like a millionaire to make one of the persons staying with him fetch the guests for dinner, instead of using his own chauffeur, but now I'm glad Magnus was running true to form. Do you live in London?'

'Yes—and you?'

'We're at Sunningdale.'

'Isn't that where Stringham's mother, Mrs Foxe, has a house?'

'Charles Stringham—I haven't thought of him for years.'

'Does she still live there?'

'She does, as a matter of fact. We don't know them. Rather too grand for us. Odd you should mention Stringham. It wasn't quite true when I said I hadn't thought of him for years, because, as it happened, I ran across Mrs Foxe's naval-officer husband at a golf tournament handicap not so long ago who said something about him.'

'Stringham was knocking it back pretty hard when I last saw him. What did Buster Foxe say? They don't much care for each other.'

'Don't they? I gather from Commander Foxe they were great pals. Now, what did he say? Gone right out of my head. No, I know—Stringham is living at Glimber, the house Mrs Foxe inherited from her first husband. It's huge, uninhabitable, entailed, nobody wants to rent it. Stringham looks after it apparently. He has a former secretary of his mother's to help him. It's like being an agent, I suppose.'

'Sounds rather grim.'

'Oh, I don't know. Stately home, and all that. Commander Foxe said Charles liked it. Now you come to mention it, he did say something, too, about giving up the bottle. I hadn't realised Stringham's drinking had reached the headline category.'

'He used to hit it fairly hard. The secretary you mention is called Miss Weedon—Tuffy to her intimates. Rather a frightening lady. She has always taken a great hand in arranging Charles's life. In fact, she had more or less undertaken to stop his drinking at one moment. They even lived in the same flat.'

'Wasn't she the Medusa-like figure who appeared at

that party Mrs Foxe gave for my symphony?' said Moreland.

'She was. Charles Stringham is Mrs Foxe's son.'

'It was Miss Weedon who hauled him off home when he was so tight.'

'It was a very enjoyable party, anyway,' said Matilda.

I remembered that it had ended by Moreland's disappearing with Isobel's sister, Priscilla. Templer showed no interest at all in these reminiscences. They were not, perhaps, very absorbing in themselves, but he might have been expected to have given them more attention inasmuch as they referred to so old a friend as Stringham.

'Talking of people we knew at school,' he said, 'Kenneth will be at Stourwater this evening.'

'Kenneth who?'

'Kenneth Widmerpool.'

'Oh, yes.'

'You're a friend of his, aren't you?' said Templer, evidently surprised at my not grasping immediately whom he meant. 'I've heard him speak of you. His mother has a cottage near here.'

I saw that it was no longer a question of Stringham and Widmerpool having drawn level as friends in Templer's mind; the fact was that Widmerpool was now miles ahead. That was clear from Templer's tone. There was not a flicker of laughter or irony in his employment of Widmerpool's Christian name, as there had certainly been when I had last seen them together at Dicky Umfraville's night-club. There was, of course, absolutely no reason why Templer should adopt a satirical tone towards Widmerpool, who had as much right as anyone else to make friends with—if necessary, even to dominate—persons like Templer, who had made fun of him as a schoolboy. It was the juxtaposition of his complete acceptance of Widmerpool with Templer's equally complete indifference to his old crony, Stringham, that gave the two things an emphasis that certainly jarred a little. Templer had probably not set eyes on him since the day when he had arrived in Stringham's college room, later driven us all into the ditch in his newly bought car. If it came to that, I never saw Stringham these days myself, while Templer, doing business with Widmerpool for a long time now, had naturally come to regard him as a personal friend. By that time we were entering the park of Stourwater.

'Look, the castle,' said Isobel. 'Nobody warned me it was made of cardboard.'

Cardboard was certainly the material of which walls and keep seemed to be built, as we rounded the final sweep of the drive, coming within sight of a large castellated pile, standing with absurd unreality against a background of oaks, tortured by their antiquity into elephantine and grotesque shapes. From the higher ground at the back, grass, close-cropped by sheep, rolled down towards the greenish pools of the moat. All was veiled in the faint haze of autumn.

'I told you it was Wagnerian,' said Moreland.

'When we wind the horn at the gate, will a sullen dwarf usher us in,' said Isobel, 'like Beckford's at Fonthill or the Castle of Joyous Gard in the *Morte d' Arthur*?'

'A female dwarf, perhaps,' said Moreland, rather maliciously.

'Don't miss the black swans,' said Matilda, disregarding him.

'An anachronism, I fear,' said Moreland. 'Sir Magnus admitted as much to me in an unguarded moment. They come from Australia. Doesn't it all look as if the safety curtain would descend any moment amid bursts of applause?'

Stourwater was certainly dramatic; yet how unhaunted, how much less ghost-ridden than Stonehurst; though perhaps Sir Magnus himself might leave a spectre behind him. In my memory, the place had been larger, more forbidding, not so elaborately restored. In fact, I was far less impressed than formerly, even experiencing a certain feeling of disappointment. Memory, imagination, time, all building up on that brief visit, had left a magician's castle (brought into being by some loftier Dr Trelawney), weird and prodigious, peopled by beings impossible to relate to everyday life. Now, Stourwater seemed nearer to being an architectural abortion, a piece of monumental vulgarity, a house where something had gone very seriously wrong. We crossed the glittering water by a causeway, drove under the portcullis and through the outer courtyard, entering the inner court, where a fountain stood in the centre of a sunken garden surrounded by a stone balustrade. Here, in the days when he had been first ingratiating himself with Sir Magnus, Widmerpool had backed his car into one of the ornamental urns filled with flowers.

'Is Kenneth Widmerpool staying in the house?' I asked, thinking of that incident.

'Just driving over after dinner,' said Templer. 'Some sort of business to clear up. I'm involved to a small extent, because it's about my ex-brother-in-law, Bob Duport. Between you and me, I think I've been asked partly because Magnus wants me to know what is going on for his own purposes.'

'What are his own purposes?'

'I don't know for certain. Perhaps he wants this particular scheme given a little discreet publicity.'

We had drawn up by the wing of the castle that was used for residence. The girls and Moreland had left the car by then, and were making their way up the steps to the front door. Templer had paused for a moment to fiddle with one of the knobs of the dashboard which for some reason seemed to dissatisfy him. This seemed a good opportunity for learning privately what had happened to Jean; for although by then I no longer thought about her, there is always a morbid interest in following the subsequent career of a woman with whom one has once been in love. That I should have been in this position *vis-à-vis* his sister, Templer himself, I felt pretty sure, had no idea.

'Duport is an *ex*-brother-in-law now?'

'Jean finally got a divorce from him. They lived apart for quite a time when Bob was running round with Bijou Ardglass. Then they joined up again and went to South America together. However, it didn't last. You never really knew Jean, did you?'

'I met her when I stayed with your family years ago—a few times later. What's happened to her now?'

'She married a South American—an army officer.'

'And Bob Duport?'

'There is some question of his going to Turkey for Magnus. Kenneth has been fixing it.'

'On business?'

'Magnus is interested in chromite.'

'What's that?'

'Used for hardening steel.'

By that time we were half-way up the steps, at the top of which the others were waiting.

'Shall I lead the way?' said Templer. 'Magnus was in the Bailiff's Room when last seen.'

If the outside of Stourwater made a less favourable impression than when I had come there with the Walpole-Wilsons, improvements within were undeniable. Ten years before, the exuberance of the armour, tapestries, pictures, china, furniture, had been altogether too much for the austere aesthetic ideals to which I then subscribed. Time had no doubt modified the uninstructed severity of my own early twenties. Less ascetic, intellectually speaking, more corrupt, perhaps, I could now recognise that individuals live in different ways. They must be taken as they come,

Sir Magnus Donners, everyone else. If Sir Magnus liked to make his house like a museum, that was his affair; one must treat it as a museum. In any case, there could be no doubt that protégés like Moreland and Barnby, mistresses like Baby Wentworth and Matilda, had played their part in the castle's redecoration. Certainly it was now arranged in a manner more in keeping with contemporary fashion. Sir Magnus had cleared out some of the more cumbersome of his belongings, although much remained that was unviable enough.

'It's all rather wonderful, Nick, isn't it?' said Matilda in a whisper, as we passed through the main hall. 'Whatever Hugh may say about the Donners taste. How would you like to own it all?'

'How would you?'

'I nearly did.'

I laughed, surprised by her directness, always attractive in women. Entering a panelled gallery, Templer opened a door and indicated we were to go in. The room overlooked the garden. Between bookshelves hung drawings: Conder, Steer, John, a couple of Sickerts. Barnby's nude of Norma, the waitress from Casanova's Chinese Restaurant, was beside the fireplace, above which stood a florid china statuette of *Cupid Chastised*. Just as the last of our party crossed the threshold, one of the bookcases on the far side of the room swung forward, revealing itself as an additional door covered with the spines of dummy volumes, through which Sir Magnus Donners himself appeared to greet his guests at exactly the same moment. I wondered whether he had been watching at a peephole. It was like the stage entrance of a famous actor, the conscious modesty of which is designed, by its absolute ease and lack of emphasis, both to prevent the performance from being disturbed at some anti-climax of the play by too deafening a round of applause, at the same time to confirm—what everyone in the theatre knows already—the complete mastery he possesses of his art. The manner in which Sir Magnus held out his hand also suggested brilliant miming of a distinguished man feeling a little uncomfortable about something.

'You did not tell me I was to collect one of my oldest friends, Magnus,' said Templer, addressing his host as if he were on the most familiar terms with him, in spite of any differences between them of age and eminence. 'Nick and I were at school together.

Sir Magnus did not answer. He only raised his eyebrows and smiled. Introductions began. While he was shaking hands with Isobel, I observed, from out of the corner of my eye, a woman—whom I assumed to be Templer's wife—sitting in an armchair with its back towards us in the corner of the room. She was reading a newspaper, which she did not lower at our entry. Sir Magnus shook hands all round, behaving as if he had never before met the Morelands, giving, when he reached me, that curious pump-handle motion to his handshake, terminated by a sudden upward jerk (as if suddenly shutting off from the main a valuable current of good will, of which not a volt too much must be expended), a form of greeting common to many persons with a long habit of public life. Ten years left little mark on him. Possibly the neat grey hair receded a trifle more; the line on one side of the mouth might have been a shade deeper; the eyes—greenish, like Matilda's—were clear and very cold. Sir Magnus's mouth was his least comfortable feature. Tall, holding himself squarely, he still possessed the air, conveyed to me when I first set eyes on him, of an athletic bishop or clerical headmaster. This impression was dispelled when he spoke, because he had none of the urbane manner usual to such persons. Unlike Roddy Cutts or Fettiplace-Jones, he was entirely without the patter of the professional politician, even appearing to find difficulty in making 'small talk' of any kind whatsoever. When he spoke, it was as if he had forced himself by sheer effort of will into manufacturing a few stereotyped sentences to tide over the trackless wilderness of social life. Such colourless phrases as he achieved were produced with a difficulty, a hesitancy, simulated perhaps, but decidedly effective in their unconcealed ineptness. While he uttered these verbal formalities, the side of his mouth twitched slightly. Like more successful men, he had turned this apparent disadvantage into a powerful weapon of offence and defence, in the way that the sledge-hammer impact of his comment left, by its banality, every other speaker at a standstill, giving him as a rule complete mastery of the conversational field. A vast capacity for imposing boredom, a sense of immensely powerful stuffiness, emanated from him, sapping every drop of vitality from weaker spirits.

'So you were at school together,' he said slowly.

He regarded Templer and myself as if the fact we had been at school together was an important piece of evidence in assessing our capabilities, both as individuals and as a team. He paused. There was an awkward silence.

'Well, I suppose you sometimes think of those days with regret,' Sir Magnus continued at last. 'I know I do. Only in later life does one learn what a jewel is youth.'

He smiled apologetically at having been compelled to use such a high-flown phrase. Matilda, laughing, took his arm. 'Dear Donners,' she said, 'what a thing to tell us. You don't suppose we believe you for a moment. Of course you much prefer living in your lovely castle to being back at school.'

Sir Magnus smiled. However, he was not to be jockeyed so easily from his serious mood.

'Believe me,' he said, 'I would at least give what I have to live again my time at the Sorbonne. One is not a student twice in a lifetime.'

'One is never a student at all in England,' said Moreland, in a tone that showed he was still in no mood to be tractable, 'except possibly a medical student or an art student. I suppose you might say I was myself a student, in one sense, when I was at the Royal College of Music. I never felt in the least like one. Besides, with that sort of student, you enter an area of specialisation, which hardly counts for what I mean. Undergraduates in this country are quite different from students. Not that I was ever even an undergraduate myself, but my observation shows me that undergraduates have nothing in common with what is understood abroad by the word students—young men for ever rioting, undertaking political assassination, overturning governments.'

Sir Magnus smiled a little uncertainly, as if only too familiar with these dissertations of Moreland's on fugitive subjects; as if aware, too, that it was no good hoping to introduce any other matter unless such aimless ramblings had been brought by Moreland himself to a close. Moreland stopped speaking and laughed, seeing what was in Sir Magnus's mind. Sir Magnus began a sentence, but, before he could get the words out, the woman sitting in the corner of the room threw down her newspaper and jumped to her feet. She came hurriedly towards us. She was quite pretty, very untidy, with reddish hair and elaborately blued eyelids. Far from being Templer's wife—unless, by some extraordinary freak, they had married and the news had never come my way—this was Lady Anne Stepney, sister of Peggy Stepney (now divorced and remarried) who had been Stringham's former wife. Anne Stepney was also a *divorcée* —in fact, she was Anne Umfraville, having married that raffish figure, Dicky Umfraville, at least twenty years older than herself, as his third or fourth wife. That marriage, too, had broken up. There had been a time, just before meeting Dicky Umfraville, when Anne had been closely associated with Barnby. Now her manner suggested that she regarded Sir Magnus as her own property.

'I really do agree with you about students,' she said, speaking a torrent of words addressed to Moreland. 'Why is it we don't have any in England? It would liven things up so. I wish the students would do something to prevent all the awful things that have been happening in Czecho-slovakia. I do apologise for my rudeness in not coming to talk to you before now. I was so utterly engrossed in what I was reading, I really had to finish the article. It's by J. G. Quiggin. He says we ought to have fought. I can't think about *anything* but Czechoslovakia. Why can't one of the Germans do in Hitler? Those German students, who are so proud of the duelling scars on their faces, take it like lambs when it comes to being bossed about by a man like that.'

'*The Times* says that the Lord Mayor's Fund for the relief of the Czechs has evoked a wide response,' said Sir Magnus mildly.

Lady Anne made an angry movement.

'But you must all be longing for a drink,' she said, as if in despair. 'I didn't know you were going to sit in here, Magnus. I told them to put the drink tray in the Chinese Room. Shall I ring and have it transferred here?'

It was clear that she regarded herself as holding an estab-lished position at Stourwater. Sir Magnus continued to look embarrassed, but whether on account of this outburst, the distressing situation in Central Europe, or the problem of where to consume our drinks, was not apparent. He was probably far from anxious to embark, there and then, on the rights and wrongs of Munich, the practical issues of which were certainly at that time occupying the foremost place in his mind. Roddy Cutts had indicated that when we had talked of Sir Magnus again, after Fettiplace-Jones and his wife had gone home.

'Donners is in close touch with some of the seedy business-men one or two of the Cabinet think worth cultivating,' said Roddy, who appeared to have kept his own artillery masked while speaking with Fettiplace-Jones, 'but he is alleged to be absolutely out of sympathy with the Chamberlain policy. He is playing a waiting game, perhaps a wise one from his point of view.'

The explosive undertones introduced by Anne Umfraville were deadened at that moment by the entry of another woman, whose arrival immediately altered the atmosphere of the room, without greatly relieving its tensions. She, too, was pretty, with the looks sometimes described as 'porcelain', fragile and delicate, slim and blonde. She gave the impression of being not so much an actress, as the sort of girl an actress often tries to portray on the stage in some play making few demands on the mind: the 'nice' girl in a farce or detective story. A typical Templer girl, I thought, feeling sure she must be Peter's wife, then remembering she was the woman with him at Dicky Umfraville's night-club.

'A Mrs Taylor or Porter,' he had said, 'I can't remember which. Rather a peach, isn't she?'

Presumably Templer had removed her from Mr Taylor or Porter. As she came through the door, Templer's own expression altered slightly. It was as if his features contracted for a brief instant with a sudden spasm of toothache, an agony over almost as soon as felt. The woman moved slowly, shyly, towards us. Sir Magnus stopped looking at Anne Umfraville, following this new arrival with his eyes, as if she were walking a tight-rope and he feared she might at any moment make a false step, fall into the net below, ruin the act, possibly break her neck. Templer watched her too. She came to a standstill.

'This is Betty,' Templer said.

He spoke as if long past despair. Sir Magnus nodded in resigned, though ever hopeful, agreement that this was indeed Betty. Betty stood for a moment gazing round the room in a dazed, almost terrified, manner, suggesting sudden emergence into the light of day after long hours spent behind drawn curtains. I suddenly thought of the tour of Stourwater's 'dungeons' (strenuously asserted by Miss Janet Walpole-Wilson, on my previous visit, to be mere granaries), when Sir Magnus had remarked with sensuous ogreishness, '*I sometimes think that is where we should put the girls who don't behave.*' Could it be that Betty Templer, with her husband's connivance—an explanation of Templer's uneasy air—had been imprisoned in the course of some partly high-spirited, partly sadistic, rompings to gratify their host's strange whims? Of course, I did not seriously suppose such a thing, but for a split second the grotesque notion presented itself. However, setting fantasy aside, I saw at once that something was 'wrong' with Betty Templer, not realising, until I came to shake hands with her, how badly 'wrong' things were. It was like trying to shake hands with Ophelia while she was strewing flowers. Betty Templer was 'dotty'. She was as 'dotty' as my sister-in-law, Blanche Tolland—far 'dottier', because people met Blanche, talked with her at parties, had dealings with her about her charities, without ever guessing about her 'dottiness'. Indeed, in the world of 'good works' she was a rather well known, certainly a respected, figure. Blanche's strangeness, when examined, mainly took the shape of lacking any desire to engage herself in life, to have friends, to marry, to bear children, to go out into the world. Within, so to speak, her chosen alcove, she appeared perfectly happy, at least not actively unhappy. The same could certainly not be said for Betty Templer. Betty Templer, on the contrary, was painfully disorientated, at her wits' end, not happy at all. It was dreadful. I saw that the situation required reassessment. After my failure at shaking hands with her, I made some remark about the weather. She looked at me without speaking, as if horrified at my words.

'Perhaps it would be better to go to the Chinese Room,' said Sir Magnus, 'if the drinks are really there.'

He spoke in that curiously despondent, even threatening, manner sometimes adopted by very rich people towards their guests, especially where food and drink are concerned, a tone suggesting considerable danger that drinks would not be found in the Chinese Room or, indeed, anywhere else at Stourwater Castle; that we should be lucky if we were given anything to drink at all—or to eat, too, if it came to that—during the evening that lay ahead of us.

'Will you lead the way, Anne?' he said, with determined cheerfulness. 'I shall have to speak to you later about trying to keep us from our drinks. Deliberate naughtiness on your part, I fear. Have you heard the New Hungarian String Quartet, Hugh? I haven't been myself. I was at *Faust* the other night, and a little disappointed at some of the singing.'

We followed through the door, crossing the hall again, while I wondered what on earth had happened to Templer's wife to give her this air of having been struck by lightning. Contact between us was broken for the moment, because, while drinks were being dispensed in the Chinese Room, I found myself talking to Anne Umfraville. By the fireplace there, as if left by some visiting photographer, was a camera on a tripod, beside which stood two adjustable lamps.

'What's all this, Donners?' asked Matilda. 'Have you taken up photography?'

'It is my new hobby,' said Sir Magnus, speaking apologetically, as if this time, at least, he agreed with other people in thinking his own habits a shade undesirable. 'I find it impossible to persuade professionals to take pictures of my collections in the way I want them taken. That was why I decided to do it myself. The results, although I say it, are as good, if not better. I have been photographing some of the Nymphenburg. That is why the apparatus is in here.'

'Do you ever photograph people?' asked Moreland.

'I had not thought of that,' said Sir Magnus, smiling rather wolfishly. 'I suppose I might rise to people.'

'Happy snaps,' said Matilda.

'Or unhappy ones,' said Moreland, 'just for a change.'

Dinner was announced. We found ourselves among those scenes in blue, yellow and crimson, the tapestries illustrating the Seven Deadly Sins, which surrounded the dining-room, remembered so well from my earlier visit. Then, I had sat next to Jean Duport. We had talked about the imagery of the incidents depicted in the tapestries. Suitably enough our place had been just below the sequences of *Luxuria*.

'Of course they are newly married . . .' she had said.

That all seemed a long time ago. I glanced round the room. If the rest of Stourwater had proved disappointing —certainly less overpowering in ornate magnificence—these fantastic tapestries, on the other hand, had gained in magnitude. More gorgeous, more extravagant than ever, they engulfed my imagination again in their enchanting colours, grotesque episodes, symbolic moods, making me forget once more the persons on either side of me, just as I had been unaware of Jean when she had spoken on that day, telling me we had met before. Thinking of that, I indulged in a brief moment of sentimentality permissible before social duties intervened. Then, I collected myself. I was between Matilda and Betty Templer—we were sitting at a table greatly reduced in size from that in use on the day when Prince Theodoric had been entertained at Stourwater—and, abandoning the tapestries, I became aware that Templer was chatting in his easy way to Matilda, while I myself had made no effort to engage his wife in conversation. Beyond Betty Templer, Moreland was already administering a tremendous scolding to Anne Umfraville, who, as soon as they sat down, had ventured to express some musical opinion which outraged him, an easy enough thing to do. Sir Magnus, on the other side, had begun to recount to Isobel the history of the castle.

'Have you been to Stourwater before?' I asked Betty Templer.

She stared at me with big, frightened eyes.

'No.'

'It's rather a wonderful house, isn't it?'

'How—how do you mean?'

That question brought me up short. To like Stourwater, to disapprove, were both tenable opinions, but, as residence, the castle could hardly be regarded as anything except unusual. If Betty Templer had noticed none of its uncommon characteristics, pictures and furniture were not a subject to embark upon.

'Do you know this part of the world at all?'

'No,' she said, after some hesitation.

'Peter told me you lived at Sunningdale.'

'Yes.'

'Have you been there long?'

'Since we married.'

'Good for getting up and down to London.'

'I don't go to London much.'

'I suppose Peter gets back for dinner.'

'Sometimes.'

She looked as if she might begin to cry. It was an imbecile remark on my part, the worst possible subject to bring up, talking to the wife of a man like Templer.

'I expect it is all rather nice there, anyway,' I said.

I knew I was losing my head, that she would soon reduce me to as desperate a state, conversationally speaking, as herself.

'Yes,' she admitted.

'It was extraordinary Peter's bringing us over in the car this evening. I hadn't seen him for ages. We used to know each other so well at school.'

'He knows such a lot of people,' she said.

Her eyes filled with tears. There could be no doubt of it. I wondered what was going to happen next, fearing the worst. However, she made a tremendous effort.

'Do you live in London?' she asked.

'Yes, we——'

'I used to live in London when I was married to my first husband.'

'Oh, yes.'

'He was in—in jute.'

'Was he?'

For the moment I saw no way of utilising this opening.

'Are you a stockbroker?' she asked.

'No . . . I . . .'

I suddenly felt unable to explain what I did, what I was. The difficulties seemed, for some reason, insuperable. Fortunately no explanation was necessary. She required of me no alternative profession.

'Most of Peter's friends are stockbrokers,' she said, speaking rather more calmly, as if that thought brought some small balm to her soul, adding, a moment later, 'Some of them live at Sunningdale.'

The situation was relieved at that moment by Matilda's causing conversation to become general by returning to the subject of Sir Magnus and his photography.

'You were talking about photographing people, Donners,' she said. 'Why don't you begin on us after dinner? What could be nicer to photograph than the present company?'

'What a good idea,' said Anne Umfraville. 'Do let's do that, Magnus. It would be fun.'

She was greatly improved, far less truculent, than in the days when I had first met her. If Dicky Umfraville could not be said exactly to have knocked the nonsense out of her, marriage to him had certainly effected a change. At least the nonsense was, so to speak, rearranged in a manner less irksome to those with whom she came in contact. She no longer contradicted, as a matter of principle, every word spoken to her; her demeanour was friendly, rather than the reverse. Soon after our arrival at Stourwater, she had reminded Isobel that they were distant cousins; her musical blunder with Moreland was due to ignorance, not desire to exacerbate him; she was well disposed even to Matilda, who, as a former 'girl' of Sir Magnus's, might well have incurred her antagonism. I thought she had obviously taken a fancy to Templer, and he to her. That might explain her excellent humour. It might also explain, at least in part, his wife's 'state'.

'Oh, are we going to be photographed?' Betty Templer whispered at that moment in an agonised voice.

I concluded she had been reduced to her unhappy condition largely by Templer's goings-on. Her own prettiness, silliness, adoration of himself must have brought Templer to the point of deciding to remove her from the husband who 'bored her by talking of money all the time'. At a period when Templer was no doubt still smarting from his own abandonment by Mona, Betty had re-established his confidence by accepting him so absolutely. In marrying her, Templer had shown himself determined to make no such mistake a second time, to choose a wife unquestionably devoted to him, one possessing, besides, not too much life of her own. Mona, by the time she came Templer's way, had had too many adventures. In Betty, he had certainly found adoration (throughout dinner, she continually cast tortured glances in his direction), but the price had been a high one. In short, Templer had picked a girl probably not quite 'all there' even at the beginning of their married life; then, by his rackety conduct, he had sent her never very stable faculties off their balance. Betty Templer was simply not equipped to cope with her husband, to stand up to Templer's armour-plated egotism as a 'ladies' man'. The qualities that had bowled her over before marriage—that bowled her over, so far as that went, still—had also driven her to the borders of sanity. Never very bright in the head, she had been shattered by the unequal battle. The exercise of powerful 'charm' is, in any case, more appreciated in public than in private life, exacting, as it does, almost as heavy demands on the receiver as the transmitter, demands often too onerous to be weighed satisfactorily against the many other, all too delicate, requirements of married life. No doubt affairs with other women played their part as well. In the circumstances, it was inconceivable that Templer did not have affairs with other women. That, at least, was my own reading of the situation. Anyway, whatever the cause, there could be no doubt Betty Templer's spirit was broken, that she was near the end of her tether. Templer must have been aware of that himself. In fact, his perpetual awareness of it explained my own consciousness of some horror in the background when he had stepped from his car that evening. He was always kind, I noticed, when he spoke to Betty, would probably have done anything in his power—short of altering his own way of life, which perhaps no one can truly do—to alleviate this painful situation. It was a gruesome predicament. I thought how ironic that Templer, my first friend to speak with assurance of 'women' and their ways, should have been caught up in this dire matrimonial trap. These impressions shot across the mind, disquieting, evanescent, like forked lightning. Sir Magnus, who had been silent for a minute or two, now leaned forward over the dinner-table, as if to carry us all with him at some all important board meeting—at a Cabinet itself—in the pursuance of an onerous project he had in mind.

'By all means let us take some photographs after dinner,' he said. 'What a good idea.'

Highlights showed on his greenish eyes. No doubt he saw escape from dishing up 'Munich' for the thousandth time, not only with Anne Umfraville, but also with a handful of guests whose views he could not reasonably be expected to take seriously. Like so many men who have made a successful career through the will, it was hard to guess how much, or how little, Sir Magnus took in of what was going on immediately round him. Did he know that his own sexual habits were a source of constant speculation and jocularity; that Moreland was tortured by the thought of Matilda's former status in the house; that Betty Templer made the party a very uncomfortable one; or was he indifferent to these things, and many others as well? It was impossible to say. Perhaps Sir Magnus, through his antennae, was even more keenly apprised of surrounding circumstances than the rest of us; perhaps, on the other hand, he was able to dismiss them completely from his consciousness as absolutely unessential elements in his own tranquil progress through life.

'Let's pose some tableaux,' said Matilda. 'Donners can photograph us in groups.'

'Historical events or something of that sort,' said Anne Umfraville. 'The history of the castle? We could use some of the armour. Ladies watching a tournament?'

Moreland had shown signs of being dreadfully bored until that moment, expressing his own lack of enjoyment by yawns and occasional tart remarks. Now he began to cheer up. The latest proposal not only pointed to the kind of evening he liked, it also opened up new possibilties of teasing Sir Magnus, a project certainly uppermost at that moment in his mind. Anne Umfraville seemed to some extent to share this wish to torment her host.

'Let's do scenes from the career of Sir Magnus,' said Moreland. 'His eventual rise to being dictator of the world.'

'No, no,' said Sir Magnus, laughing. 'That I cannot allow. It would have a bad effect on my photography. You must remember I am only a beginner. Myself as a subject would make me nervous.'

'Hitler and Chamberlain at Godesberg?' suggested Templer.

That proposal, certainly banal enough, was at once dismissed, not only as introducing too sinister, too depressing a note, but also as a scene devoid of attractive and colourful characters of both sexes.

'What about some mythological incident?' said Moreland. 'Andromeda chained to her rock, or the flaying of Marsyas?'

'Or famous pictures?' said Anne Umfraville. 'A man once told me I looked like Mona Lisa. I admit he'd drunk a lot of Martinis. We want something that will bring everyone in.'

'Rubens's *Rape of the Sabine Women*,' said Moreland, 'or *The Garden of Earthly Delights* by Hieronymus Bosch. We might even be highbrows, while we're about it, and do *Les demoiselles d'Avignon*. What's against a little practical cubism?'

Sir Magnus nodded approvingly.

'We girls don't want to die of cold,' said Anne Umfraville. 'Nothing too rough, either. I'm not feeling particularly cubistic tonight.'

'Or too highbrow,' said Templer. 'Nick will get out of hand. I know him of old. Let's stick to good straightforward stuff, don't you agree, Magnus—Anne doing a strip-tease, for instance.'

'Nothing sordid,' said Anne Umfraville, her attention distinctly engaged by this last suggestion. 'It must all be at a high intellectual level, or I shan't play.'

'Well-known verses, then,' said Moreland.

> 'I was a king in Babylon,
> And you were a Christian slave. . . .

—not that I can ever see how the couple in question managed to be those utterly disparate things at the same moment in history—or, to change the mood entirely:

> Now all strange hours and all strange loves are over,
> Dreams and desires and sombre songs and sweet . . .

There is good material in both of those. The last would be convenient for including everyone.'

My own mind was still on the tapestries. What could be better than variations on the spectacle these already offered?

'Why not the Seven Deadly Sins?'

'Oh, yes,' said Anne Umfraville.

'Modern version,' said Moreland.

'A good idea,' agreed Sir Magnus. 'A very good idea indeed.'

He nodded his head in support of the Board's—the Cabinet's—proposal. That was the tone of his words. He glanced round to talk. There was no dissentient voice.

'I shall look forward to seeing some first-rate acting after dinner,' he said.

He nodded his head again. Everything he did had about it heavy, sonorous overtones. He was entirely free from gaiety. Nothing of that kind could ever have troubled him. There was suddenly a tremendous gasp from Betty Templer, who had been quite silent while all this discussion was taking place.

'Oh, we haven't got to act, have we?' she now cried out in a voice of despair. 'I can't act. I never was able to. Need we really?'

'Oh, don't be so silly, darling,' said Templer, addressing her for the first time that evening rather sharply. 'It's only a game. Nothing much will be expected of you. Don't try and wreck everything from the start.'

'But I *can't* act.'

'It will be all right.'

'Oh, I wish I hadn't come.'

'Pull yourself together, Betty.'

This call to order made her lips tremble. Again, I thought there were going to be tears. However, once more she recovered herself. She was more determined than one might suppose.

'Yes, you must certainly play your part, Betty,' said Sir Magnus, with just a hint, just the smallest suggestion, of conscious cruelty. 'We are exactly seven, so everyone must do his or her bit.'

'We're eight,' said Moreland. 'Surely you yourself are not going to be sinless?'

'I shall only be the photographer,' said Sir Magnus, smiling firmly.

'What are the Seven Deadly Sins, anyway?' said Anne Umfraville. 'I can never remember. Lust, of course—we all know that one—but the others, Pride——'

'Anger—Avarice—Envy—Sloth—Gluttony,' said Isobel.

'They are represented all round us,' said Sir Magnus, making a gesture towards the walls, at the same time wiping his lips very carefully with a napkin, as if in fear of contamination, 'sometimes pictured rather whimsically.'

He seemed cheered as Moreland by what lay ahead. He must also have decided either that a little more drink would improve the tableaux, or that the measure of wine up to then provided was insufficient to clear him unequivocally of the sin of Avarice, because he said in an aside to the butler: 'I think we shall need some more of that claret.'

'How are we to decide what everyone is going to do?'

said Anne Umfraville. 'Obviously Lust is the star part.'

'Do you think so, Anne?' said Sir Magnus, feigning ponderous reproof. 'Then to prevent argument, I must decide for you all. It will be my privilege as host. I shall allot everyone a Sin. Then they will be allowed their own team to act it. Peter, I think we can rely on you to take charge of Lust—which for some reason Anne seems to suppose so acceptable to everyone—for I don't think we can offer such a sin to a lady. Perhaps, Anne, you would yourself undertake Anger—no, no, not a word. I must insist. Matilda—Envy. Not suit you? Certainly I think it would suit you. Lady Isobel, no one could object to Pride. Betty, I am going to ask you to portray Avarice. It is a very easy one, making no demand on your powers as an actress. Nonsense, Betty, you will do it very well. We will all help you. Hugh, don't be offended if I ask you to present Gluttony. I have often heard you praise the pleasures of the table above all others. Mr Jenkins, I fear there is nothing left for you but Sloth. There are, of course, no personal implications. I am sure it is quite inappropriate, but like Avarice, it makes no great demands on the actor.'

If the administrative capacity of Sir Magnus Donners had ever been at all in question before that moment, his ability to make decisions—and have them obeyed—was now amply demonstrated. Naturally, a certain amount of grumbling took place about the allotment of Sins, but only superficial. No vital objection was raised. In the end everyone bowed to the Donners ruling. Even Betty Templer made only a feeble repetition of the statement that she could not act at all. It was brushed aside for the last time. Moreland was especially delighted with the idea of portraying Gluttony.

'Can we do them in here?' he asked, 'everyone in front of his or her appropriate Sin?'

'Certainly,' said Sir Magnus, 'certainly. We will return after coffee.'

He had become more than ever like an energetic, dominating headmaster, organising extempore indoor exercise for his pupils on an afternoon too wet for outdoor games. A faint suggestion of repressed, slightly feverish excitement under his calm, added to this air, like some pedagogue confronted with aspects of his duties that gratify him almost to the point of aberration. The rest of dinner passed with much argument as to how best the Sins were to be depicted. All of us drank a lot, especially Moreland, Templer and Anne Umfraville, only Sir Magnus showing his usual moderation. The extravagance of the project offered temporary relief from personal problems, from the European scene. I had not expected the evening to turn out this way. There could be no doubt that Sir Magnus, genuinely exhilarated, was, as much as anyone, casting aside his worries. While the table was cleared, we had coffee in the Chinese Room, drawing lots as to the order in which the Sins should be presented. Camera and arc lamps were moved into the dining-room.

'Do you want any companions, Hugh?' asked Sir Magnus.

'Gluttony at its most enjoyable dispenses with companionship,' said Moreland, who was to lead off.

He had surrounded himself with dishes of fruit and liqueur bottles, from both of which he was helping himself liberally.

'Be prepared for the flash,' said Sir Magnus.

Moreland, not prepared, upset a glass of Kümmel. He must have been photographed half-sprawled across the table. It was agreed to have been a good performance.

'I shall continue to act the Sin for the rest of the evening,' he said, pouring out more Kümmel, this time into a tumbler.

Isobel was next as Pride. She chose Anne Umfraville as her 'feed'. With these two a different note was struck.

Moreland's 'turn' was something individual to himself, an artist—in this case a musician—displaying considerable attainment in a medium not his own. With Isobel and Anne Umfraville, on the other hand, the performance was of quite another order. The two of them had gone off together to find suitable 'properties', returning with a metal receptacle for fire irons, more or less golden in material, the legs of which, when inverted, formed the spikes of a crown. They had also amassed a collection of necklaces and beads, rugs and capes of fur. With the crown on her head, loaded with jewels, fur hanging in a triangular pattern from her sleeves, Isobel looked the personification of Pride. Anne Umfraville, having removed her dress, wore over her underclothes a tattered motor rug, pinned across with a huge brooch that might have come from a sporran. She had partially blacked her face; her hair hung in rats' tails over her forehead; her feet were bare, enamelled toenails the only visible remnant of a more ornamented form of existence. Here, before us, in these two, was displayed the nursery and playroom life of generations of 'great houses': the abounding physical vitality of big aristocratic families, their absolute disregard for personal dignity in uninhibited delight in 'dressing up', that passionate return to childhood, never released so fully in any other country, or, even in this country, so completely by any other class. Sir Magnus was enchanted.

'You are a naughty girl, Anne,' he said, with warm approval. 'You've made yourself look an absolute little scamp, a bundle of mischief. I congratulate you, too, Lady Isobel. You should always wear fur. Fur really becomes you.'

'My turn next,' said Anne Umfraville now breathless with excitement. 'Isobel and I can do Anger just as we are. It fits perfectly. Wait a second.'

She went off to the hall, returning a moment later with

a long two-handed sword, snatched from the wall, or from one of the figures in armour. With this, as Anger provoked by Pride, she cut Isobel down in her finery.

'That should make a splendid picture,' said Sir Magnus, from behind the camera.

My own enactment of Sloth required no histrionic ability beyond lying on the table supported by piles of cushions. It was quickly over.

'Leave the cushions there, Nick,' said Templer, 'I shall need them all for Lust.'

Matilda's turn, good as it was in some ways, noticeably lowered the temperature of the entertainment. Once again the whole tone of the miming changed. I had the impression that, if Anne Umfraville was unexpectedly tolerant of Matilda, Matilda was less prepared to accept Anne Umfraville. Certainly Matilda was determined to show that she, as a professional actress, had a reputation to sustain. She had draped herself in a long green robe—possibly one of Sir Magnus's dressing gowns, since Matilda's familiarity with the castle rooms had been of help in collecting costumes and 'props'—a dress that entirely concealed her trousers. In this she stood, with no supporting cast, against the panel of the tapestry representing Envy. Everything was to be done by expression of the features. She stood absolutely upright, her face contorted. The glance, inasmuch as it was canalised, seemed aimed in the direction of Anne Umfraville. So far as it went, the performance was good; it might even be said to show considerable talent. On the other hand, the professional note, the contrast with what had gone before, somewhat chilled the party. There was some clapping. There appeared to be no other way of bringing Matilda back to earth.

'Jolly good, Matty,' said Moreland. 'I shall know now what's happened when I next see you looking like that.'

There was still Betty Templer to be hustled through Avarice, before her husband sustained the role of Lust, the final Sin, which, it was agreed, would make a cheerful termination to the spectacle. I was interested to see what would happen when Betty Templer's turn came: whether Sir Magnus would take charge, or Templer. It was Templer.

'Come on, Betty,' he said in a soothing voice. 'I can be a beggar by the side of the road and you can be walking past with your nose in the air.'

That was obviously a simple, kindly solution to Betty Templer's diffidence about acting, to which no objection could possibly be taken. There was assistance from Anne Umfraville and Isobel in providing a suitably rich-looking bag, and various garments, to increase the contrast between riches and poverty. Templer himself had by then removed some of his clothes, so that only a few touches were required to turn him into an all but naked beggar seeking alms. His wife stood smiling unhappily for a second or two, taut and miserable, but carried through, in spite of everything, by her looks. She was undeniably very pretty indeed. In the unpropitious circumstances, she might be said to have acquitted herself well. Now that the ordeal was over, she would no doubt feel better. I thought that the danger of a total breakdown on her part—by no means to be disregarded until that moment—could now be dismissed from the mind. Indeed, having been forced against her will to 'act', Betty Templer would probably discover that she was quite pleased with herself after carrying things off with such comparative success.

'Good, Betty,' said Sir Magnus, perhaps himself a little relieved. 'Now Lust, Peter. Do you want any help?'

'Yes, of course, I do, old boy,' said Templer, now rather tight. 'Really, that is a most insulting remark, Magnus. I shouldn't have thought it of you. I want all the girls I'm not married to. Married Lust isn't decent. I'd like to do some different forms of Lust. You can photograph the one you think best.'

'No reason not to photograph them all,' said Sir Magnus. 'There is plenty of film.'

'Why not do the three ages of Lust?' said Moreland, 'Young, Middle-aged, Elderly?'

'A splendid idea,' said Templer. 'Perhaps Lady Isobel and Mrs Moreland would assist me in the first two, and Anne in the last.'

He began to prepare a corner of the table, upon which the cushions of Sloth still remained. Templer had now entirely thrown off the distant, almost formal air he had shown earlier in the day. He was more like himself when I had known him years before. His first scene, Youthful Lust, as he saw it—an old-fashioned conception, very typical of Templer himself—was to take place in the private room of a restaurant, where a debutante had been lured by a lustful undergratuate: Isobel, in long white gloves (which Sir Magnus produced, as if by magic), with three ostrich feathers in her hair; Templer, in vaguely sporting attire, shorts and a scarf playing some part. Then, Middle-aged Lust; Matilda for some reason wearing sun-spectacles, was a married woman repelling the advances of a lustful clergy-man, Templer in this role wearing an evening collar back-to-front. Neither of these two tableaux was specially memorable. For the third scene, Elderly Lust, a lustful octogenarian entertained to dinner a ballet girl—another typically nineteenth-century Templer concept—an opera-hat being produced from somewhere, white blotting paper from the writing-table in the morning-room providing a stiff shirt. Anne Umfraville had constructed some sort of a ballet skirt, but was wearing by then little else. In his presentation of senile lust, Templer excelled himself, a theatrical performance he could never have achieved in the past. His acting might almost be regarded as one of those cases where unhappiness and frustration seem to force something like art from persons normally concerned with only the material side of life. Anne Umfraville, as the ballet girl, fell not far short of him in excellence.

'Give me that fly-whisk,' said Templer.

At the height of the act, amid much laughter from the audience, I suddenly heard next to me a muffled howl. It was the noise a dog makes when accidentally trodden on. I turned to see what had happened. The sound came from Betty Templer. Tears were coursing down her cheeks. Up to that moment she had been sitting silent on one of the dining-room chairs, watching the show, apparently fairly happy now that her own turn was passed. I thought she was even finding these antics a little amusing. Now, as I looked at her, she jumped up and rushed from the room. The door slammed. Templer and Anne Umfraville, both by then more or less recumbent on the cushions littering the table, in a dramatic and convincing representation of impotent desire, now separated one from the other. Templer slid to his feet. Sir Magnus looked up from the camera.

'Oh, dear,' he said mildly, 'I'm afraid Betty is not feeling well again. Perhaps she should not have sat up so late.'

For some reason my mind was carried back at that moment to Stonehurst and the Billson incident. This was all the same kind of thing. Betty wanted Templer's love, just as Billson wanted Albert's; Albert's marriage had precipitated a breakdown in just the same way as Templer's extravagances with Anne Umfraville. Here, unfortunately, was no General Conyers to take charge of the situation, to quieten Betty Templer. Certainly her husband showed no immediate sign of wanting to accept that job. However, before an extreme moral discomfort could further immerse all of us, a diversion took place. The door of the dining-room, so recently slammed, opened again. A man stood on the threshold. He was in uniform. He appeared to be standing at attention, a sinister, threatening figure, calling the world to arms. It was Widmerpool.

'Good evening,' he said.

Sir Magnus, who had been fiddling with the camera, smiling quietly to himself, as if he had not entirely failed to extract a passing thrill of pleasure from Betty Templer's *crise*, looked up. Then he advanced across the room, his hand outstretched.

'Kenneth,' he said, 'I did not expect to see you at this late hour. I thought you must have decided to drive straight to London. We have been taking some photographs.'

By that date, when the country had lived for some time under the threat of war, the traditional, the almost complete professional anonymity of the army in England had been already abrogated. Orders enacting that officers were never to be seen in London wearing uniform—certainly on no social occasion, nor, as a rule, even when there on duty—being to some extent relaxed, it was now not unknown for a Territorial, for example, to appear in khaki in unmilitary surroundings because he was on his way to or from a brief period of training. Something of the sort must have caused Widmerpool's form of dress. His arrival at this hour was, in any case, surprising enough. The sight of him in uniform struck a chill through my bones. Nothing, up to that date, had so much brought home to me the imminence, the certitude, of war. That was not because Widmerpool himself looked innately military. On the contrary, he had almost the air of being ⌐bout to perform a music-hall turn, sing a patriotic song or burlesque, with 'patter', an army officer. Perhaps that was only because the rest of the party were more or less in fancy dress. Even so, uniform, for some reason, brings out character, physique, class, even sex, in a curious manner. I had never before thought of Widmerpool as possessing physical characteristics at all feminine in disposition, but now his bulky, awkward shape, buttoned up and held together by a Sam Browne belt, recalled Heather Hopkins got up as an admiral in some act at the Merry Thought. Widmerpool was evidently at a loss, hopelessly at a loss, to know what was happening. He put his cap, leather gloves and a swagger stick bound in leather on the sideboard, having for some reason brought all these with him, instead of leaving them in the hall; possibly to make a more dramatic appearance. Sir Magnus introduced the Morelands. Widmerpool began to assert himself.

'I have heard my medical man, Brandreth, speak of you, Mr Moreland,' he said. 'Don't you play the piano? I think so. Now I recall, I believe, that we met in a nursing home where I was confined for a time with those vexatious boils. I found you in the passage one day, talking to Nicholas here. I believe you are one of Brandreth's patients, too. He is an able fellow, Brandreth, if something of a gossip.'

'I say, Kenneth, old boy,' said Templer, who, in surprise at seeing Widmerpool at this moment in such an outfit, seemed to have forgotten, at least dismissed from his mind, his wife's hysterical outburst, 'are you going to make us all form fours?'

'You are not very up to date, Peter,' said Widmerpool, smiling at such a pitiful error. 'The army no longer forms fours. You should surely know that. We have not done so for several years now. I cannot name the precise date of the Army Council Regulation. It is certainly by no means recent.'

'Sorry,' said Templer. 'You must give us some squad drill later.'

'You are very fortunate not to be faced with squad drill

in any case,' said Widmerpool severely, 'it was touch and go. You may count yourself lucky that the recent formula was reached.'

Templer brought his heels together with a click. Widmerpool ignored this facetiousness. He turned to me.

'Well, Nicholas,' he said, 'I did not know you were a Stourwater visitor. Can you explain to me why everyone is clad—or unclad—in this extraordinary manner?'

Sir Magnus took charge of him.

'I am glad you were able to look in, Kenneth,' he said. 'We were taking a few photographs after dinner. Just the Seven Deadly Sins, you know. Like yourself, I am a believer in relaxation in these troublous times. It is absolutely necessary. You look very military, my dear fellow.'

'I have been staying at my mother's cottage,' said Widmerpool, evidently gratified by Sir Magnus's conciliatory tone. 'I spent most of the afternoon with one of the other units in my Territorial division. I was doing a rather special job for our CO. There seemed no point in changing back into mufti. I find, too, that uniform makes a good impression these days. A sign of the times. However, I merely looked in to tell you, Magnus, that arrangements about the Swiss company are all but completed. There were no complications.'

'This is old Bob's affair, is it?' said Templer. 'I saw him last week. He was complaining about the markets. God knows, they're awful.'

Templer, at that moment, was sitting on the edge of the dining-room table, with the opera-hat tipped to the back of his head. Having removed most of his clothes, he had wrapped a heavy rug around him, so that he might have been wearing some garment like an Inverness cape. He looked like a contemporary picture of a Victorian businessman on a journey.

'Steel made a modest recovery,' said Widmerpool, apparently mesmerised by this semi-professional garb of Templer's into talking general business. 'Then Copper has been receiving a fair amount of support. Also the Zinc-Lead group, with certain specific Tin shares. Still, it's a sorry state of affairs. I'm keeping an eye on this calling-in of funds by non-clearing lenders.'

Even Sir Magnus himself was unable to resist this sudden switch to money-matters at Widmerpool's entrance.

'The discount houses are getting sixty-nine per cent of their applications for bills dated any day next week except Saturday at a price equal to a discount rate of practically twenty-five thirty-seconds per cent,' he said.

'What do you think about the rumours of Roosevelt devaluing the dollar, Magnus?' asked Templer. 'You don't mind if I put a few more clothes on, here and now? It's getting a shade chilly.'

'I see the flight of funds to Wall Street as continuing,' said Sir Magnus, speaking very quietly, 'even though we have avoided war for the time being.'

That was an opinion I should have been prepared to hazard myself without laying claim to financial wizardry. Sir Magnus must have been unwilling to commit himself in front of Widmerpool. His words also carried the unmistakable note of implication that we should all go home.

'Well, we have avoided war,' said Widmerpool. 'That is the important point. I myself think we are safe for five years at least. But—to get back to Duport—everything is going through the subsidiary company, as agreed. Duport will collect the material from the Turkish sellers on his own responsibility, and wire the Swiss company when he has enough ores for shipment.'

'This ought to keep old Bob quiet for a bit,' said Templer. 'He does a job well when he's at it, but goes to pieces if unemployed. He brought off some smart deals in manganese when he was in South America, so he is always telling me.

Chromite is the main source of manganese, isn't it? I'm no expert.'

'Chromite——' began Widmerpool.

'And payments?' asked Sir Magnus, not without emphasis.

'I've opened an account for him through a local bank,' said Widmerpool, 'since you asked me to handle the credit formalities. That is agreeable to you, I hope. Duport can thereby undertake down-payments. We shall have to keep an eye on the European situation. In my opinion, as I said just now, it is going to steady up.'

'Very good, Kenneth,' said Sir Magnus, in a voice that closed the matter.

He began to fold up the stand of the flash lamp. The evening, for Sir Magnus's visitors, was at an end. The girls, who had already gone off to clean themselves up, were now returning. There was some muttering between Templer and Anne Umfraville. Then she said good night all round, and retired from the dining-room.

'I think I'd better go up too,' said Templer. 'See how Betty is getting on.'

He too said good night. There was a sound of laughter from the stairs, suggesting that Anne Umfraville had not yet reached her room.

'Kenneth,' said Sir Magnus, 'I am going to ask you to take these friends of mine back in your car. It is not out of your way.'

'Where do they live?' asked Widmerpool, without bothering to assume even the most superficial veneer of pleasure, even resignation, at this prospect. 'I was intending to take the short cut through the park.'

'Peter kindly fetched them,' said Sir Magnus, 'but Betty is not feeling well this evening. Naturally he wants to attend to her.'

He was absolutely firm.

'Come on, then,' said Widmerpool, without geniality.

We thanked Sir Magnus profusely. He bowed us out. There was not much room in Widmerpool's car. We charged insecurely through murky lanes.

'What happened to Peter's wife?' asked Widmerpool. 'She is rather delicate, isn't she? I have hardly met her.'

We gave him some account of the Stourwater evening.

'You seem all to have behaved in an extraordinary manner,' said Widmerpool. 'There is a side of Magnus of which I cannot altogether approve, his taste for buffoonery of that kind. I don't like it myself, and you would be surprised at the stories such goings-on give rise to. Disgusting stories. Totally untrue, of course, but mud sticks. You know Magnus will sit up working now until two or three in the morning. I know his habits.'

'What is wrong with Betty Templer?' I asked.

'I have been told that Peter neglects her,' said Widmerpool. 'I understand she has always been rather a silly girl. Someone should have thought of that before she became involved in your ragging. It was her husband's place to look after her.'

We arrived at the Morelands' cottage.

'Come in and have a drink,' said Moreland.

'I never touch alcohol when I'm driving,' said Widmerpool, 'more especially when in uniform.'

'A soft drink?'

'Thanks, no.'

'I'll make you a cup of tea,' said Matilda.

'No, Mrs Moreland, I will push on.'

The car's headlights illuminated a stretch of road; then the glare disappeared from sight. We moved into the house.

'Who was that awful man?' said Moreland.

'You met him with me once in a nursing home.'

'No recollection.'

'What a party,' said Isobel. 'Some of it was rather enjoyable, all the same.'

'What do you think of Stourwater?' asked Matilda. 'I find it really rather wonderful, in spite of everything.'

'*Eldorado banal de tous les vieux garçons,*' said Moreland.

'But that was Cythera,' said Isobel, 'the island of love. Do you think love flourishes at Stourwater?'

'I don't know,' said Moreland. 'Love means such different things to different people.'

THREE

Every Christmas, as I have said, Albert used to send my mother a letter drafted in a bold, sloping, dowager's hand, the mauve ink of the broad nib-strokes sinking deep, spreading, into the porous surface of the thick, creamy writing paper with scalloped edge. He had kept that up for years. This missive, composed in the tone of a dispatch from a distant outpost of empire, would contain a detailed account of his recent life, state of health, plans for the future. Albert expressed himself well on paper, with careful formality. In addition to these annual letters, he would, every three or four years, pay my mother a visit on his 'day off'. These visits became rarer as he grew older. During the twenty-five years or so after we left Stonehurst, I saw him on such occasions twice, perhaps three times; one of these meetings was soon after the war, when I was still a schoolboy; another, just before 'coming down' from the university. Perhaps there was a third. I cannot be sure. Certainly, at our last encounter, I remember thinking Albert remarkably unchanged from Stonehurst days: fatter, undeniably, though on the whole additional flesh suited him. He had now settled down to be a fat man, with the professional fat man's privileges and far from negligible status in life. He still supported a chronic weariness of spirit with an irony quite brutal in its unvarnished view of things. His dark-blue suit, assumed ceremonially for the call, gave him a rather distinguished appearance, brown canvas, rubber-soled shoes temporarily substituted for the traditional felt slippers (which one pictured as never renovated or renewed), adding a seedy, nearly sinister touch. He could have passed for a depressed, incurably indolent member of some royal house (there was a look of Prince Theodoric) in hopeless exile. The 'girl from Bristol' had taken him in hand, no doubt bullied him a bit, at the same time arranged a life in general tolerable for both of them. She had caused him to find employment in hotels where good wages were paid, good cooking relatively appreciated. There were two children, a boy and a girl. Albert himself was never greatly interested in either of them, while admitting they 'meant a lot' to his wife. It had been largely with a view to the children's health and education that she had at last decided on moving to a seaside town (the resort, as it happened, where Moreland had once conducted the municipal orchestra), when opportunity was offered there to undertake the management of a small 'private hotel'. Albert was, in principle, to do the cooking, his wife look after the housekeeping. It was a species of retirement, reflecting the 'girl from Bristol's' energetic spirit.

To this establishment—which was called the Bellevue—Uncle Giles inevitably gravitated. Even if he had never heard of Albert, Uncle Giles would probably have turned up there sooner or later. His life was spent in such places —the Ufford, his *pied-à-terre* in Bayswater, the prototype—a phenomenal number of which must have housed him at one time or another through different parts of the United Kingdom.

'Battered caravanserais,' Uncle Giles used to say. 'That's what a fellow I met on board ship used to call the pubs he stayed in. From Omar Khayyám, you know. Not a bad name for 'em. Well-read man in his way. Wrote for the papers. Bit of a bounder. Stingy, too. Won the ship's sweep and nobody saw a halfpenny back in hospitality.'

The position of Albert at the Bellevue offered a family connexion not to be disregarded, one to support a reasonable demand for that special treatment always felt by Uncle Giles to be unjustly denied him by fate and the malign efforts of 'people who want to push themselves to the front'. Besides, the Bellevue offered a precinct where he could grumble to his heart's content about his own family to someone who knew them personally. That was a rare treat. In addition, when Uncle Giles next saw any members of his family, he could equally grumble about Albert, complaining that his cooking had deteriorated, his manners become 'offhand'. Uncle Giles did not visit the Bellevue often. Probably Albert, who had his own vicissitudes of temperament to contend with, did not care—family connexion or no family connexion—to accommodate so cantankerous a client there too frequently. He may have made intermittent excuses that the hotel was full to capacity. Whatever the reason, these occasional sojourns at the Bellevue were spaced out, for the most part, between Uncle Giles's recurrent changes of employment, which grew no less frequent with the years. He continued to enjoy irritating his relations.

'I like the little man they've got in Germany now,' he would remark, quite casually.

This view, apparently so perverse in the light of Uncle Giles's often declared biblical principles, was in a measure the logical consequence of them. Dating to some extent from the post-war period, when to support Germany against France was the mark of liberal opinion, it had somehow merged with his approval of all action inimical to established institutions. National Socialism represented revolution; to that extent the movement gained the support, at any rate temporary support, of Uncle Giles. Besides, he shared Hitler's sense of personal persecution, conviction that the world was against him. This was in marked contrast to the feeling of my brother-in-law, Erridge, also a declared enemy of established institutions, who devoted much of his energies to assisting propaganda against current German policies.

Erridge, however, in his drift away from orthodox Communism after his own experiences in Spain, had become an increasingly keen 'pacifist', so that he was, in practice, as unwilling to oppose Germany by force of arms as Uncle Giles himself.

'We don't want guns,' Erridge used to say. 'We want to make the League of Nations effective.'

The death of the Tollands' stepmother, Lady Warminster, a year or two before, with the consequent closing down of Hyde Park Gardens as an establishment, caused a re-grouping of the members of the Tolland family who had lived there. This had indirectly affected Erridge, not as a rule greatly concerned with the lives of his brothers and sisters. When Lady Warminster's household came to an end, Blanche, Robert and Hugo Tolland had to find somewhere else to live, a major physical upheaval for them. Even for the rest of the family, Lady Warminster's death snapped a link with the past that set the state of childhood at a further perspective, forced her stepchildren to look at life in rather a different manner. Ties with their stepmother, on the whole affectionate, had never been close in her lifetime. Death emphasised their comparative strength: Norah Tolland, especially, who had never 'got on' very well with Lady Warminster, now losing no opportunity of asserting —with truth—that she had possessed splendid qualities. Although widow of two relatively rich men, Lady Warminster left little or no money of her own. There were some small bequests to relations, friends and servants. Blanche Tolland received the residue. She had always been the favourite of her stepmother, who may have felt that Blanche's 'dottiness' required all financial support available. However, when the point of departure came, Blanche's future posed no problem. Erridge suggested she should keep house for him at Thrubworth. His butler, Smith, had also died at about that moment—'in rather horrible circumstances', Erridge wrote—and he had decided that he needed a woman's help in running the place.

'Smith is the second butler Erry has killed under him,' said Norah. 'You'd better take care, Blanchie.'

Since his brief adventure with Mona, Erridge had shown no further sign of wanting to marry, even to associate himself with another woman at all intimately. That may have been partly because his health had never wholly recovered from the dysentery incurred in Spain: another reason why his sister's care was required. This poor state of health Erridge—always tending to hypochondria—now seemed to welcome, perhaps feeling that to become as speedily as possible a chronic invalid would be some insurance against the need to take a decision in the insoluble problem of how to behave if hostilities with Germany were to break out.

'I have become a sick man,' he used to say, on the rare occasion when any of his family visited Thrubworth. 'I don't know at all how long I am going to last.'

Robert Tolland had lived in his stepmother's house, partly through laziness, partly from an ingrained taste for economy; at least those were the reasons attributed by his brothers and sisters. At her death, Robert took a series of small flats on his own, accommodation he constantly changed, so that often no one knew in the least where he was to be found. In short, Robert's life became more mysterious than ever. Hitherto, he had been seen from time to time at Hyde Park Gardens Sunday luncheon-parties; now, except for a chance glimpse at a theatre or a picture gallery, he disappeared from sight entirely, personal relationship with him in general reduced to an occasional telephone call. Hugo Tolland, the youngest brother, also passed irretrievably into a world of his own. He continued to be rather successful as assistant to Mrs Baldwyn Hodges in her second-hand furniture and decorating business, where, one afternoon, he sold a set of ormolu candlesticks to Max Pilgrim, the pianist and cabaret entertainer, who was moving into a new flat. When Hyde Park Gardens closed down, Hugo announced that he was going to share this flat. There was even a suggestion—since engagements of the kind in which he had made his name were less available than formerly—that Pilgrim might put some money into Mrs Baldwyn Hodge's firm and himself join the business.

Among her small bequests, Lady Warminster left her sister, Molly Jeavons, the marquetry cabinet in which she kept the material for her books, those rambling, unreviewed, though not entirely unreadable, historical studies of dominating women. The Maria Theresa manuscript, last of these biographies upon which she had worked, remained uncompleted, because Lady Warminster admitted—expressing the matter, of course, in her own impenetrably oblique manner —she had taken a sudden dislike to the Empress on reading for the first time of her heartless treatment of prostitutes. Although they used to see relatively little of each other, Molly Jeavons was greatly distressed at her sister's death. No greater contrast could be imagined than the staid, even rather despondent atmosphere of Hyde Park Gardens, and the devastating muddle and hustle of the Jeavons house in South Kensington, but it was mistaken to suppose these antitheses precisely reproduced the opposing characters of the two sisters. Lady Warminster had a side that took pleasure in the tumbledown aspects of life: journeys to obscure fortune-tellers in the suburbs, visits out of season to dowdy seaside hotels. It was, indeed, remarkable that she had never found her way to the Bellevue. Molly Jeavons, on the other hand, might pass her days happily enough with a husband as broken down, as unemployable, as untailored, as Ted Jeavons, while she ran a kind of free hotel for her relations, a rest-home for cats, dogs and other animals that could impose themselves on her good nature; Molly, too, was capable of enjoying other sides of life. She had had occasional bursts of magnificence as Marchioness of Sleaford, whatever her first marriage may have lacked in other respects.

'The first year they were married,' Chips Lovell said, 'the local Hunt Ball was held at Dogdene. Molly, aged eighteen or nineteen, livened up the proceedings by wearing the Sleaford tiara—which I doubt if Aunt Alice has ever so much as tried on—and the necklace belonging to Tippoo Sahib that Uncle Geoffrey's grandfather bought for his Spanish mistress when he outbid Lord Hertford on that famous occasion.'

For some reason there was a great deal of fuss about moving the marquetry cabinet from Hyde Park Gardens to South Kensington. The reason for these difficulties was obscure, although it was true that not an inch remained in the Jeavons house for the accommodation of an additional piece of furniture.

'Looks as if I shall have to push the thing round myself on a barrow,' said Jeavons, speaking gloomily of this problem.

Then, one day in the summer after 'Munich', when German pressure on Poland was at its height, Uncle Giles died too—quite suddenly of a stroke—while staying at the Bellevue.

'Awkward to the end,' my father said, 'though I suppose one should not speak in that way.'

It was certainly an inconvenient moment to choose. During the year that had almost passed since Isobel and I had stayed with the Morelands, everyday life had become increasingly concerned with preparations for war: expansion of the services, air-raid precautions, the problems of evacuation; no one talked of anything else. My father, in poor health after being invalided out of the army a dozen years before (indirect result of the wound incurred in Mesopotamia), already racked with worry by the well-justified fear that he would be unfit for re-employment if war came, was at that moment in no state to oversee his brother's cremation. I found myself charged with that duty. There was, indeed, no one else to do the job. By universal consent, Uncle Giles was to be cremated, rather than buried. In the first place, no specially apposite spot awaited his coffin; in the second, a crematorium was at hand in the town where he died. Possibly another feeling, too, though unspoken, influenced that decision: a feeling that fire was the element appropriate to his obsequies, the funeral pyre traditional to the nomad.

I travelled down to the seaside town in the afternoon. Isobel was not feeling well. She was starting a baby. Circumstances were not ideal for a pregnancy. Apart from unsettled international conditions, the weather was hot, too hot. I felt jumpy, irritable. In short, to be forced to undertake this journey in order to dispose of the remains of Uncle Giles seemed the last straw in making life tedious, disagreeable, threatening, through no apparent fault of one's own. I had never seen much of Uncle Giles, felt no more than formal regret that he was no longer among us. There seemed no justice in the fact that fate had willed this duty to fall on myself. At the same time, I had to admit things might have been worse. Albert—more probably his wife—had made preliminary arrangements for the funeral, after informing my father of Uncle Giles's death. I should stay at the Bellevue, where I was known; where, far more important, Uncle Giles was known. He probably owed money, but there would be no uneasiness. Albert would have no fears about eventual payment. It was true that some embarrassing fact might be revealed: with Uncle Giles, to be prepared for the unexpected in some more or less disagreeable form was always advisable. Albert, burdened with few illusions on any subject, certainly possessed none about Uncle Giles; he would grasp the situation even if there were complexities. I could do what clearing up was required, attend the funeral, return the following morning. There was no real excuse for grumbling. All the same, I felt a certain faint-heartedness at the prospect of meeting Albert again after all these years, a fear—rather a base one—that he might produce embarrassing reminiscences of my own childhood. That was very contemptible. A moment's serious thought would have shown me that nothing was less likely. Albert was interested in himself, not in other people. That did not then occur to me. My trepidation was increased by the fact that I had never yet set eyes on the 'girl from Bristol', of whom her husband had always painted so alarming a picture. She was called 'Mrs Creech', because Albert, strange as it might seem, was named 'Albert Creech'. The suffix 'Creech' sounded to my ears unreal, incongruous, rather impertinent, like suddenly attaching a surname to one of the mythical figures of Miss Orchard's stories of the gods and goddesses, or Mr Deacon's paintings of the Hellenic scene. Albert, I thought, was like Sisyphus or Charon, one of those beings committed eternally to undesired and burdensome labours. Charon was more appropriate, since Albert had, as it were, recently ferried Uncle Giles over the Styx. I do not attempt to excuse these frivolous, perhaps rather heartless, reflections on my own part as I was carried along in the train.

On arrival, I went straight to the undertaker's to find out what arrangements had already been made. Later, when the Bellevue hove into sight—the nautical phrase is deliberately chosen—I saw at once that, during his visits there, Uncle Giles had irrevocably imposed his own personality upon the hotel. Standing at the corner of a short, bleak, anonymous street some little way from the sea-front, this corner house, although much smaller in size, was otherwise scarcely to be distinguished from the Ufford, his London *pied-à-terre*. Like the Ufford, its exterior was painted battleship-grey, the angle of the building conveying just the same sense of a hopelessly unseaworthy, though less heavily built vessel, resolutely attempting to set out to sea. This foolhardy attempt of the Bellevue to court shipwreck, emphasised by the distant splash of surf, seemed somehow Uncle Giles's fault. It was just the way he behaved himself. Perhaps I attributed too much to his powers of will. The physical surroundings of most individuals, left to their own choice, vary little wherever they happen to live. No doubt that was the explanation. I was in the presence of one of those triumphs of mind over matter, like the photographer's power of imposing his own personal visual demands on the subject photographed. Nevertheless, even though I ought to have been prepared for a house of more or less the same sort, this miniature, shrunken version of the Ufford surprised me by its absolute consistency of type, almost as much as if the Ufford itself had at last shipped anchor and floated on the sluggish Bayswater tide to this quiet roadstead. Had the Ufford done that? Did the altered name, the new cut of jib, hint at mutiny, barratry, piracy, final revolt on the high seas—for clearly the Bellevue was only awaiting a favourable breeze to set sail—of that ship's company of well brought up souls driven to violence at last by their unjustly straitened circumstances?

Here, at any rate, Uncle Giles had died. By the summer sea, death had claimed him, in one of his own palaces, amongst his own people, the proud, anonymous, secretive race that dwell in residential hotels. I went up the steps of the Bellevue. Inside, again on a much smaller scale, resemblance to the Ufford was repeated: the deserted hall; yellowing letters on the criss-cross ribbons of a board; a faint smell of clean sheets. Striking into the inner fastnesses of its precinct, I came suddenly upon Albert himself. He was pulling down the blinds of some windows that looked on to a sort of yard, just as if he were back putting up the shutters at Stonehurst, for it was still daylight.

'Why, Mr Nick . . .'

Albert, dreadfully ashamed at being caught in this act, in case I might suppose him habitually to lend a hand about the house, began to explain at once that he was occupied in that fashion only because, on this particular evening, his wife was in bed with influenza. He did not hide that he considered her succumbing in this way to be an act of disloyalty.

'I don't think she'll be up and about for another day or two,' he said, 'what with the news on the wireless night after night, it isn't a very cheerful prospect.'

It was absurd to have worried about awkward adjustments where Albert was concerned. Talking to him was just as easy, just as natural, as ever. All his old fears and prejudices remained untouched by time, the Germans—scarcely more ominous—taking the place of the suffragettes. He was older, of course, what was left of his hair, grey and grizzled; fat, though not outrageously fatter than when I had last seen him; breathing a shade more heavily, if that were possible. All the same, he had never become an old man. In essential aspects, he was hardly altered at all: the same timorous, self-centred, sceptical artist-cook he had always been, with the same spirit of endurance, battling his way through life in carpet-slippers. Once the humiliation of being caught doing 'housework' was forgotten, he seemed pleased to see me. He launched at once into an elaborate account of Uncle Giles's last hours, making no attempt to minimise the fearful lineaments of death. In the end, with a view to terminating this catalogue of macabre detail, which I did not at all enjoy and seemed to have continued long enough, however much pleasure the narrative might afford Albert himself in the telling, I found myself invoking the past. This seemed the only avenue of escape. I spoke of Uncle Giles's visit to Stonehurst just before the outbreak of war. Albert was hazy about it.

'Do you remember Bracey?'

'Bracey?'

'Bracey—the soldier servant.'

Albert's face was blank for a moment; then he made a great effort of memory.

'Little fellow with a moustache?'

'Yes.'

'Used to come on a bicycle?'

'That was him.'

'Ignorant sort of man?'

'He had his Funny Days.'

Albert looked blank again. The phrase, once so heavy with ominous import at Stonehurst, had been completely erased from his mind.

'Can't recollect.'

'Surely you must remember—when Bracey used to sulk.'

'Did he go out with the Captain—with the Colonel, that is—when the army went abroad?'

'He was killed at Mons.'

'And which of us is going to keep alive, I wonder, when the next one starts?' said Albert, dismissing, without sentiment, the passing of Bracey. 'It won't be long now, the way I see it. If the government takes over the Bellevue, as they looks like doing, we'll be in a fix. Be just as bad, if we stay. They say the big guns they have nowadays will reach this place easy. They've come on a lot from what they was in 1914.'

'And Billson?' I said.

I was now determined to re-create Stonehurst, the very subject I had dreaded in the train on the way to meet Albert again. I suppose by then I had some idea of working up, by easy stages, to the famous Billson episode with General Conyers. I should certainly have liked to hear Albert's con-

sidered judgment after all these years. Once again, he
showed no sign of recognition.

'Billson?'

'The parlourmaid at Stonehurst.'

'Small girl, was she—always having trouble with her
teeth?'

'No, that was another one.'

I recognised that it was no good attempting to rebuild the
red tiles, the elongated façade of the bungalow. If Albert
supposed Billson to be short and dark, she must have
passed from his mind without leaving a trace of her own
passion. That was cruel. All the same, I made a final shot.

'You don't remember when she gave the slice of seed-cake
to the little boy from Dr Trelawney's?'

The question struck a spark. This concluding bid to
unclog the floods of memory had an immediate, a wholly
unexpected effect.

'I knew there was something else I wanted to tell you,
sir,' said Albert. 'It just went out of my head till you
reminded me. That's the very gentleman—Dr Trelawney—
been staying here quite a long time. Came through a
friend of your uncle's, a lady. I puzzled and puzzled where
I'd seen him before. Captain Jenkins said something one
day how Dr Trelawney had lived near Stonehurst one time.
Then the name came back to me.'

'Does he still wear a beard and take his people out
running?'

'Still got a beard,' said Albert, 'but he lives very quiet
now. Not so young as he was, like the rest of us. Has a
lot of meals in his room. Quite a bit of trouble, he is. I get
worried about him now and then. So does the wife. Not
too quick at settling the account. Then he does say some
queer things. Not everyone in the hotel likes it. Of course,
we have to have all sorts here. Can't pick and choose.
Dr Trelawney's health ain't all that good neither. Suffers

155

terrible from asthma. Something awful. I get frightened when he's got the fit on him.'

It was clear that Albert, too well-behaved to say so explicitly, would have been glad to eject Dr Trelawney from the Bellevue. That was not surprising. I longed to set eyes on the Doctor again. It would be a splendid story to tell Moreland, with whom I had been out of any close contact since we had stayed at the cottage.

'Used my uncle to see much of Dr Trelawney?'

'They'd pass the time of day,' said Albert. 'The lady knew both of them, of course. They'd sometimes all three go out together on the pier and such like. Captain Jenkins used to get riled with some of the Doctor's talk about spirits and that. I've heard him say as much.'

'Was the lady called Mrs Erdleigh?' I asked.

Uncle Giles had once been suspected of being about to marry this fortune-telling friend of his. It was likely that she was the link between himself and Dr Trelawney.

'That's the name,' said Albert. 'Lives in the town here. Tells fortunes, so they say. Used to come here quite a lot. In fact, she rang up and offered to help after Captain Jenkins died, but I thought I'd better wait instructions. As it was, we just put all the clothing from the drawers tidy on the bed, so the things would be easy to pack. We haven't touched the Gladstone bag. Captain Jenkins didn't have much with him at the end. Kept most of his stuff in London, so I believe.'

Albert sniffed. He evidently held a low opinion of the Ufford.

'I'll just give you your uncle's keys, sir,' he said. 'If you'll excuse me, I must see the wife now. She takes on if I don't keep her informed about veg. Those silly girls never bring her what she wants neither. One of them's having time off, extra like, old Mrs Telford persuading her to go to an ambulance class or some such. I don't know what the young women of today are about. Making sheep's eyes most of the time, that's what it comes to.'

He moved off laboriously to Mrs Creech's sick-bed. I thought the best system would be to deal with Uncle Giles's residue straight away, then dine. The news of Dr Trelawney's installation at the Bellevue aroused a cloud of memories. That he had not passed into oblivion like so many others Albert had met was a tribute to the Doctor's personality. Even he would have been forgotten, if Uncle Giles had not recalled him to mind. That was strange because, as a rule, where others were concerned, Uncle Giles's memory was scarcely more retentive than Albert's. I wondered what life would be like lived in this largely memoryless condition. Better? Worse? Not greatly different? It was an interesting question. The reapparance of Mrs Erdleigh was also a matter of note. This fairly well known clairvoyante (whom Lady Warminster had consulted in her day) had once 'put out the cards' for me at the Ufford, prophesying my love affair with Jean Duport, for a time occupying so much of my life, now like an episode in another existence. Later, characteristically, Uncle Giles had pretended never to have heard of Mrs Erdleigh. However, rumours persisted at a later date to the effect that they still saw each other. There must have been a reconciliation. I wondered whether she would turn up at the funeral, what had been her relations with Uncle Giles, what with Dr Trelawney.

I had told Albert I would find my own way to the bedroom, which was some floors up. It was small, dingy, facing inland. The sea was in any case visible from the Bellevue—in spite of its name—only from the attic windows, glimpsed through a gap between two larger hotels, though the waves could be heard clattering against the shingle. Laid out on the bed were a couple of well-worn suits; three or four shirts, frayed at the cuff; half a dozen discreet, often-knotted ties;

darned socks (who had darned them?); handkerchiefs embroidered with the initials GDJ (who had embroidered them?) thick woollen underclothes; two pairs of pyjamas of unattractive pattern; two pairs of shoes, black and brown; bedroom slippers worthy of Albert; a raglan overcoat; a hat; an unrolled umbrella; several small boxes containing equipment such as studs and razor blades. That was what Uncle Giles had left behind him. No doubt there was more of the same sort of thing at the Ufford. The display was a shade depressing. Dust was returning to dust with dreadful speed. I looked under the bed. There lay the suitcase into which these things were to be packed, beside it, the Gladstone bag to which Albert had referred, a large example of its kind, infinitely ancient, perhaps the very one with which Uncle Giles had arrived at Stonehurst on the day of the Archduke's assassination. I dragged these two pieces out. One of the keys on the ring committed to me by Albert fitted this primitive, shapeless survival of antique luggage, suitable for a conjuror or comedian.

At first examination, the Gladstone bag appeared to be filled with nothing but company reports. I began to go through the papers. Endless financial projects were adumbrated; gratifying prospects; inevitable losses; hopeful figures, in spite of past disappointments. The whole panorama of the money-market lay before one—as it must once have burgeoned under the eyes of Uncle Giles—like the kingdoms of the world and the glory of them. Hardly a venture quoted on the Stock Exchange seemed omitted; several that were not. There were two or three share certificates marked 'valueless' that might have been stock from the South Sea Bubble. Uncle Giles's financial investigations had been extensive. Then a smaller envelope turned out to be something different. One of the sheets of paper contained there showed a circle with figures and symbols noted within its circumference. It was a horoscope, presumably that of Uncle Giles himself.

He had been born under Aries—the Ram—making him ambitious, impulsive, often irritable. He had secret enemies, because Saturn was in the Twelfth House. I remembered Mrs Erdleigh remarking that handicap when I met her with Uncle Giles at the Ufford. Mars and Venus were in bad aspect so far as dealings with money were concerned. However, Uncle Giles was drawn to hazards such as the company reports revealed by the conjunction of Jupiter. Moreover Jupiter, afflicting Mercury, caused people to find 'the native'—Uncle Giles—unreliable. That could not be denied. Certainly none of his own family would contradict the judgment. Unusual experiences with the opposite sex (I thought of Sir Magnus Donners) were given by Uranus in the Seventh House, a position at the same time unfavourable to marriage. It had to be admitted that all gave a pretty good, if rough-and-ready, account of my uncle and his habits.

Underneath the envelope containing the horoscope was correspondence, held together by a paper-clip, with a firm of stockbrokers. Then came Uncle Giles's pass-book. The bank statements of the previous year showed him to have been overdrawn, though somewhat better off than was commonly supposed. The whole question of Uncle Giles's money affairs was a mysterious one, far more mysterious than anything revealed about him astrologically. Speculation as to the extent of his capital took place from time to time, speculation even as to whether he possessed any capital at all. The stockbroker's letters and bank statements came to an end. The next item in the Gladstone bag appeared to be a surgical appliance of some sort. I pulled it out. The piece of tubing was for the administration of an enema. I threw the object into the wastepaper-basket, with the company reports. Below again—the whole business was like research into an excavated tomb—lay a roll of parchment tied in a bow with red tape.

'VICTORIA by the Grace of God, of the United Kingdom of Great Britain and Ireland, Queen, Defender of the Faith, Empress of India &c. To Our Trusty and well-beloved *Giles Delahay Jenkins, Gentleman*, Greeting. We, reposing especial Trust and Confidence in your Loyalty, Courage and good Conduct, do by these Presents Constitute and Appoint you to be an Officer in Our *Land* Forces . . .'

Trusty and well-beloved were not the terms in which his own kith and kin had thought of Uncle Giles for a long time now. Indeed, the Queen's good-heartedness in herself greeting him so warmly was as touching as her error of judgment was startling. There was something positively ingenuous in singling out Uncle Giles for the repose of confidence, accepting him so wholly at his own valuation. No doubt the Queen had been badly advised in the first instance. She must have been vexed and disappointed.

'. . . You are therefore carefully and diligently to discharge your Duty as such in the Rank of *2nd Lieutenant* or in such higher Rank as we may from time to time hereafter be pleased to promote or appoint you to . . .'

The Queen's faith in human nature appeared boundless for, extraordinary as the royal whim might seem, she had indeed been pleased to appoint Uncle Giles to higher rank, instead of quietly—and far more wisely—dispensing with his services at the very first available opportunity. Perhaps such an opportunity had not arisen so immediately as might have been expected; perhaps Uncle Giles had assumed the higher rank without reference to the Queen. Certainly he was always styled 'Captain' Jenkins, so that there must have been at least a presumption of a once held captaincy of some sort, however 'temporary', 'acting' or 'local' that rank might in practice have been. No doubt her reliance would have been lessened by the knowledge that Mercury was afflicting Jupiter at the hour of Uncle Giles's birth.

'. . . and you are at all times to exercise and well discipline in Arms both the inferior Officers and Men serving under you and use your best endeavours to keep them in good Order and Discipline. And we do hereby command them to Obey you as their superior Officer . . . according to the Rules and Discipline of War, in pursuance of the Trust hereby reposed in you . . .'

The great rolling phrases, so compelling in their beauty and simplicity, might be thought inadmissible for the most heedless, the most cynical, to disregard, so moderate, so obviously right in the circumstances, were their requirements, so friendly—even to the point of intimacy—the manner in which the Sovereign outlined the principles of her honourable service. Uncle Giles, it must be agreed, had not risen to the occasion. So far as loyalty to herself was concerned, he had been heard on more than one occasion to refer to her as 'that old Tartar at Osborne', to express without restraint his own leanings towards a republican form of government. His Conduct, in the army or out of it, could not possibly be described as Good. In devotion to duty, for example, he could not be compared with Bracey, a man no less pursued, so far as that went, by Furies. There remained Uncle Giles's Courage. That, so far as was known, remained untarnished, although—again so far as was known—never put to any particularly severe test. Certainly it could be urged that he had the Courage of his own opinions; the Queen had to be satisfied with that. In short, the only one of her admonitions Uncle Giles had ever shown the least sign of taking to heart was the charge to command his subordinates to obey him. Even after his own return to civilian life, Uncle Giles tried his best to carry out this injunction in relation to all who could possibly be regarded as subordinate to him. Being 'a bit of a radical' never prevented that; the Sign of Aries investing him with the will to command, adding that touch of irritability of disposition as an additional spur to obedience.

While I thus considered, rather frivolously, Uncle Giles's actual career in contrast with the ideal one envisaged by the terms of his Commission, I could not help thinking at the same time that facile irony at my uncle's expense could go too far. No doubt irony, facile or otherwise, can often go too far. In this particular instance, for example, it was fitting to wonder what sort of a figure I should myself cut as a soldier. The question was no longer purely hypothetical, a grotesque fantasy, a romantic daydream, the career one had supposed to lie ahead as a child at Stonehurst. There was every reason to think that before long now the tenor of many persons' lives, my own among them, would indeed be regulated by those draconic, ineluctable laws, so mildly, so all embracingly, defined in the Commission as 'the Rules and Discipline of War'. How was it going to feel to be subject to them? My name was on the Emergency Reserve, although no one at that time knew how much, or how little, that might mean when it came to joining the army. At the back of one's mind sounded a haunting resonance, a faint disturbing buzz, that was not far from fear.

By the time these disturbing thoughts had descended on me, I had begun to near the bottom of the Gladstone bag. There was another layer of correspondence, this time in a green cardboard file, on the subject of a taxi-cab's collision with a lorry, an accident with regard to which Uncle Giles had been subpoenaed as witness. It went into the waste-paper-basket, a case—as Moreland would have said—in which there was 'nothing of the spirit'. That brought an end to the contents, except for a book. This was bound in grubby vellum, the letterpress of mauve ink, like that used by Albert in his correspondence. I glanced at the highly decorated capitals of the title page:

The Perfumed Garden
of the Sheik Nefzaoui
or
The Arab Art of Love

I had often heard of this work, never, as it happened, come across a copy. Uncle Giles was an unexpected vehicle to bring it to hand. The present edition—'Cosmopoli: 1886'—was stated to be published 'For Private Circulation Only', the English translation from a French version of the sixteenth-century Arabic manuscript made by a 'Staff Officer in the French Army in Algeria'.

I pictured this French Staff Officer sitting at his desk. The sun was streaming into the room through green latticed windows of Moorish design, an oil sketch by Fromentin or J. F. Lewis. Dressed in a light-blue frogged coatee and scarlet peg-topped trousers buttoning under the boot, he wore a pointed moustache and imperial. Beside him on the table stood his shako, high and narrowing to the plume, the white puggaree falling across the scabbard of his discarded sabre. He was absolutely detached, a man who had tasted the sensual pleasures of the Second Empire and Third Republic to their dregs, indeed, come to North Africa to escape such insistent banalities. Now, he was examining their qualities and defects in absolute calm. Here, with the parched wind blowing in from the desert, he had found a kindred spirit in the Sheik Nefzaoui, to whose sixteenth-century Arabic he was determined to do justice in the language of Racine and Voltaire. Perhaps that picture was totally wide of the mark: the reality quite another one. The Staff Officer was a family man, snatching

a few minutes at his beloved translation between the
endearments of his wife, the rompings of a dozen children.
. . . Rimbaud's father, perhaps, who had served in North
Africa, made translations from the Arabic. . . . The 'Rules
and Discipline of War' must in some degree have been
relaxed to allow spare time for these literary labours.
Possibly he worked only on leave. I turned the pages idly.
The Sheik's tone was authoritative, absolutely self-assured
—for that reason, a trifle forbidding—the chapter headings
enigmatic:

'. . . Concerning Praiseworthy Men . . . Concerning
Women who deserve to be Praised . . . Of Matters Injuri-
ous to the Act of Generation . . . On the Deceits and
Treacheries of Women . . . Concerning Sundry Observations
useful to Know for Men and Women . . .'

On the Deceits and Treacheries of Women? The whole
subject was obviously very fully covered. Sincere and
scholarly, there was also something more than a little
oppressive about the investigation, moments when the
author seemed to labour the point, to induce a feeling of
surfeit in the reader. All the same, I felt rather ashamed
of my own lack of appreciation, because I could see that
much of the advice was good. Disinclination to continue
reading I recognised as a basic unwillingness to face facts,
rather than any innate fastidiousness to be regarded as a
matter for self-congratulation. I felt greatly inferior to the
French Staff Officer, whatever his personal condition, who
saw this severely technical sociological study, by its nature
aseptic, even chilling in deliberate avoidance of false
sentiment and specious charm, as a refreshing antidote to
Parisian canons of sensuality.

Uncle Giles's acquisition of this book must have been one
of the minor consequences of having Uranus in the Seventh
House; that was the best that could be said for him. It reminded him perhaps of ladies like the garage proprietor's

widow, manicurist at Reading, once thought to be under consideration as his future wife; possibly it was used as a handbook in those far off, careless days. In any case, there was no reason to suppose Uncle Giles to have become more strait-laced as he grew older. I put the volume aside to reconsider. There was work to be done. The clothes were packed away at last in the suitcase, the papers spared from the waste-paper basket, returned to the Gladstone bag, the two pieces of luggage placed side by side to await removal. As Albert had remarked, Uncle Giles had not left much behind, even though further items would be found at the Ufford. By that time the gong had sounded for dinner.

I took the Sheik Nefzaoui's treatise with me to the dining-room, which was fairly full, single white-haired ladies predominating, here and there an elderly couple. No doubt the seasons made little difference to the Bellevue, the bulk of its population living there all the year round, winter and summer, solstice to solstice. I was given a table in the corner, near the hatch through which food was thrust by Albert. The table next to mine was laid for one person. Upon it stood a half-consumed bottle of whisky, a room-number pencilled on the label. I wondered whether my neighbour would turn out to be Dr Trelawney. That would provide an excitement. I hoped, in any case, that I should catch a glimpse of the Doctor before leaving the hotel, contrive some anecdote over which Moreland and I could afterwards laugh. I had nearly finished my soup —which recalled only in a muted form Albert's ancient skill—when a tall man, about my own age or a year or two older, entered the dining-room. He strode jauntily through the doorway, looking neither to the right nor left, making straight for the table with the whisky bottle. Hope vanished of enjoying near me Dr Trelawney's mysterious presence. This man was thin, with fair to reddish hair, pink-faced, pale eyebrows raised in an aggressive expression, as if he would welcome a row at the least provocation. He wore a country suit, somehow rather too elegant for the Bellevue's dining-room. I experienced that immediate awareness, which can descend all of a sudden like the sky becoming overcast, of the close proximity of a person I knew and did not like, someone who made me, at the same time, in some way morally uncomfortable. For a second, I thought this impression one of those sensations of dislike as difficult to rationalise as the contrasting feelings of sudden sympathy; a moment later realising that Bob Duport was sitting next to me, that there was excuse for this onset of tingling antipathy.

I had not set eyes on Duport since I was an undergraduate, since the night, in fact, when Templer had driven us all into the ditch in his new car. A whole sequence of memories and sensations, luxuriant, tender, painful, ludicrous, wearisome, rolled up, enveloping like a fog. Moreland, as I have said, liked talking of the variations of sexual jealousy, the different effect produced by men with whom a woman has been 'shared'.

'Some of them hardly matter at all,' he had said. 'Others you can't even bear to think about. Very mention of their name poisons the whole relationship—the whole atmosphere. Again you get to like—almost to love—certain ones, husbands or cast-off lovers, I mean. You feel dreadfully sorry for them, at least, try to make their wives or ex-mistresses behave better to them. It becomes a matter of one's own self-respect.'

Duport, so far as I was concerned, had been a case in point. I had once loved his wife, Jean, and, although I loved her no longer, our relationship had secreted this distasteful residue, an unalterable, if hidden, tie with her ex-husband. It was a kind of retribution. I might not like the way Duport behaved, either to Jean or towards the world in general, but what I had done had made him, at least in some small degree, part of my own life. I was bound to him throughout eternity. Moreover, I was, for the same reason, in no position to be censorious. I had undermined my own critical standing. Duport's emergence in this manner cut a savage incision across Time. Templer's Vauxhall seemed to have crashed into the ditch only yesterday; I could almost feel my nose aching from the blow received by the sudden impact of Ena's knee, hear Templer's fat friend, Brent, swearing, the grinding, ghastly snorts of the expiring engine, Stringham's sardonic comments as we clambered out of the capsized car. It had all seemed rather an adventure at the time. I reflected how dreadfully boring such an experience would be now, the very thought fatiguing. However, an immediate decision had to be taken about Duport. I made up my mind to pretend not to recognise him, although the years I had loved Jean made him horribly, unnaturally familiar to me, as if I had been seeing Duport, too, all the time I had been seeing her. Indeed, he seemed now almost more familiar than repellent.

The thought that Duport had been Jean's husband, that she had had a child by him, that no doubt she had once loved him, had not, for some reason, greatly worried me while she and I had been close to each other. Duport had never—I cannot think why—seemed to be in competition with myself where she was concerned. For Jean to have married him, still, so to speak, to own him, although living apart, was like a bad habit (Uncle Giles poring in secret over *The Perfumed Garden*), no more than that; something one might prefer her to be without, to give up, nothing that could remotely affect our feeling for each other. Anyway, I thought, those days are long past; they can be considered with complete equanimity. Duport and I had met only once, fourteen or fifteen years before. He could safely be regarded as the kind of person to whom the past, certainly such a chance encounter, would mean little or nothing, in fact be completely forgotten. No doubt since then new friends of his had driven him scores of times into the ditch with new cars full of new girls. He was that sort of man. Such were my ill-judged, unfriendly, rather priggish speculations. They turned out to be hopelessly wide of the mark.

Duport's first act on sitting down at the table was to pour out a stiffish whisky, add a splash of soda from the syphon also standing on the table, and gulp the drink down. Then he looked contemptuously round the room. Obviously my own presence had materially altered the background he expected of the dining-room at the Bellevue. He stared hard. Soup was set in front of him. I supposed he would turn to it. Instead, he continued to stare. I pretended to be engrossed with my fish. There was something of the old Albert in the sauce. Then Duport spoke. He had a hard, perfectly assured, absolutely ingratiating voice.

'We've met before,' he said.

'Have we?'

'Somewhere.'

'Where could that have been?'

'Certain of it. I can't remember your name. Mine's Duport—Bob.'

'Nicholas Jenkins.'

'Aren't you a friend of my former brother-in-law, Peter Templer?'

'A very old friend.'

'And he drove us both into the ditch in some bloody fast second-hand car he had just bought. Years ago. A whole row of chaps and a couple of girls. The party included a fat swab called Brent.'

'He did, indeed. That was where we met. Of course I remember you.'

'I thought so. Do you ever see Peter these days?'

'Hadn't for ages. Then we met about a year ago—just after "Munich", as a matter of fact.'

'I've heard him talk about you. I used to be married to his sister, Jean, you know. I believe I've heard her speak of you, too.'

'I met her staying with the Templers.'

'When was that?'

'Years ago—when I had just left school.'

'Ever see her later?'

'Yes, several times.'

'Probably when she and I were living apart. That is when Jean seems to have made most of her friends.'

'When I last saw Peter, he was talking about some new job of yours.'

I judged it best to change the subject of Jean—also remembering the talk about Duport between Sir Magnus Donners and Widmerpool. Up to then, I had thought of Duport only in an earlier incarnation, never considered the possibility of running into him again.

'Was he, indeed? Where did you meet him?'

'Stourwater.'

'Did you, by God? What do you do?'

I tried to give some account, at once brief and intelligible, of the literary profession : writing; editing; reviewing; the miscellaneous odd jobs to which I was subject, never, for some reason, very easy to define to persons not themselves in the world. To my relief, Duport showed no interest whatever in such activities, apparently finding them neither eccentric nor important.

'Shouldn't think it brings in much dough,' he said. 'But how do you come to know Donners?'

'We were taken over by some friends who live in the neighbourhood.'

'You're married?'

'Yes.'

'How do you like being married?'

'Support it all right.'

'You're lucky. I find it a great relief not to be married
—though I was quite stuck on Jean when we were first
wed. But what on earth are you doing in this dump?'

I explained about Uncle Giles, about Albert.

'So that's the answer,' said Duport. 'Of course I used to
see your uncle cruising about here. Bad-tempered old
fellow. Didn't know he'd dropped off the hooks. They like
to keep death quiet in places like this. Look here, when
you were staying with Donners, was an absolute bugger
called Widmerpool there too?'

'Widmerpool wasn't staying there. He just looked in.
Wanted to say something about your business affairs, I
think. I know Widmerpool of old.'

'A hundred per cent bastard—word's too good for him.'

'I know some people think so.'

'Don't you?'

'He and I rub along all right. By the way are *you* living at
the Bellevue?'

'Keeping out of the immediate view of the more enter-
prising of my creditors. I only wish my stay here were going
to be as brief as yours.'

'How did you find the place?'

'Odd chance, as a matter of fact. I once brought a girl
down to the Royal for the week-end—one of those bitches
you want to have and get out of your system and never set
eyes on again. While we were there I made friends with
the barman. He's called Fred and a very decent sort of
chap. When I found, not so long ago, that I'd better go
into comparative hiding, I decided this town would be as
good a place as any other to put myself out of commission
for a week or two. I left my bags at the station and
dropped in to the Royal bar to ask Fred the best place to

make an economical stay. He sent me straight to the Bellevue.'

'How do you like Albert?'

'Get along with Albert, as you call him, like a house on fire—but it's a pretty dead-and-alive hole to live in, I can tell you. It's the sort of town where you feel hellishly randy all the time. I've got quite a bit of work to do in the way of sorting out my own affairs. That keeps me going during the day. But there's nothing whatever to do in the evenings. I go to a flick sometimes. The girls are a nightmare. We'd better go out and get drunk together tonight. Make you forget about your uncle. Has he left you anything?'

'Doubt if he'd anything to leave.'

'Never mind. You'll get over it. I'd like to have a talk with you about Widmerpool.'

This intermittent conversation had taken us through most of dinner. I felt scarcely more drawn to Duport than on the day we first met. He was like Peter Templer, with all sympathetic characteristics removed. There was even a slight physical resemblance between the two of them. I wondered if one of those curious, semi-incestuous instincts of attraction had brought Jean to Duport in the first place, or whether Templer and Duport had become alike by seeing a good deal of each other as brothers-in-law and in the City. Duport, I knew, suffered financial crises from time to time. For a period he would live luxuriously, then all his money would disappear. This capacity for making money, combined with inability to keep it, was mysterious to me. I had once said something of the sort to Templer, when he complained of his brother-in-law's instability.

'Oh, Bob knows he will be able to recoup in quite a short time,' Templer had said. 'Doesn't worry him, any more than it worries you that you will be able to write the review of some book when it appears next year. You'll have something to say, Bob'll find a way of making money. It's only momentary inconvenience, due to his own idiocy. It's not making the money presents the difficulty, it's keeping his schemes in bounds—not landing in jail.'

I could see the force of these words. They probably explained Duport's present situation. From what Templer used to say of him—from what Jean used to say of him—I knew quite a lot of Duport. At the same time, there were other things I should not at all have minded hearing about, which only Duport could tell me. I was aware that to probe in this manner was to play with fire, that it would probably be wiser to remain in ignorance of the kind of thing which I was curious to know. However, I saw, too, there was really no escape. I was fated to spend an evening in Duport's company. While I was about it, I might as well hear what I wanted to hear, no matter what the risk. Like Uncle Giles's failings, all was no doubt written in the stars.

'Where shall we go?'

'The bar of the Royal.'

For a time we walked in silence towards the sea-front, the warm night hinting at more seductive pursuits than drinking with Duport.

'News doesn't look very good,' I said. 'Do you think the Germans are going into Poland?'

There seemed no particular object in avoiding banality from the start, as the evening showed every sign of developing into a banal one.

'There's bloody well going to be a war,' said Duport, 'you can ease your mind about that. If I'd been in South America, I'd have sweated it out there. Might in any case. Still, I suppose currency restrictions would make things difficult. I've always been interested in British Guiana aluminium. That might offer something. I'll recount some of my recent adventures in regard to the international situation when

172

we've had some drinks. Did you meet Peter Templer's wife at Stourwater?'

'Yes.'

'What did you think of her?'

'Something's gone a bit adrift, hasn't it?'

'Peter has driven her off her rocker. Nothing else. Used to be a very pretty little thing married to an oaf of a man who bored her to death.'

'What went wrong?'

'She was mad about Peter—still is—and he got too much of her. He always had various items on the side, of course. Then he started up with Lady Anne Something-or-Other, who is always about with Donners.'

'Anne Umfraville.'

'That's the one.'

'There was rather a scene when we were there.'

I gave a brief account of the Masque of the Seven Deadly Sins. Duport listened without interest.

'Donners never seems to mind about other people getting off with his girls,' he said. 'I've heard it said he is a *voyeur*. No accounting for tastes. I don't think Peter cares what he does now. Something of the sort may have upset Betty—though whether she herself, or Anne, was involved, you can't say.'

'I found Peter quietened down on the whole.'

'Quite right. He is in a way. Used to be more cheerful in the days of the slump, when he was down the drain like the rest of us. Then he turned to, and made it all up. Very successful, I'd say. But he never recovered from it. Slowed him up for good, so far as being a pal for a night on the tiles. Prefers now to read the *Financial Times* over a glass of port. However, that need not apply to his private life—may have developed special tastes, just as Donners has. Very intensive womanising sometimes leads to that kind of thing, and you can't say Peter hasn't been intensive.'

By this time we had reached the Royal. Duport led the way to the bar. It was empty, except for the barman, a beefy, talkative fellow, who evidently knew Duport pretty well.

'Fred will fix you up with a girl, if you want one,' said Duport, while drinks were being poured out. 'I don't recommend it.'

'Come off it, Mr Duport.'

'You know you can, Fred. Don't be so coy about it. Where are we going to sit? How do you feel about availing yourself of Fred's good offices?'

'Not tonight.'

'Why not?'

'Not in the mood.'

'Sure?'

'Certain.'

'Don't make a decision you'll regret later.'

'I won't.'

'Do you play poker?'

'Not a great hand at it.'

'Bores you?'

'Never seem to hold a card.'

'Golf?'

'No.'

I felt I was not cutting a very dashing figure, even if I did not accept all this big talk about women as necessarily giving an exact picture of Duport's own life. No doubt women played a considerable part in his existence, but at the same time he seemed over keen on making an impression on that score. He probably talked about them, I thought, more than concerning himself with incessant action in that direction. He was not at all put out that I should fall so far short of the dissipations suggested by him. All he wanted was a companion with whom to drink. Life at the Bellevue must certainly be boring enough.

'I was going to tell you about that swine Widmerpool,' he said.

This seemed no occasion for an outward display of loyalty to Widmerpool by taking offence at such a description. I had stated earlier that Widmerpool and I were on reasonably good terms. That would have to be sufficient. In any case, I had no illusions about Widmerpool's behaviour. All the same, this abuse sounded ungrateful, for what I knew of their connexion indicated that more than once Widmerpool had been instrumental in finding a job for Duport when hard up. It was a Widmerpool job for Duport that had finally severed me from Jean.

'Why do you dislike Widmerpool so much?'

'Listen to this,' said Duport. 'Some years ago, when I was on my uppers, Widmerpool arranged for me to buy metal ores for a firm in South America. When that was fixed, I suggested to my wife, Jean, that we might as well link up again. Rather to my surprise, she agreed. Question of the child and so on. Made things easier.'

Duport paused.

'I'll tell you about Jean later,' he said. 'The Widmerpool story first. I don't expect you've ever heard of chromite?'

'The word was being bandied about at Stourwater.'

'Of course. I'd forgotten you'd been there at the critical moment.'

'What was the critical moment?'

'Donners got into his head that he would be well advised to get a foothold in the Turkish chromite market. He'd already talked to Widmerpool about it, when I arrived in London from South America. I'd left South America for reasons I'll explain later. I found a message from Widmerpool, with whom I was of course in touch, telling me to come and see him. I went along to his office. He suggested I should push off to Turkey and buy chromite. It was for Donners-Brebner, but negotiated through a Swiss subsidiary company. What about a refill?'

We ordered some more drinks.

'Widmerpool opened a credit for me through a Turkish bank,' said Duport. 'I was to buy the ores myself and send a shipment as soon as I had enough. I sent one shipment, was getting to work good and proper on the second shipment, when, a week or two ago, do you know what happened?'

'I'm floored.'

'Widmerpool,' said Duport slowly, 'without informing me, cancelled the credit. He did that on his own responsibility, because he didn't like the look of the European situation.'

'Can't you apply to Donners?'

'He is in France, doing a tour of the Maginot Line or something of the sort—making French contacts and having a bit of a holiday at the same time. I was bloody well left holding the baby. The sellers were looking for me for payments impossible for me to make. Of course I shall see Donners the moment he returns. Even if he re-opens the credit, there's been an irreparable balls-up.'

'And you'd go back?'

'If the international situation allows. It may not. I've no quarrel with Widmerpool about the likelihood of war. I quite agree. That is why Donners wants chromite. Widmerpool seems to have missed that small point.'

'Why does Donners specially want chromite if there's war?'

'Corner the Turkish market. The more there is talk of war, the more Donners-Brebner will need chromite. Donners gives out that it is for some special process he is interested in. That was why Peter Templer was asked to Stourwater—so that he would gossip afterwards about that. Not a word of truth. Donners had quite other reasons. He is not going to give away his plans to a fool like Widmerpool, even when it suits his book to use Widmerpool. Widmerpool talks a lot of balls about "reducing the firm's commitments". He's missed the whole bloody point.'

I was not sure that I saw the point myself. It presumably turned on whether or not there was a war—Sir Magnus thinking there would be, Widmerpool undecided how to act if there were. All that was clear was that Duport had been put into an unenviable position.

'So you see,' he said, 'Widmerpool isn't a great favourite with me at the moment.'

'You were going to tell me why you left South America.'

'I was,' said Duport, speaking as if it were a relief to abandon the subject of Widmerpool and chromite. 'Since you know Peter Templer, did you ever meet another ex-brother-in-law of mine. Jimmy Stripling, who was married to Peter's other sister, Babs? He used to have quite a name as a racing driver.'

'Stripling was at the Templers' when I stayed there years ago. I met him once since.'

'Jimmy and Babs got a divorce. Jimmy—who has always been pretty cracked in some ways—took up with a strange lady called Mrs Erdleigh, who tells fortunes. Incidentally, she sometimes came to the Bellevue to see your uncle. I remembered her. Looks as if she kept a high-class knocking-shop. There is another queer fish living at the Bellevue—old boy with a beard. He and Mrs Erdleigh and your late lamented uncle used sometimes to have tea together.'

'I know about Mrs Erdleigh—and Dr Trelawney too.'

'You do? Trelawney tried to bring off a touch last time we talked. I explained I was as broke as himself. No ill feeling. That's beside the point. Also the fact that Myra Erdleigh milked Jimmy Stripling to quite a tune. All I want to know is: what did you think of Jimmy when you met him?'

'Pretty awful—but I never knew him well. He may be all right.'

'Not a bit of it,' said Duport. 'He is awful. Couldn't be worse. Kept out of the war himself and ran away with Babs when her husband was at the front. Double-dealing, stingy, conceited, bad tempered, half cracked. I went to him to try and get a bit of help during my last pre-South American *débâcle*. Not on your life. Nothing doing with Jimmy. I might have starved in the gutter for all Jimmy cared. Now, you say you knew Jean, my ex-wife?'

'She was at Peter's Maidenhead house once when I went there.'

'Nice girl, didn't you think?'

'Yes, I did.'

'Reasonably attractive?'

'I'd certainly have said so.'

'Wouldn't have any difficulty in getting hold of the right sort of chap?'

'It wouldn't be polite to express doubt on that point, since she married you.'

I did not manage to impart all the jocularity fittingly required to give lively savour to this comment. Duport, in any case, brushed it aside as irrelevant.

'Leave me out of it by all means,' he said. 'Just speaking in general, would you think Jean would have any difficulty in getting hold of a decent sort of chap? Yes or no.'

'No.'

'Neither should I,' said Duport. 'But the fact remains that she slept with Jimmy Stripling.'

I made some suitable acknowledgment, tempered, I hoped, by polite surprise. I well remembered the frightful moment when Jean herself had first informed me, quite gratuitously, of having undergone the experience to which Duport referred. I could recall even now how painful that information had been at the time, as one might remember a physical accident long past. The matter no longer worried me, primarily because I no longer loved Jean, also because the whole Stripling question had, so to speak, been resolved between Jean and myself at the time. All the same, the incident had been a disagreeable one. That had to be admitted. One does not want to dwell on some racking visit to the dentist, however many years have rolled on since that day. Perhaps I would have preferred to have remained even then unreminded of Jean and Stripling. However, present recital could in no way affect the past. That was history.

'Can you beat it?'

I acknowledged inability to offer a parallel instance.

'Well, I can,' said Duport. 'I don't set up as behaving perticularly well myself, but, when it comes to behaving badly, women can give you a point or two every time. I just tell you about Jimmy Stripling by the way. He is not the cream of the jest. As I mentioned before, I thought things would be easier if Jean and I joined up again. I found I was wrong.'

'Why was that?'

'Not surprisingly, Jean had been having a bit of a run around while we were living apart,' said Duport. 'I suppose that was to be expected.'

I began to feel decidedly uncomfortable. So far as I knew, neither Duport, nor anyone else, had the smallest reason to guess anything of what had passed between Jean and myself. All the same, his words suggested he was aware of more than I might suppose.

'The point turned out to be this,' said Duport. 'Jean only wanted to link up with me again to make things easier for herself in carrying on one of her little affairs.'

'But how could joining up with you possibly help? Surely things were much easier when she was on her own?'

Duport did not answer that question.

'Guess who the chap was?' he said.

'How could I possibly?'

'Somebody known to you.'

'Are you sure?'

'Seen you and him at the same time.'

Duport grinned horribly. At least I guiltily thought his grin horrible, because I supposed him to be teasing me. It was unlikely, most unlikely, that Jean had told him about ourselves, although, since she had told both of us about Stripling, such a confession could not be regarded as out of the question. Perhaps someone else, unknown to us, had passed the story on to Duport. In either case, the situation was odious. I greatly regretted having agreed to come out drinking with him, even more of having encouraged him to speak of his own troubles. My curiosity had put me in this position. I had no one but myself to blame. It was just in Duport's character, I felt, to discompose me in this manner. If he chose to make himself unpleasant about what had happened, I was in no position to object. Things would have to be brazened out. All the same, I could not understand what he meant by saying that Jean had come back to him in order to 'make things more convenient'. Her return to her husband, their journey together to South America, had been the moment when we had been forced finally to say good-bye to each other. Since then, I had neither seen nor heard of her.

'Just have a shot at who it was,' said Duport, 'bearing in mind Jimmy Stripling as the standard of what a lover should be.'

'Did he look like Stripling?'

I felt safe, at least, in the respect that, apart from any difference in age, no two people could look less alike than Stripling and myself.

'Even more of a lout,' said Duport, 'if you can believe that.'

'In what way?'

There was a ghastly fascination in seeing how far he would go.

'Wetter, for one thing.'

'I give it up.'

'Come on.'

'No good.'

I knew I must be red in the face. By this time we had had some more drinks, to which heightened colouring might reasonably be attributed.

'I'll tell you.'

I nerved myself.

'It was another Jimmy,' said Duport. 'Perhaps Jimmy is just a name she likes. Call a man Jimmy and she gets hot pants at once, I shouldn't wonder. Anyway, it was Jimmy Brent.'

'Brent?'

At first the name conveyed nothing to me.

'The fat slob who was in the Vauxhall when Peter drove us all into the hedge. You must remember him.'

'I do remember him now.'

Even in retrospect, this was a frightful piece of information.

'Jimmy Brent—always being ditched by tarts in night-clubs.'

I felt as if someone had suddenly kicked my legs from under me, so that I had landed on the other side of the room, not exactly hurt, but thoroughly ruffled, with all the breath knocked out of me.

'Nice discovery, wasn't it?' said Duport.

'Had this business with Brent been going on long?'

'Quite a month or two. Took the place of something else, I gather. In fact there was a period when she was running both at the same time. That's what I have good reason to believe. The point was that Brent was going to

South America too. It suited Jean's book for me to buy her ticket. We all three crossed on the same boat. Then she continued to carry on with him over there.'

'But are you sure this is true? She can't really have been in love with Brent.'

This naïve comment might have caught the attention of someone more interested than Duport in the emotions of other people. It was, in short, a complete give-away. No one was likely to use that phrase about a woman he scarcely knew, as I had allowed Duport to suppose about Jean and myself. As it was, he merely showed justifiable contempt for my lack of grasp, no awareness that the impact of his story had struck a shower of sparks.

'Who's to say when a woman's in love?' he said.

I thought how often I had made that kind of remark myself, when other people were concerned.

'I've no reason to suppose she wasn't speaking the truth when she told me she'd slept with him,' Duport said. 'She informed me in bed, appropriately enough. You're not going to tell me any woman would boast of having slept with Jimmy Brent, if she hadn't. The same applies to Jimmy Stripling. It's one of the characteristics the two Jimmies have in common. Both actions strike me as even odder to admit to than to do, if that was possible.'

'I see.'

'Nothing like facing facts when you've been had for a mug in a big way,' said Duport. 'I was thinking that this morning when I was working out some freight charges. The best one can say is that Jimmy and the third party —if there was a third party—were probably had for mugs too.'

I agreed. There was nothing like facing facts. They blew into the face hard, like a stiff, exhilarating, decidedly gritty breeze, which brought sanity with it, even though sanity might be unwelcome.

'What made you think there was another chap too?' I asked, from sheer lack of self-control.

'Something Jean herself let fall.'

It is always a temptation to tell one's own story. However, I saw that would be only to show oneself, without the least necessity, in a doubly unflattering light to someone I did not like, someone who could not, in the circumstances, reasonably be expected to be in the least sympathetic. I tried to sort out what had happened. Only a short while earlier, I had thought of myself as standing in an uneasy position *vis-à-vis* Duport, although at the same time a somewhat more advantageous one. Now, I saw that I, even more than he, had been made a fool of. At least Duport seemed to have begun the discord in his own married life—although, again, who can state with certainty the cause of such beginnings?—while I had supposed myself finally parting with Jean only in order that her own matrimonial situation might be patched up. That charming love affair, which had formerly seemed to drift to a close through my own ineffectiveness, had, in reality, been terminated by the deliberate manœuvre of Jean herself for her own purposes, certainly to the detriment of my self-esteem. I thought of that grave, gothic beauty that once I had loved so much, which found fulfilment in such men. The remembered moaning in pleasure of someone once loved always haunts the memory, even when love itself is over. Perhaps, I thought, her men are gothic too, beings carved on the niches and corbels of a mediaeval cathedral to arouse at once laughter and horror. In any case, I had been one of them. If her lovers were horrifying, I too had been out of their order. That had to be admitted.

'It is no good pontificating,' Mr Deacon used to say, 'about other people's sexual tastes.'

For the moment, angry, yet at the same time half inclined to laugh, I could not make up my mind what I thought.

This was yet another example of the tricks that Time can play within its own folds, tricks that emphasise the insecurity of those who trust themselves over much to that treacherous concept. I suddenly found what I had regarded as immutable—the not entirely unsublime past—roughly reshaped by the rude hands of Duport. That was justice, I thought, if you like.

'What happened after?'

'After what?'

'Did she marry Brent?'

Duport's story had made me forget entirely that Templer had already told me his sister had made a second marriage.

'Not she,' said Duport. 'Ditched Brent too. Can't blame her for that. Nobody could stick Jimmy for long—either of them. She married a local Don Juan some years younger than herself—in the army. Nephew of the President. I've just met him. He looks like Rudolph Valentino on an off day. Change from Brent, anyway. It takes all sorts to make a lover. Probably keep her in order, I should think. More than I ever managed.'

He stretched.

'I could do with a woman now,' he said.

'Why not have one of Fred's?'

'Fred hasn't got what I want. Besides, it's too late in the evening. Fred likes about an hour's notice. You know, I'll tell you something else, as I seem to be telling you all about my marital affairs. My wife wasn't really much of a grind. That was why I went elsewhere. All the same, she had something. I wasn't sorry when we started up again.'

I loathed him. I still carried with me *The Perfumed Garden*. Now seemed a suitable moment to seek a home for the Sheik Nefzaoui's study. Room could no doubt be found for it in the Duport library. To present him with the book would be small, secret amends for having had a love affair with his wife, a token of gratitude for having brought home to me in so uncompromising a fashion the transitory nature of love. It would be better not to draw his attention to the chapter on the Deceits and Treacheries of Women. He could find that for himself.

'Ever read this?'

Duport glanced at the title, then turned the pages.

'*The Arab Art of Love*,' he said. 'Are you always armed with this sort of literature? I did not realise you meant that kind of thing when you said you reviewed books.'

'I found it among my uncle's things.'

'The old devil.'

'What do you think of it?'

'They say you're never too old to learn.'

'Would you like it?'

'How much?'

'I'll make a present of it.'

'Might give me a few new ideas,' said Duport. 'I'll accept it as a gift. Not otherwise.'

'It's yours then.'

'Got to draw your attention to the clock, Mr Duport,' said the barman, who was beginning to tidy up in preparation for closing the bar.

'We're being kicked out,' said Duport. 'Just time for a final one.'

The bar closed. We said good night to Fred.

'Nothing for it but go back to the Bellevue,' said Duport. 'I've got a bottle of whisky in my room.'

'What about the pier?'

'Shut by now.'

'Let's walk round by the Front.'

'All right.'

The wind had got up by that time. The sea thudded over the breakwaters in a series of regular, dull explosions, like a cannonade of old-fashioned artillery. I felt thoroughly annoyed. We turned inland and made for the Bellevue.

The front door was shut, but not locked. We were crossing the hall, when Albert came hurrying down the stairs. He was evidently dreadfully disturbed about some matter. His movements, comparatively rapid for him, indicated consternation. He was pale and breathless. When he saw us, he showed no surprise that Duport and I should have spent an evening together. Our arrival in each other's company seemed almost expected by him, the very thing he was hoping for at that moment.

'There's been a proper kettle of fish,' he said. 'I'm glad to see you back, Mr Nick—and you too, Mr Duport.'

'What's happened?'

'Dr Trelawney.'

'What's he done?'

'Gone and locked himself in the bathroom. Can't get out. Now he's having one of his asthma attacks. With the wife queer herself, I don't want to get her out of bed at this time of night. I'd be glad of you gentlemen's help. There's no one else in the house that's less than in their seventies and it ain't no good asking those silly girls. I'm all that sorry to trouble you.'

'What,' said Duport, 'the good Dr Trelawney, the bearded one? We'll have him out in a trice. Lead us to him.'

This sudden crisis cheered Duport enormously. Action was what he needed. I thought of Moreland's remarks about men of action, wondering whether Duport would qualify. This was not how I had expected to meet Dr Trelawney again. We hurried along the passages behind Albert, slip-slopping in his ancient felt slippers. There were many stairs to climb. At last we reached the bathroom door. There it became clear that the rescue of Dr Trelawney presented difficulties. In fact it was hard to know how best to set about his release. From within the bathroom, rising and falling like the vibrations of a small but powerful engine, could be heard the alarming pant of the asthma victim. Dr

Trelawney sounded in extremity. Something must be done quickly. There was no doubt of that. Albert bent forward and put his mouth to the keyhole.

'Try again, Dr Trelawney,' he shouted.

The awful panting continued for a minute or two; then, very weak and shaky, came Dr Trelawney's thin, insistent, voice.

'I am not strong enough,' he said.

Albert turned towards us and shook his head.

'He's done this before,' he said in a lower tone. 'It's my belief he just wants to get attention. He was angry when your uncle died, Mr Nick, and the wife and I had to see about that, and not about him for a change. It can't go on. I won't put up with it. He'll have to go. I've said so before. It's too much. Flesh and blood won't stand it.'

'Shall we bust the door down?' said Duport. 'I could if I took a run at it, but there isn't quite enough space to do that here.'

That was true. The bathroom door stood at an angle by the end of the passage, built in such a way that violent attack of that kind upon it was scarcely possible. Dr Trelawney's hoarse, trembling voice came again.

'Telephone to Mrs Erdleigh,' he said. 'Tell her to bring my pills. I must have my pills.'

This request seemed to bring some relief to Albert.

'I'll do that right away, sir,' he shouted through the keyhole.

'What on earth can Mrs Erdleigh do?' said Duport.

Albert, with an old-fashioned gesture, touched the side of his nose with his forefinger.

'I know what he wants now,' he said. 'One of his special pills. I might have thought of Mrs Erdleigh before. We'll have him out when she comes. She'll do it.'

'What pills are they?'

'Better not ask, sir,' said Albert.

'Drugs, do you mean?'

'I've never pressed the matter, sir, nor where they come from.'

Duport and I were left alone in the passage.

'I suppose we could smash the panel,' he said. 'Shall I try to find an instrument?'

'Better not break the house up. Anyway, not until Albert returns. Besides, it would wake everybody. We don't want a bevy of old ladies to appear.'

'Try taking the key out, Dr Trelawney,' said Duport in an authoritative voice, 'then put it back again and have another turn. That sometimes works. I know that particular key. I thought I was stuck in the bloody hole myself yesterday, but managed to get out that way.'

At first there was no answer. When at last he replied, Dr Trelawney sounded suspicious.

'Who is that?' he asked. 'Where has Mr Creech gone?'

'It's Duport. You know, we sometimes talk in the lounge. You borrowed my *Financial Times* the other morning. Creech has gone to ring Mrs Erdleigh.'

There was another long silence, during which Dr Trelawney's breathing grew a little less heavy. Evidently he was making a great effort to bring himself under control, now that he found that people, in addition to Albert, were at work on his rescue. Then the ritual sentence sounded through the door:

'The Essence of the All is the Godhead of the True.

Duport turned to me and shook his head.

'We often get that,' he said.

This seemed the moment, now or never, when the spell must prove its worth. I leant towards his keyhole and spoke the concordant rejoinder:

'The Vision of Visions heals the Blindness of Sight.'

Duport laughed.

'What on earth are you talking about?' he said.

188

'That's the right answer.'

'How on earth did you know?'

We heard the sound of Dr Trelawney heaving himself up with difficulty from wherever he was sitting. He must have staggered across the bathroom, for he made a great deal of noise as he came violently into contact with objects obstructive to his passage. Then he reached the door and began to fumble with the key. He removed it from the lock; after a moment or two he tried once more to insert it in the keyhole. Several of these attempts failed. Then, suddenly, quite unexpectedly, came a hard scraping sound; the key could be heard turning slowly; there was a click; the door stood ajar. Dr Trelawney was before us on the threshold.

'I told you that would work,' said Duport.

Except for the beard, hardly a trace remained of the Dr Trelawney I dimly remembered. All was changed. Even the beard, straggling, dirty grey, stained yellow in places like the patches of broom on the common beyond Stonehurst, had lost all resemblance to that worn by the athletic, vigorous prophet of those distant days. Once broad and luxuriant, it was now shrivelled almost to a goatee. He no longer seemed to have stepped down from a stained-glass window or ikon. His skin was dry and blotched. Dark spectacles covered his eyes, his dressing-gown a long blue oriental robe that swept the ground. He really looked rather frightening. Although so altered from the Stonehurst era, he still gave me the same chilly feeling of inner uneasiness that I had known as a child when I watched him and his flock trailing across the heather. I remembered Moreland, when we had once talked of Dr Trelawney, quoting the lines from *Marmion*, where the king consults the wizard lord:

> 'Dire dealings with the fiendish race
> Had mark'd strange lines upon his face;

Vigil and fast had worn him grim,
His eyesight dazzled seem'd and dim . . .'

That just about described Dr Trelawney as he supported
himself against the doorpost, seized with another fearful
fit of coughing. I do not know what Duport and I would
have done with him, if Albert had not reappeared at that
moment. Albert was relieved, certainly, but did not seem
greatly surprised that we had somehow brought about this
liberation.

'Mrs Erdleigh promised she'd be along as quick as possible,' he said, 'but there were a few things she had to do
first. I'm glad you was able to get the door open at last, sir.
Mrs Creech must have that door seen to. I've spoken to
her about it before. Might be better if you used the other
bathroom in future, Dr Trelawney, we don't want such a
business another night.'

Dr Trelawney did not reply to this suggestion, perhaps
because Albert spoke in what was, for him, almost a disre-
spectful tone, certainly a severe one. Instead, he held out his
arms on either side of him, the hands open, as if in preparation for crucifixion.

'I must ask you two gentlemen to assist me to my room,'
he said. 'I am too weak to walk unaided. That sounds like
the beginning of an evangelical hymn:

I am too weak to . . . walk unaided . . .

The fact is I must be careful of this shell I call my body,
though why I should be, I hardly know. Perhaps from mere
courtesy to my medical advisers. There have been warnings
—cerebral congestion.'

He laughed rather disagreeably. We supported him along
the passage, led by Albert. In his room, not without effort,
we established him in the bed. The exertions of Duport and

myself brought this about, not much aided by Albert, who, breathing hard, showed little taste for the job. Duport, on the other hand, had been enjoying himself thoroughly since the beginning of this to-do. Action, excitement were what he needed. They showed another side to him, Dr Trelawney, too, was enjoying himself by now. So far from being exhausted by this heaving about of the shell he called his body, he was plainly stimulated by all that had happened. He had mastered his fit of asthma, brought on, no doubt as Albert had suggested, by boredom and depression. The Bellevue must in any case have represented a low ebb in Dr Trelawney's fortunes. Plenty of attention made him almost well again. He lay back on his pillows, indicating by a movement of the hands that he wished us to stay and talk with him until the arrival of Mrs Erdleigh.

'Bring some glasses, my friend,' he said to Albert. 'We shall need four—a number portending obstacles and opposition in the symbolism of cards—yet necessary for our present purpose, if Myra Erdleigh is soon to be of our party.'

Albert, thankful to have Dr Trelawney out of the bathroom and safely in bed at so small a cost, went off to fetch the glasses without any of the peevishness to be expected of him when odd jobs were in question. Dr Trelawney's request seemed to have reference to a half-bottle of brandy, already opened, that stood on the wash-stand. I had been prepared to find myself in an alchemist's cell, where occult processes matured in retorts and cauldrons, reptiles hung from the ceiling while their venom distilled, homunculi in bottles lined the walls. However, there were no dog-eared volumes of the Cabbala to be seen, no pentagrams or tarot cards. Instead, Dr Trelawney's room was very like that formerly occupied by Uncle Giles, no bigger, just as dingy. A pile of luggage lay in one corner, some suits —certainly ancient enough—hung on coat-hangers suspended from the side of the wardrobe. The only suggestion of the Black Arts was wafted by a faint, sickly smell, not immediately identifiable: incense? hair-tonic? opium? It was hard to say whether the implications were chemical, medicinal, ritualistic; a scent vaguely disturbing, like Dr Trelawney's own personality. Albert returned with the glasses, then said good night, adding a word about latching the front door when Mrs Erdleigh left. He must have been used to her visits at a late hour. Duport and I were left alone with the Doctor. He told us to distribute the brandy—the flask was about a quarter full—allowing a share for Mrs Erdleigh herself when she arrived. Duport took charge, pouring out drink for the three of us.

'Which of you answered me through the door?' asked Dr Trelawney, when he had drunk some brandy.

'I did.'

'You know my teachings then?'

I told him I remembered the formula from Stonehurst. That was not strictly speaking true, because I should never have carried the words in my head all those years, if I had not heard Moreland and others talk of the Doctor in later life. My explanation did not altogether please Dr Trelawney, either because he wished to forget that period of his career, or because it too painfully recalled happier, younger days, when his cult was more flourishing. Possibly he felt disappointment that I should turn out to be no new, hitherto unknown, disciple, full of untapped enthusiasm, admiring from afar, who now at last found dramatic opportunity to disclose himself. He made no comment at all. There was something decidedly unpleasant about him, sinister, at the same time absurd, that combination of the ludicrous and alarming soon to be widely experienced by contact with those set in authority in wartime.

'I may be said to have come from Humiliation into Triumph,' he said, 'the traditional theme of Greek Tragedy.

The climate of this salubrious resort does not really suit me. In fact, I cannot think why I stay. Perhaps because I cannot afford to pay my bill and leave. Nor is there much company in the Bellevue calculated to revive failing health and spirts. And you, sir? Why are you enjoying the ozone here, if one may ask? Perhaps for the same reason as Mr Duport, who has confided to me some of the secrets of his own private prison-house.'

Dr Trelawney smiled, showing teeth as yellow and irregular as the stains on his beard. He was, I thought, a tremendously Edwardian figure: an Edwardian figure of fun, one might say. All the same, I remembered that a girl had thrown herself from a Welsh mountain-top on his account. Such things were to be considered in estimating his capacity. His smile was one of the worst things about him. I saw that Duport must be on closer terms with the Doctor than he had pretended. I had certainly not grasped the fact that they already knew each other well enough to have exchanged reasons for residing at the Bellevue. Indeed, Duport, while he had been drinking at the Royal, seemed almost deliberately to have obscured their comparative intimacy. There was nothing very surprising about their confiding in one another. Total strangers in bars and railway carriages will unfold the story of their lives at the least opportunity. It was probably true to say that the hotel contained no more suitable couple to make friends. The details about his married life which Duport had imparted to me showed that he was a more complicated, more introspective character than I had ever guessed. His connexion with Jean was now less mysterious to me. No doubt Jimmy Stripling's esoteric goings-on had familiarised Duport, more or less, with people of Dr Trelawney's sort. In any case, Dr Trelawney was probably pretty good at worming information out of other residents. Even during the time we had been sitting in the room I had become increasingly aware of his pervasive, quasi-hypnotic powers, possessed to a greater or lesser degree by all persons—not necessarily connected with occultism—who form little cults devoted primarily to veneration of themselves. This awareness was not because I felt myself in danger of falling under Dr Trelawney's dominion, though it conveyed an instinctive warning to be on one's guard. Perhaps the feeling was no more than a grown-up version of childish fantasies about him, perhaps a tribute to his will. I am not certain. Duport, on the other hand, appeared perfectly at ease. He sat in a broken-down armchair facing the bed, his hands in his pockets. I explained about my early associations with Albert, about Uncle Giles's funeral.

'I used to talk with your uncle,' said Dr Trelawney.

'What did you think of him?'

'A thwarted spirit, a restless soul wandering the vast surfaces of the earth.'

'He never found a job he liked.'

'Men do not gather grapes from off a thorn.'

'He told you about himself?'

'It was not necessary. Every man bears on his forehead the story of his days, an open volume to the initiate.'

'From that volume, you knew him well?'

'Who can we be said to know well? All men are mysteries.'

'There was no mystery about your uncle's grousing,' said Duport. 'The only thing he was cheerful about was saying there would not be a war. What do you think, Dr Trelawney?'

'What will be, must be.'

'Which means war, in my opinion,' said Duport.

'The sword of Mithras, who each year immolates the sacred bull, will ere long now flash from its scabbard.'

'You've said it.'

'The slayer of Osiris once again demands his grievous

tribute of blood. The Angel of Death will ride the storm.'

'Could this situation have been avoided?' I asked.

'The god, Mars, approaches the earth to lay waste. Moreover, the future is ever the consequence of the past.'

'And we ought to have knocked Hitler out when he first started making trouble?'

I remembered Ted Jeavons had held that view.

'The Four Horsemen are at the gate. The Kaiser went to war for shame of his withered arm. Hitler will go to war because at official receptions the tails of his evening coat sweep the floor like a clown's.'

'Seems an inadequate reason,' said Duport.

'Such things are a paradox to the uninstructed—to the adept they are clear as morning light.'

'I must be one of the uninstructed,' said Duport.

'You are not alone in that.'

'Just one of the crowd?'

'Reason is given to all men, but all men do not know how to use it. Liberty is offered to each one of us, but few learn to be free. Such gifts are, in any case, a right to be earned, not a privilege for the shiftless.'

'How do you recommend earning it?' asked Duport, stretching out his long legs in front of him, slumping down into the depths of the armchair. 'I've got to rebuild my business connexions. I could do with a few hints.'

'The education of the will is the end of human life.'

'You think so?'

'I know.'

'But can you always apply the will?' said Duport. 'Could I have renewed my severed credits by the will?'

'I am concerned with the absolute.'

'So am I. An absolute balance at the bank.'

'You speak of material trifles. The great Eliphas Lévi, whose precepts I quote to you, said that one who is afraid of fire will never command salamanders.'

195

'I don't need to command salamanders. I want to shake the metal market.'

'To know, to dare, to will, to keep silence, those are the things required.'

'And what's the bonus for these surplus profits?'

'You have spoken your modest needs.'

'But what else can the magicians offer?'

'To be for ever rich, for ever young, never to die.'

'Do they, indeed?'

'Such was in every age the dream of the alchemist.'

'Not a bad programme—let's have the blue-prints.'

'To attain these things, as I have said, you must emancipate the will from servitude, instruct it in the art of domination.'

'You should meet a mutual friend of ours called Widmerpool,' said Duport. 'He would agree with you. He's very keen on domination. Don't you think so, Jenkins? Anyway, Dr Trelawney, what action do you recommend to make a start?'

'Power does not surrender itself. Like a woman, it must be seized.'

Duport jerked his head in my direction.

'I offered him a woman in the bar of the Royal this evening,' he said, 'but he declined. He wouldn't seize one. I must admit Fred never has much on hand.'

'Cohabitation with antipathetic beings is torment,' said Dr Trelawney. 'Has that never struck you, my dear friend?'

'Time and again,' said Duport, laughing loudly. 'Perfect hell. I've done quite a bit of it in my day. Would you like to hear some of my experiences?'

'Why should we wish to ruminate on your most secret orgies?' said Dr Trelawney. 'What profit for us to muse on your nights in the lupanar, your diabolical couplings with the brides of debauch, more culpable than those phantasms of the incubi that racks the dreams of young girls, or

196

the libidinous gymnastics of the goat-god whose ice-cold sperm fathers monsters on writhing witches in coven?'

Duport shook with laughter. I saw that one of Dr Trelawney's weapons was flattery, though flattery of no trite kind, in fact the best of all flattery, the sort disguised as disagreement or rebuke.

'So you don't want a sketch of my love life in its less successful moments?' said Duport.

Dr Trelawney shook his head.

'There have been some good moments too,' said Duport. 'Don't get me wrong.'

'He alone can truly possess the pleasures of love,' said Dr Trelawney, 'who has gloriously vanquished the love of pleasure.'

'Is that your technique?'

'If you would possess, do not give.'

'I've known plenty of girls who thought that, my wife among them.'

'Continual caressing begets satiety.'

'She thought that too. You should meet. However, if what you said about a war coming is true—and it's what I think myself—why bother? We shall soon be as dead as Jenkins's uncle.'

Duport had a way of switching from banter to savage melancholy.

'There is no death in Nature,' said Dr Trelawney, 'only transition, blending, synthesis, mutation.'

'All the same,' said Duport, 'to take this uncle of Jenkins's again, you must admit, from his point of view, it was different sitting in the Bellevue lounge, from lying in a coffin at the crematorium, his present whereabouts, as I understand from his nephew.'

'Those who no longer walk beside us on the void expanses of this fleeting empire of created light have no more reached the absolute end of their journey than birth was for them the absolute beginning. They have merely performed their fugitive pilgrimage from embryo to ashes. They are in the world no longer. That is all we can say.'

'But what more can anyone say?' said Duport. 'You're put in a box and stowed away underground, or cremated in the Jenkins manner. In other words, you're dead.'

'Death is a mere phantom of ignorance,' said Dr Trelawney. 'It does not exist. The flesh is the raiment of the soul. When that raiment has grown threadbare or is torn asunder by violent hands, it must be abandoned. There is witness without end. When men know how to live, they will no longer die, no more cry with Faustus:

O lente, lente currite, noctis equi!'

Dr Trelawney and Duport were an odd couple arguing together about the nature of existence, the immortality of the soul, survival after death. The antithetical point of view each represented was emphasised by their personal appearance. This rather bizarre discussion was brought to an end by a knock on the door.

'Enter,' said Dr Trelawney.

He spoke in a voice of command. Mrs Erdleigh came into the room. Dr Trelawney raised himself into a sitting position, leaning back on his elbows.

'The Essence of the All is the Godhead of the True.'

'The Vision of Visions heals the Blindness of Sight.'

While she pronounced the incantation, Mrs Erdleigh smiled in a faintly deprecatory manner, like a grown-up who, out of pure good nature, humours the whim of a child. I remembered the same expression coming into her face when speaking to Uncle Giles. Dr Trelawney made a dramatic gesture of introduction, showing his fangs again in one of those awful grins as he lay back on the pillow.

'Mr Duport, you've met, Myra,' he said. 'This gentleman

here is the late Captain Jenkins's nephew, bearing the same name.'

He rolled his eyes in my direction, indicating Mrs Erdleigh.

'*Connaissez-vous la vieille souveraine du monde,*' he said, '*qui marche toujours, et ne se fatigue jamais?* In this incarnation, she passes under the name of Mrs Erdleigh.'

'Mr Jenkins and I know each other already,' she said, with a smile.

'I might have guessed,' said Dr Trelawney. 'She knows all.'

'And your introduction was not very polite,' said Mrs Erdleigh. 'I am not as old as she to whom the Abbé referred.'

'Be not offended, priestess of Isis. You have escaped far beyond the puny fingers of Time.'

She turned from him, holding out her hand to me.

'I knew you were here,' she said.

'Did Albert say I was coming?'

'It was not necessary. I know such things. Your poor uncle passed over peacefully. More peacefully than might have been expected.'

She wore a black coat with a high fur collar, a tricorne hat, also black, riding on the summit of grey curls. These had taken the place of the steep bank of dark-reddish tresses of the time when I had met her at the Ufford with Uncle Giles seven or eight years before. Then, I had imagined her nearing fifty. Lunching with the Templers eighteen months later (when she had arrived with Jimmy Stripling), I decided she was younger. Now, she was not so much aged as an entirely different woman—what my brother-in-law, Hugo Tolland, used to call (apropos of his employer, Mrs Baldwyn Hodges) a 'blue-rinse marquise'. This new method of doing her hair, the tone and texture of which suggested a wig, together with the three-cornered hat,

recalled Longhi, the Venetian ridotto. You felt Mrs Erdleigh had just removed her mask before paying this visit
to Cagliostro—or, as it turned out with no great difference, to Dr Trelawney.

'Sad that your mother-in-law, Lady Warminster, passed
over too,' said Mrs Erdleigh. 'She had not consulted me
for some years, but I foretold both her marriages. I
warned her that her second husband should beware of
the Eagle—symbol of the East, you know—and of the
Equinox of Spring. Lord Warminster died in Kashmir at
just that season.'

'She is greatly missed in the family.'

'Lady Warminster was a woman among women,' said
Mrs Erdleigh. 'I shall never forget her gratitude when I
revealed to her that Tuesday was the best day for the
operation of revenge.'

Dr Trelawney was becoming restive, either because
Mrs Erdleigh had made herself the centre of attention,
or because his own 'treatment' had been delayed too long.

'We think we should have our . . . er . . . pill, ha-ha,' he
said, trying to laugh, but beginning to twitch dreadfully.
'We do not wish to cut short so pleasurable an evening. I
am eternally grateful to you, gentlemen—though to name
eternity is redundant, since we all perforce have our being
within it—and I hope we shall meet again, if only in the
place where the last are said to be first, though, for my own
part, I shall not be surprised if the first are first there too.'

'We shall have to turn in as well,' said Duport, rising,
'or I shall have no head for figures tomorrow.'

I thought Duport did not much care for Mrs Erdleigh,
certainly disliked the fact that she and I had met before.

'The gods brook no more procrastination,' said Dr
Trelawney, his hoarse voice rising sharply in key. 'I am like
one of those about to adore the demon under the figure of
a serpent, or such as make sorceries with vervain and peri-

winkle, sage, mint, ash and basil . . .'

Mrs Erdleigh had taken off her coat and hat. She was fumbling in a large black bag she had brought with her. Dr Trelawney's voice now reached an agonised screech.

'. . . votaries of the Furies who use branches of cedar, alder, hawthorn, saffron and juniper in their sacrifices of turtle doves and sheep, who pour upon the ground libations of wine and honey . . .'

Mrs Erdleigh almost hustled us through the door. There was something in her hand, a small instrument that caught the light.

'I shall be with my old friend at the last tomorrow,' she said, opening wide her huge, misty eyes.

The door closed. There was the sound of the key turning in the lock, then, as we moved off down the passage, of water poured into a basin.

'You see what living at the Bellevue is like,' said Duport.

'I'm surprised you find it boring. Have you still got *The Perfumed Garden*?'

'What's that?'

'The book I gave you—*The Arab Art of Love*.'

'Hell,' said Duport, 'I left it in Trelawney's room. Well, I can get it again tomorrow, if he hasn't peddled it by then.'

'Good night.'

'Good night,' said Duport. 'I don't envy you having to turn out for your uncle's funeral in the morning.'

The Bellevue mattress was a hard one. Night was disturbed by dreams. Dr Trelawney—who had shaved his head and wore RAF uniform—preached from the baroquely carved pulpit of a vast cathedral on the text that none should heed Billson's claim to be pregnant by him of a black messiah. These and other aberrant shapes made the coming of day unwelcome. I rose, beyond question impaired by the drinks consumed with Duport, all the same anxious to get through my duties. Outside, the weather was sunny, all that the seaside required. Nevertheless, I wanted only to return to London. While I dressed, I wondered whether the goings-on of the night before had disturbed other residents of the hotel. When I reached the dining-room, the air of disquiet there made me think we had made more noise than I had supposed. Certainly the murmur of conversation was uneasy at the tables of the old ladies. An atmosphere of tension made itself felt at once. Duport, unexpectedly in his place, was eating a kipper, a pile of disordered newspapers lying on the floor beside him. I made some reference to the unwisdom of terminating an evening of that sort with Dr Trelawney's brandy. Duport made a face. He ignored my comment.

'Nice news,' he said, 'isn't it?'

'What?'

'Germany and Russia.'

'What have they done? I haven't seen a paper.'

'Signed a Non-Aggression Pact with each other.'

He handed me one of the newspapers. I glanced at the headlines.

'Cheerful situation, you will agree,' said Duport.

'Makes a good start to the day.'

I felt a sinking inside me as I read.

'Molotov and Ribbentrop,' said Duport. 'Sound like the names of a pair of performing monkeys. Just the final touch to balls up my affairs.'

'It will be war all right now.'

'And Hitler will be able to buy all the chromite he wants from the Soviet.'

'So what?'

'It's good-bye to my return to Turkey, whatever happens.'

'But if there's war, shan't we want the stuff more than ever?'

'Of course we shall. Even a bloody book-reviewer, or whatever you are, can see that. It doesn't prevent Widmerpool from failing to grasp the point. The probability of war made the pre-empting of the Turkish market essential to this country.'

'Then why not still?'

'Buying chromite to prevent Germany from getting it, and buying it just for our own use, are not the same thing. All the chromite Germany wants will now be available from Russian sources—and a bloody long list of other important items too.'

'I see.'

'Donners will handle matters differently now. I shall drop out automatically. I might get another job out of him, not that one. But can you imagine Widmerpool being such a fool as to suppose the prospect of war would diminish Donners-Brebner requirements. "Cut down our commitments", indeed.'

Duport spat out some kipper-bones on to his plate. He took several deep gulps of coffee.

'Of course in a way Widmerpool turned out to be right,' he said. 'As usual, his crassness brought him luck. As a matter of fact, I wouldn't wonder if he didn't cut off my credits as much from spite as obtuseness.'

'Why should Widmerpool want to spite you?'

'Just to show who's master. I sent him one or two pretty curt telegrams. He didn't like that. Probably decided to get his own back. Anyway, I'm up a gum tree now.'

I saw he had cause to grumble. At that moment, I could not spare much sympathy. In any case, I did not care for Duport, although I had to admit he had his points. He was, in his way, a man of action. Ahead, I thought, lay plenty of opportunity for action of one kind or another. Even now, a thousand things had to be done. Then and there, the only course to follow was to oversee Uncle Giles's cremation, return home, try to make plans in the light of the new international situation.

' 'Spect they'll requisition the place now all right,' said Albert, when I saw him. 'That's if there's anything to requisition in a day or two. Hitler's not one to tell us when he's coming. Just loose a lot of bombs, I reckon. The wife's still poorly and taking on a treat about the blackout in the bedrooms.'

For a man who thoroughly disliked danger, Albert faced the prospect of total war pretty well. At best its circumstances would shatter the props of his daily life at a time when he was no longer young. All the same, the Germans, the Russians, the suffragettes were all one when it came to putting up the shutters. He might be afraid when a policeman walked up the Stonehurst drive; that trepidation was scarcely at all increased by the prospect of bombardment from the air. Indeed, his fear was really a sort of courage, fear and courage being close to each other, like love and hate.

'Mr Duport and I sat up with Dr Trelawney for a while after he went to bed last night,' I said.

Albert shook his head.

'Don't know how we're going to get rid of him now,' he said. 'Flesh and blood won't stand it much longer. If there's requisitioning, he'll be requisitioned like the rest of us, I suppose. It won't do no good talking. Well, it's been nice seeing you again, Mr Nick.'

I felt no more wish to adjudicate between Albert and Dr Trelawney than between Duport and Widmerpool. They must settle their own problems. I went on my way. The crematorium was a blaze of sunshine. I had a word with the clergyman. It looked as if I was going to be the only mourner. Then, just as the service was about to begin, Mrs Erdleigh turned up. She was shrouded in black veils that seemed almost widow's weeds. She leant towards me and whispered some greeting, then retired to a seat at the back of the little chapel. The clergyman's voice sounded as if he, too, had sat up drinking the night before, though his appearance put such a surmise out of court.

'. . . For man walketh in a vain shadow, and disquieteth himself in vain; he heapeth up riches and cannot tell who shall gather them . . .'

Uncle Giles's spirit hovered in the air. I could well imagine one of his dissertations on such a theme. The coffin slid through the trap-door with perfect precision: Uncle Giles's remains committed to a nomad's pyre. I turned to meet Mrs Erdleigh. She had already slipped away. Her evasiveness was perhaps due to delicacy, because, when Uncle Giles's will (proved at the unexpectedly large figure of seven thousand, three hundred pounds) came to light, Mrs Erdleigh turned out to be the sole legatee. Uncle Giles could not be said to have heaped up riches, but he had seen to it that his relations did not gather them. It was one of those testamentary surprises, like St John Clarke's leaving his money to Erridge. The bequest gave some offence within the family.

'Giles was always an unreliable fellow,' said my father, 'but we mustn't speak ill of him now.'

FOUR

When the sword of Mithras—to borrow Dr Trelawney's phrase—flashed at last from its scabbard, people supposed London would immediately become the target of bombs. However, the slayer of Osiris did not at first demand his grievous tribute of blood, and a tense, infinitely uneasy over-all stagnation imposed itself upon an equally uncomfortable, equally febrile, over-all activity. Everyone was on the move. The last place to find a friend or relation was the spot where he or she had lived or worked in peacetime. Only a few, here and there, discovered themselves already suitably situated for war conditions. Frederica Budd, for example, Isobel's eldest sister, as a widow with children to bring up, had not long before gone to live in the country within range of their schools. Her small house stood in a village within twenty or thirty miles of Thrubworth, upon which Frederica always liked to keep an eye. Here it was arranged that Isobel should stay, if possible, until she gave birth. Without much in common except their relationship as sisters, the temperaments of Isobel and Frederica—unlike those of Frederica and Norah—were at the same time not in active conflict. Isobel's help in running the house was as convenient to Frederica as this arrangement was acceptable to ourselves.

Thrubworth had been requisitioned as a military headquarters. In principle detesting war in all its manifestations, Erridge was reported, in practice, to enjoy the taking over of his house by the government. This unexpected attitude on his part was not, as might be thought, because of any theoretical approval of state intervention where private property was concerned, so much as on account of the legitimate grievances—indeed, series of legitimate grievances—with which the army's investment of his mansion provided him. Erridge, a rebel whose life had been exasperatingly lacking in persecution, had enjoyed independence of parental control, plenty of money, assured social position, early in life. Since leaving school he had been deprived of all the typical grudges within the grasp of most young men. Some of these grudges, it was true, he had later developed with fair success by artificial means, grudges being, in a measure, part and parcel of his political approach. At first the outbreak of war had threatened more than one of his closest interests by making them commonplace, compulsory, even vulgarly 'patriotic'. The army at Thrubworth, with the boundless inconvenience troops bring in their train, restored Erridge's inner well-being. There was no major upheaval in his own daily existence. He and Blanche, in any case, inhabited only a small corner of the house, so that domestically speaking things remained largely unchanged for him on his own ground. At the same time he was no longer tempted to abandon all his high-minded activities. Provided with a sitting target, he was able to devote himself to an unremitting campaign against militarism as represented in person by the commanding officer and staff of the formation quartered on his property. A succession of skirmishes raged round the use of the billiard-table, the grand piano, the hard tennis-court, against a background of protest, often justifiable enough, about unsightly tracks made by short cuts across lawns, objects in the house broken or defaced by carelessness and vandalism. However, these hostilities could at the same time be unremitting only so far as Erridge's own health allowed, the outbreak of war having quite genuinely transformed him from a congenital sufferer from many vague ailments into a man whose physical state bordered on that of a chronic invalid.

'Erry helped to lose the Spanish war for his own side,' said Norah. 'Thank goodness he is not going to be fit enough to lose this one for the rest of us.'

Norah herself, together with her friend, Eleanor Walpole-Wilson, had already enrolled themselves as drivers in some women's service. They could talk of nothing but the charm of their superior officer, a certain Gwen McReith. Eleanor's father, Sir Gavin Walpole-Wilson, after many years of retirement, had made a public reappearance by writing a 'turn-over' article for *The Times* on German influence in the smaller South American countries. This piece had ended with the words: 'The dogs bark: the caravan moves on.' In fact everyone, one way and another, was becoming absorbed into the leviathan of war. Its inexorable pressures were in some ways more irksome for those outside the machine than those within. I myself, for example, felt lonely and depressed. Isobel was miles away in the country; most of the people I knew had disappeared from London, or were soon to do so. They were in uniform, or some new, unusual civil occupation. In this atmosphere writing was more than ever out of the question; even reading could be attempted only at short stretches. I refused one or two jobs offered, saying I was 'on the Reserve', should soon be 'called up'. However, no calling-up took place; nor, so far as I could discover, was any likely to be enunciated in the near future. There was just the surrounding pressure of uneasy stagnation, uneasy activity.

I was not alone, of course, in this predicament. Indeed, my father, who might have been expected to be of some assistance, was, as it turned out, in worse case even than myself. He was by this time totally immersed in the problem of how to bring about his own re-employment, a preoccupation which, in spite of her very mixed feelings

208

on the subject, equally engrossed my mother, who partly feared he might succeed, partly dreaded his despair if left on the shelf. It was hard, even impossible, for my father to concentrate for even a short time on any other subject. He would talk for hours at a time about possible jobs that he might be offered. His prospects were meagre in the extreme, for his health had certainly not improved since retirement. Now, his days were spent writing letters to contemporaries who had achieved senior rank, hanging about his club trying to buttonhole them in person.

'I managed to have a word with Fat Boy Gort at the Rag yesterday,' he would say, speaking as if in a dream. 'Of course I knew he could do nothing for me himself in his exalted position, but he wasn't at all discouraging. Gave me the name of a fellow in the Adjutant-General's own secretariat who is entering my name on a special file with a few others of much the same category as myself. Something may come of it. Brownrigg's doing his best too. As a member of the Army Council, he ought to bring something off.'

Then it struck me that General Conyers might be worth approaching in my own interests. By that time my parents had almost lost touch with the General, having themselves drifted into a form of life in which they hardly ever 'saw' anybody, certainly a way of life far removed from the General's own restless curiosity about things, an energy that age was said to have done little to abate. At least that was the picture of him to be inferred from their occasional mention of his name. To tell the truth, they rather disapproved of rumours that percolated through to them that General Conyers would sometimes attend meetings of the Society for Psychical Research, or had given a lecture at one of the universities on the subject of Oriental secret societies. My parents preferred to think of General Conyers as living a life of complete retirement and inactivity since the death of his wife four or five years before. At that date he had sold their house in the country, at the same time disposing of such sporting poodles as remained in the kennels there. Now he lived all the year round in the small flat near Sloane Square, where he was still said to play Gounod on his 'cello in the afternoons.

'Poor old Aylmer,' my father would say, since he liked to think of other people existing in an unspectacular, even colourless manner. 'You know he was rather a gay spark in his youth. Never looked at another woman after he married Bertha. It must be a lonely life.'

At first I hesitated to call on General Conyers, not only on account of this forlorn picture of him, but also because great age is, in itself, a little intimidating. I had not set eyes on him since my own wedding. Finally, I decided to telephone. The General sounded immensely vigorous on the line. Like so many of his generation, he always shouted into the mouthpiece with the full force of his lungs, as if no other method would make the instrument work.

'Delighted to hear your voice, Nick. Come along. Of course, of course, of course.'

He was specific about the time I was to call on the following day. I found myself once more under his photograph in the uniform of the Body Guard I had so much admired as a child, when my mother had taken me to see Mrs Conyers not long after we had left Stonehurst. I think the General admired this picture too, because, while we were talking of people we knew in common, he suddenly pointed to this apotheosis of himself in plumed helmet bearing a halberd.

'They made me give all that up,' he said. 'Reached the age limit. Persuaded them to keep me on for quite a while longer than allowed by regulations, as a matter of fact, but they kicked me out in the end. Lot of nonsense. It's not the fellows of my age who feel the strain. We know how to hold ourselves easily on parade. It's the fellow in his fifties who has to go to bed for a week after duty at a court or levée. Tries to stand to attention all the time and be too damned regimental. Won't do at that age. Anyway, I've got plenty to occupy me. Too much, I don't mind telling you. In any case, gallivanting round in scarlet and gold doesn't arise these days.'

He shook his head emphatically, as if I might try to deny that. His face had become more than ever aquiline and ivory, the underlying structure of bone and muscle, accentuated by age, giving him an other-worldliness of expression, a look withdrawn and remote (not unlike that of Lady Warminster's features in the months before she died), as if he now lived in a dream of half-forgotten campaigns, love affairs, heterodox experiences and opinions. At the same time there was a restless strength, a rhythm, about his movements that made one think of the Michelangelo figures in the Sistine Chapel. The Cumæan Sybil with a neat moustache added? All at once he leant forward, turning with one arm over the back of his chair, his head slightly bent, pointing to another picture hanging on the wall. I saw he was an unbearded Jehovah inspiring life into Adam through an extended finger.

'Sold most of the stuff when Bertha died,' he said. 'No good to Charlotte, married to a sailor, never has a home. Thought I'd keep the Troost, though. Troost? Van Troost? Can't remember which he is. Not sure that I was wise to have had it cleaned on the advice of that fellow Smethyck.'

The scene was a guard-room in the Low Countries.

'Undisciplined looking lot,' General Conyers went on. 'No joke soldiering in those days. Must have been most difficult to get your orders out to large bodies of men. Still, that's true today. Immense intricacies even about calling them up in the categories you want them.'

I told him that was the very subject about which I came to speak; in short, how best to convert registration with the

Reserve into a commission in the armed forces. Before the war, this metamorphosis had been everywhere regarded as a process to be put automatically in motion by the march of events; now, for those in their thirties, the key seemed inoperative for entry into that charmed circle. The General shook his head at once.

'If Richard Cœur de Lion came back to earth tomorrow,' he said, 'he would be able to tell you more, my dear Nick, than I can about the British Army of today. I am not much further advanced in military knowledge than those fellows Troost painted in the guard-room. Can't your father help?'

'He's trying to solve his own problem of getting back.'

'They'll never have him.'

'You think not?'

'Certainly not. Never heard such a thing.'

'Why not?'

'Health isn't good enough. Too old.'

'He doesn't believe that.'

'Of course he's too old. Much too old. Aren't you getting a shade old yourself to embark on a military career? Wars have to be fought by young men nowadays, you know, my dear Nick, not old buffers like us.'

'Still, I thought I might try.'

'Does you credit. Can't one of your own contemporaries give you a tip? Some of them must be soldiers.'

He stood for a moment to straighten out his rheumatic leg, carefully smoothing the thick dark check of the trouser as far down as the cloth top of his buttoned boot. I felt a little dashed to find suddenly that I was so old, by now good for little, my life virtually over. The General returned to his chair.

'Didn't you once tell me years ago that you know Hugh Moreland, the composer?' he asked. 'Splendid thing of his I heard on the wireless not long ago. Now, what was it called?

Tone Poem Vieux Port . . . something of the sort . . . wondered if I could get a record . . .'

He had evidently dismissed the army—the war itself—from his mind for a moment. Quite other thoughts were in his head.

'How are all Isobel's brothers and sisters?' he asked.

I gave some account of them.

'Erridge is a psychosomatic case, of course,' said the General. 'Not a doubt of it. Contradictory exterior demands of contending interior emotions. Great pity he doesn't get married.'

He looked at his watch. I made a movement to leave. As a man of action, General Conyers had failed me. He put out his hand at once.

'No, don't go yet,' he said. 'Stay just a moment more, if you can. There is someone coming I would like you to meet. That was why I asked you at this time. Got a bit of news to tell you, as a matter of fact. You can pass it on to your parents during the next day or two.'

He paused, nodding his head knowingly. He was evidently very pleased about something. I wondered what could have happened. Perhaps he had been given at long last some decoration he specially coveted. It would be late in the day to award him decorations, but such official afterthoughts are not unknown. All the same, it would be unlike General Conyers to care greatly about such things, certainly to speak of them with this enthusiasm, though one can never tell what specialised goals people will set their hearts on attaining.

'I am getting married again,' he said crisply.

I had just enough control not to laugh aloud.

'Some people might think it a mistake,' said the General, speaking now very sternly, as if he well knew how to deal in the most crushing fashion with such persons. 'I perfectly realise that. I have not the smallest doubt that a good many of my friends will say that I am making a mistake. My answer is that I do not care a damn. Not a damn. Don't you agree, Nicholas?'

'Absolutely.'

'After all, it is I who am getting married, not they.'

'Of course.'

'They can mind their own business, what?'

'Certainly.'

'That's a thing no one likes to do.'

General Conyers laughed very heartily at this thought of the horrible destiny pursuing his critics, that they would have to mind their own business, most dreaded of predicaments.

'So I should like you to stay and meet my future wife,' he said.

I wondered what my parents were going to say to this. From their point of view it would be the final nail in the coffin of Aylmer Conyers. There was nothing of which they would more disapprove. At that moment the front-door bell rang.

'Forgive me,' said the General, 'as I explained before, I have no longer any domestic staff.'

He went off to open the door. I heard a woman's voice in the hall; soft laughter, as if at a too violent embrace. I thought how furious Uncle Giles would have been had he lived to hear that General Conyers was contemplating re-marriage. Certainly the news was unexpected enough. I wondered who on earth was going to appear. A succession of possibilities, both ludicrous and conventional, presented themselves to the mind: ash-blondes of seventeen; red-wigged, middle-aged procuresses, on the lines of Mrs Erdleigh; silver-haired, still palely-beautiful widows of defunct soldiers, courtiers, noblemen. I even toyed for a moment with the fantasy that the slight asperity that had always existed between the General and my sister-in-law,

Frederica, might really have concealed love, dismissing such a possibility almost as soon as it took shape. Even that last expectation scarcely came up to the reality. I could not have guessed it in a million years. A tall, dark, beaky-nosed lady of about fifty came into the room. I rose. She was distinctly well dressed, with a businesslike, rather than frivolous, air.

'We have often met before,' she said, holding out her hand.

It was Miss Weedon.

'At Lady Molly's,' she said, 'and long before that too.'

The General took my arm between his forefinger and thumb, as if about to break it neatly just above the elbow with one sharp movement of his wrist.

'So you know each other already?' he said, not absolutely sure he was pleased by that fact. 'I might have guessed you would have met with Molly Jeavons. I'd forgotten she was an aunt of Isobel's.'

'But we knew each other in much more distant days as well,' said Miss Weedon, speaking in a gayer tone than I had ever heard her use before.

She looked enormously delighted at what was happening to her.

'I ran into Jeavons the other day in Sloane Street,' said General Conyers. 'Have you seen him lately, Nick?'

'Not for a month or two. There has been such a lot to do about Isobel going to the country and so on. We haven't been to Molly's house for ages. How are they?'

'Jeavons is an air-raid warden,' said the General. 'We had quite a talk. I like Jeavons. Don't know him well. Hear some people complain he is a bore. I don't think so. He put me on to a first-rate place to buy cheap shirts many years ago. Shopped there ever since.'

'I believe Lady Molly is going back to Dogdene,' said Miss Weedon. 'They have evacuated a girls' school to the house. She may help to run it—not teach, of course. How strange to return after being châtelaine of the place.'

'Of course, she was once married to that pompous fellow, John Sleaford, wasn't she?' said the General. 'One forgets things. Sleaford must be dead these twenty years. How King Edward abominated him.'

'I don't think the present marchioness will be too pleased to find her former sister-in-law in residence at Dogdene again,' said Miss Weedon, with one of those icy, malicious smiles I well remembered. 'Lady Molly has always been so funny about what she calls "the latest Dogdene economy".'

'Poor Alice Sleaford,' said the General. 'You must not be unkind to her, Geraldine.'

I had never before heard Miss Weedon addressed as 'Geraldine'. When secretary to Stringham's mother, Mrs Foxe, she had always been 'Tuffy'. That was what Molly Jeavons called her, too. I wanted to ask about Stringham, but, in the existing circumstances, hesitated to do so. As bride of General Conyers, Miss Weedon had suddenly become such a very different sort of person, almost girlish in her manner, far from the Medusa she had once been designated by Moreland. At the same time, she still retained some of her secretary's formality in speaking of people. However, she herself must have decided that her present position would be weakened, rather than strengthened, by all avoidance of the subject of Stringham, which, certain to turn up sooner or later, was best put at once on a solid basis. She now raised it herself.

'I expect you want to hear about Charles,' she said, very cheerfully.

'Of course. How is he?'

'Quite all right now.'

'Really?'

'Absolutely.'

'Charles is the fellow you were helping to look after his mother's house, is he?' asked General Conyers, speaking

216

with that small touch of impatience, permissible, even to be applauded, in the light of his own engagement. 'You knew Charles Stringham, did you, Nicholas? At school with him, were you? I hear he drank too much, but has given it up. Good thing.'

'Is he still at Glimber?'

'Glimber has been taken over as an evacuated government office. Charles is in London now, looking for a job. He wants to get into the army. Of course his health isn't very good, even though he has stopped drinking. It isn't going to be easy. There have been money troubles too. His father died in Kenya and left such money as he had to his French wife. Mrs Foxe is not nearly so rich as she was. Commander Foxe is so terribly extravagant. He has gone back to the navy, of course.'

'Good old Buster.'

Miss Weedon laughed. She deeply detested Buster Foxe.

'Nicholas wants to get into the army too,' said General Conyers, anxious to dismiss the subject of Stringham and his relations. 'He is also having difficulties. Didn't you say so, Nicholas? Now, tell me, don't I remember a former servant of your parents manages a hotel somewhere? Some seaside place. Very good cook, wasn't he? I remember his soufflés. Thought we might perhaps honeymoon at his hotel. Not going to make it a long affair. Just a week or ten days. Quite enough.'

'They have probably requisitioned the place. I was down there a month or two ago for Uncle Giles's funeral.'

'Saw his death in the paper. Made rather a mess of his life, didn't he? Don't think I set eyes on him since a week or two before the earlier war broke out.'

'Do you remember Dr Trelawney? He was staying in the hotel.'

'That old scoundrel. Was he, indeed? How is he?'

'He got locked in the bathroom.'

'Did he, did he?' said the General thoughtfully. 'The Essence of the All is the Godhead of the True . . . may be something in it. Always meant to go and have a look at Trelawney on his own ground . . . all that stuff about the Astral Plane . . .'

He pondered; then, with an effort, brought himself back to earth, when I said that I must be going.

'Sorry not to have been more use about your own problem, Nick. Have another talk with your father. Better still, get some young fellow to help you. No good trying too high up. Somebody quite junior, like a lieutenant-colonel. That's the kind of fellow. Very nice to have seen you. You must come and visit us after we get back. Don't know where we shall go yet.'

I left them together, discussing that question, Miss Weedon still looking immensely pleased about everything. As the flat door closed, I heard her laughter, now quite shrill, begin again. She had reason to be pleased. Stringham, so it appeared, had been cured by her of 'drink'; now she had captured General Conyers. The one achievement was as remarkable as the other. They were perhaps not so disparate as might at first sight appear. There was a kind of dash about Stringham comparable with the General's manner of facing the world; at the same time, the General's advanced age, like Stringham's taste for the bottle, gave Miss Weedon something ponderable upon which to exercise her talent for 'looking after' people, her taste, in short, for power. General Conyers had seemed as enchanted with Miss Weedon as she with him. I wondered what other men—in addition to Stringham—had been 'in her life', as Mrs Erdleigh would have said; what, for that matter, had been Miss Weedon's true relationship with Stringham. One passes through the world knowing few, if any, of the important things about even the people with whom one has been from time to time in the closest intimacy.

'Valéry asks why one has been summoned to this carnival,' Moreland once said, 'but it's more like blind man's buff. One reels through the carnival in question, blundering into persons one can't see, and, without much success, trying to keep hold of a few of them.'

There could be no doubt that General Conyers had taken on a formidable woman; equally no doubt that he was a formidable man. If he could handle Billson naked, he could probably handle Miss Weedon clothed—or naked, too, if it came to that. I felt admiration for his energy, his determination to cling to life. There was nothing defeatist about him. However, my parents, as I had expected, were not at all pleased by the news. They had, of course, never heard of Miss Weedon. The engagement was, indeed, quite a shock to them. In fact, the whole affair made my father very cross. Now that Uncle Giles was no more, he may have felt himself permitted a greater freedom of expression in openly criticising General Conyers. He did so in just the terms the General had himself envisaged.

'No fool like an old fool,' my father said. 'I shouldn't have believed it of him, Bertha hardly cold in her grave.'

'I hope he hasn't made a silly mistake,' said my mother. 'I like old Aylmer, with all his funny ways of behaving.'

'Very awkward for his daughter too. Why, some of his grandchildren must be almost grown up.'

'Oh, no,' said my mother, who loved accuracy in such matters, 'not grown up.'

'Where did he meet this woman?'

'I really don't know.'

It turned out later that General Conyers had sat next to Miss Weedon at a concert some months before the outbreak of war. They had fallen into conversation. Finding they knew many people in common, they had arranged to meet at another concert the following week. That was how their friendship had begun. In short, General Conyers had 'picked up' Miss Weedon. There was no denying it. It was a true romance.

'Adventures only happen to adventurers,' Mr Deacon had said one evening when we were sitting drinking in the saloon bar of the Mortimer.

'That depends on what one calls adventurers,' said Moreland, who was in a hair-splitting mood. 'What you mean, Edgar, is that people to whom adventures happen are never wholly unadventurous. That is not the same thing. It's the latter class who have the real adventures—people like oneself.'

'Don't be pedantic, Moreland,' Mr Deacon had answered.

Certainly General Conyers was not unadventurous. Was he an adventurer? I considered his advice about the army. Then the answer came to me. I must get in touch with Widmerpool. I wondered why I had not thought of that earlier. I telephoned to his office. They put me through to a secretary.

'Captain Widmerpool is embodied,' she said in an un-friendly voice.

I could tell from her tone, efficient, charmless, un-imaginative, that she had been given special instructions by Widmerpool himself to use the term 'embodied' in describing his military condition. I asked where he was to be found. It was a secret. At last, not without pressure on my own part, she gave me a telephone number. This turned out to be that of his Territorial battalion's headquarters. I rang him up.

'Come and see me by all means, my boy,' he boomed down the wire in a new, enormously hearty voice, 'but bring your own beer. There won't be much I can do for you. I'm up to my arse in bumph and don't expect I shall be able to spare you more than a minute or two for waffling.'

I was annoyed by the phrase 'bring your own beer', also

by being addressed as 'my boy' by Widmerpool. They were terms he had never, so to speak, earned the right to use, certainly not to me. However, I recognised that a world war was going to produce worse situations than Widmerpool's getting above himself and using a coarsely military boisterousness of tone to which his civilian personality could make no claim. I accepted his invitation; he named a time. The following day, after finishing my article for the paper and looking at some books I had to review, I set out for the Territorial headquarters, which was situated in a fairly inaccessible district of London. I reached there at last, feeling in the depths of gloom. Entry into the most arcane recesses of the Secret Service could not have been made more difficult. Finally an NCO admitted me to Widmerpool's presence. He was sitting, surrounded by files, in a small, horribly stuffy office, which was at the same time freezingly cold. I was still unused to the sight of him in uniform. He looked anything but an army officer—a railway official, perhaps, of some obscure country.

'Been left in charge of details consequent on the unit's move to a training area,' he said brusquely, as I entered the room. 'Suppose I shouldn't have told you that. Security —security—and then security. Everyone must learn that. Well, my lad, what can I do for you? You need not stand. Take a pew.'

I sat on a kitchen chair with a broken back, and outlined my situation.

'The fact is,' said Widmerpool, glaring through his spectacles and puffing out his cheeks, as if rehearsing a tremendous blowing up he was going to give some subordinate in the very near future, 'you ought to have joined the Territorials before war broke out.'

'I know.'

'No good just entering your name on the Reserve.'

'There were difficulties about age.'

'Only after you'd left it too late.'

'It was only a matter of months.'

'Never mind. Think how long I've been a Territorial officer. You should have looked ahead.'

'You said there wasn't going to be a war after "Munich".'

'You thought there was, so you were even more foolish.'

There was truth in that.

'I only want to know the best thing to do,' I said.

'You misjudged things, didn't you?'

'I did.'

'No vacancies now.'

'How can I put that right?'

'The eldest of our last intake of commissioned subalterns was twenty-one. The whole lot of them had done at least eighteen months in the ranks—*at least*.'

'Even so, the army will have to expand in due course.'

'Officers will be drawn from the younger fellows coming up.'

'You think there is nothing for me to do at present?'

'You could enlist in the ranks.'

'But the object of joining the Reserve—being accepted for it—was to be dealt with immediately as a potential officer.'

'Then I can't help you.'

'Well, thanks for seeing me.'

'I will keep an eye out for you,' said Widmerpool, rather less severely. 'As a matter of fact, I may be in a position well placed for doing so before many moons have waned.'

'Why?'

'I am probably to be sent to the Staff College.'

'Oh?'

'Again, for security reasons, that should not be mentioned beyond these four walls.'

He began to gather up his multitudinous papers, stowing some away in a safe, transferring others to a brief-case.

'I shall be coming back to this office again after dinner,' he said. 'Lucky if I get away before midnight. It's all got to be cleared up somehow, if the war is to be won. I gave my word to the Brigade-Major. He's a very sharp fellow called Farebrother. City acquaintance of mine.'

'Sunny Farebrother?'

'Have you met him?'

'Years ago.'

Widmerpool gave a semi-circular movement of his arm, as if to convey the crushing responsibility his promise to the Brigade-Major comprehended. He locked the safe. Putting the key in his trouser-pocket after attaching it to a chain hanging from his braces, he spoke again, this time in an entirely changed tone.

'Nicholas,' he said, 'I am going to ask you to do something.'

'Yes?'

'Let me explain very briefly. As you know, my mother lives in a cottage not very far from Stourwater. We call it a cottage, it is really a little house. She has made it very exquisite.'

'I remember your telling me.'

'Since she lives by herself, there has been pressure—rather severe pressure—applied to her by the authorities to have evacuees there.'

'Oh, yes.'

'Now I do not wish my lady mother to be plagued by evacuees.'

That seemed a reasonable enough sentiment. Nobody wanted evacuees, even if they accepted the fact that evacuees must be endured. Why should they? I could not see, how-ever, in Mrs Widmerpool's case, that I could help in pre-venting such a situation from arising. I realised at the same time that Widmerpool had suddenly effected in himself one of those drastic changes of policy in which, for example, from acting an all-powerful tyrant, he would suddenly become a humble suppliant. I understood very clearly that something was required of me, but could not guess what I was expected to do. Some persons, knowing that they were later going to ask a favour, would have made themselves more agreeable when a favour was being asked of them. That was not Widmerpool's way. I almost admired him for making so little effort to conceal his lack of interest in my own affairs, while waiting his time to demand something of myself.

'The point is this,' he said, 'up to date, my mother has had an old friend—Miss Janet Walpole-Wilson, sister of that ineffective diplomat, Sir Gavin—staying with her, so the question of evacuees, until now, has not arisen. Now Miss Walpole-Wilson's work with the Women's Voluntary Service takes her elsewhere. The danger of evacuees is acute.'

I thought how Miss Janet Walpole-Wilson's ordinary clothes must have merged imperceptibly into the uniform of her service. It was as if she had been preparing all her life for that particular dress.

'But how can I help?'

'Some relation of Lady Molly Jeavons—a relative of her husband's, to be more precise—wants accommodation in the country. A place not too far from London. Miss Walpole-Wilson heard about this herself. She told us.'

'Why not ring up the Jeavonses?'

'I have done so. In fact, I am meeting my mother at Lady Molly's tonight.'

Widmerpool was still oppressed by some unsolved problem, which he found difficulty about putting into words. He cleared his throat, swallowed several times.

'I wondered whether you would come along to the Jeavonses tonight,' he said. 'It might be easier.'

'What might?'

Widmerpool went red below his temples, under the line made by his spectacles. He began to sweat in spite of the low temperature of the room.

'You remember that rather unfortunate business when I was engaged to Mildred Haycock?'

'Yes.'

'I haven't really seen anything of the Jeavonses since then.'

'You came to the party Molly gave for Isobel just before we were married.'

'I know,' said Widmerpool, 'but there were quite a lot of people there then. It was an occasion. It's rather different going there tonight to discuss something like my mother's cottage. Lady Molly has never seen my mother.'

'I am sure it will be all right. Molly loves making arrangements.'

'All the same, I feel certain embarrassments.'

'No need to with the Jeavonses.'

'I thought that, since Molly Jeavons is an aunt of your wife's, things might be easier if you were to accompany me. Will you do that?'

'All right.'

'You will come?'

'Yes, if you wish.'

I had not visited the Jeavonses for some little time—not since Isobel had gone to stay with Frederica—so that I was quite glad to make this, as it were, an excuse for calling on them. Isobel would certainly enjoy news of the Jeavons household.

'Very well, then,' said Widmerpool, now returning at once to his former peremptory tone, 'we'll move off forthwith. It is five minutes to the bus. Come along. Party, quick march.'

He gave some final instructions in the adjoining room to a gloomy corporal sitting before a typewriter, surrounded, like Widmerpool himself, with huge stacks of documents. We went out into the street, where the afternoon light was beginning to fade. Widmerpool, his leather-bound stick caught tight beneath his armpit, marched along beside me, tramp-tramp-tramp, eventually falling into step, since I had not taken my pace from his.

'I didn't know what Jeavons's relative will be like,' he said. 'I don't feel absolutely confident she will be the sort my mother will like.'

I felt more apprehension for the person who had to share a cottage with Mrs Widmerpool.

'I saw Bob Duport just before war broke out.'

I said that partly to see what Widmerpool would answer, partly because I thought he had been unhelpful about the army, tiresome about the Jeavonses. I hoped the information would displease him. The surmise was correct. He stiffened, strutting now so fiercely that he could almost be said to have broken into the goosestep.

'Did you? Where?'

'He was staying in a hotel where an uncle of mine died. I had to see about the funeral and ran across Duport there.'

'Oh.'

'I hadn't seen him for years.'

'He is a bad mannered fellow, Duport. Ungrateful, too.'

'What is he ungrateful about?'

'I got him a job in Turkey. You may remember we were talking about Duport's affairs at Stourwater, when I saw you and your wife there about a year or more ago—just after "Munich".'

'He'd recently come back from Turkey when we met.'

'He had been working for me there.'

'So he said.'

'I had to deal rather summarily with Duport in the end,' said Widmerpool. 'He showed no grasp of the inter-

226

national situation. He is insolent, too. So he mentioned my name?'

'He did.'

'Not very favourably, I expect.'

'Not very.'

'I don't know what will happen to Duport,' said Widmerpool. 'He must be in a difficult position financially, owing to his reckless conduct. However, anybody can earn three pounds a week these days as an air-raid warden. Even Jeavons does. So Duport will not starve.'

He sounded rather sorry that Duport was not threatened with that fate.

'He thought Sir Magnus Donners might find him something.'

'Not if I know it.'

'Do you think Donners will be asked to join the Government, if there is a Cabinet reshuffle?'

'The papers speak of him as likely for office,' said Widmerpool, not without condescension. 'In some ways Magnus would make an excellent minister in time of war. In others, I am not so sure. He has certain undesirable traits for a public man in modern days. As you probably know, people speak of—well, mistresses. I am no prude. Let a man lead his own life, say I—but, if he is a public man, let him be careful. More than these allegedly bad morals, I object in Magnus to something you would never guess if you met him casually. I mean a kind of hidden frivolity. Now, what a lamentable scene that was when I looked in on Stourwater when you were there. Suppose some journalist had got hold of it.'

Widmerpool was about to enlarge on the Masque of the Seven Deadly Sins as played in the Stourwater dining-room, when his attention—and my own—was caught by a small crowd of people loitering in the half-light at the corner of a side street. Some sort of a meeting was in progress. From the traditional soapbox, a haggard middle-aged man in spectacles and a cloth cap was addressing fifteen or twenty persons, including several children. The group was apathetic enough, except for the children, who were playing a game that involved swinging their gas-mask cases at each other by the string, then running quickly away. Two women in trousers were hawking a newspaper or pamphlet. Widmerpool and I paused. The orator, his face gnarled and blotched by a lifetime of haranguing crowds out of doors in all weathers, seemed to be coming to the end of his discourse. He used that peculiarly unctuous, coaxing, almost beseeching manner of address adopted by some political speakers, reminding me a little of my brother-in-law, Roddy Cutts, whose voice would some-times take on that same pleading note when he made a public appeal for a cause in which he was interested.

'. . . why didn't the so-called British Government of the day clinch the Anglo-Soviet alliance when they had the chance . . . get something done . . . Comrade Stalin's invitation to a round-table conference at Bucharest . . . consistent moral policy . . . effective forces of socialism . . . necessary new alignments . . . USSR prestige first and foremost . . .'

The speech came to an end, the listeners demonstrating neither approval nor the reverse. The haggard man stepped down from the soapbox, wiped his spectacles, loosened the peak of his cap from his forehead, lit a cigarette. The children's gas-mask game reached a pitch of frenzied inten-sity, so that in their scamperings one of the women selling newspapers almost had the packet knocked from her hand. Widmerpool turned to me. He was about to comment, when our attention was engaged by a new speaker. This was the second newspaper-selling woman, who, having now handed over her papers to the man with the cloth cap, herself

228

jumped on to the soapbox. In a harsh clear voice she opened a tremendous tirade, quite different in approach from the quieter, more reasoned appeal of the spectacled man.

'. . . blooming bloody hypocrisy . . . anybody wants this war except a few crackpots . . . see a chance of seizing world power and grinding the last miserable halfpence from the frozen fingers of stricken mankind . . . lot of Fascist, terroristic, anti-semitic, war-mongering, exploiting White Guards and traitors to the masses . . .'

It was Gypsy Jones. I had not set eyes on her since the days when we used to meet in Mr Deacon's antique shop. She had lost a front tooth, otherwise did not look greatly changed from what she had been in the Mr Deacon period: older, harder, angrier, further than ever from her last bath, but essentially the same. Her hair was still cut short like a boy's, her fists clenched, her legs set wide apart. Over her trousers she wore a man's overcoat, far from new, the aggressive inelegance of the ensemble expressing to perfection her own revolutionary, destructive state of mind. In the old days she had worked for Howard Craggs at the Vox Populi Press, was said to be his mistress. Craggs had moved a long way since the Vox Populi Press. Lately, he had been appointed to a high post in the Ministry of Information. I recalled the night when Gypsy Jones had been dressed as Eve in order to accompany Craggs, as Adam, to the Merry Thought fancy-dress party: the encounter we had had at the back of Mr Deacon's shop. There had been a certain grubby charm about her. I felt no regrets. Love had played no part. There was nothing painful to recall. Then Widmerpool had fallen for her, had pursued her, had paid for her 'operation'. Such things seemed like another incarnation.

'. . . not appealing to a lot of half-baked Bloomsbury intellectuals and Hampstead ideologues . . . bourgeois scabs and parlour-socialist nancy boys . . . scum of weak-

229

kneed Trotskyite flunkeys . . . betraying the workers and anyone else it suits their filthy bloody blackleg book to betray . . . I'm talking about politics—socialism—reality —adaptability . . .'

I felt my arm caught tightly. It was Widmerpool. I turned towards him. He had gone quite pale. His thick lips were trembling a little. The sight of Gypsy Jones, rousing vague memories in myself, had caused him to react far more violently. To Widmerpool, she was not the mere handmaid of memory, she was a spectre of horror, the ghastly reminder of failure, misery, degradation. He dragged at my arm.

'For God's sake, come away,' he said.

We continued our course down the street, over which dusk was falling, Widmerpool walking at a much sharper pace, but without any of his former bravura, the stick now gripped in his hand as if to ward off actual physical attack.

'You realised who it was?' he said, as we hurried along.

'Of course.'

'How soon did you see her?'

'Only after she had begun to speak.'

'Me, too. What an escape. It was a near thing.'

'What was?'

'She might have noticed me.'

'Would that have mattered?'

Widmerpool stopped dead.

'What do you mean?' he asked abruptly.

'Supposing she had seen us, even said something to us?'

'I didn't say us, I said *me*.'

'You then?'

'Of course it would have mattered. It would have been disastrous.'

'Why?'

'How can you ask such a question? There are all kind of reasons why it should matter. You know something of my past with that woman. Can't you understand how painful the sight of her is to me? Besides, you heard what she was shouting. She is a Communist. Did you not understand what the words meant? Your denseness is unbelievable. She is attacking the prosecution of the war. Haven't you grasped that Russia is now Hitler's ally? Suppose that woman had suddenly addressed herself to me. That would have been a fine thing. You don't realise what it means to be in an official position. Let me explain. I am not only an army officer, I am a man with heavy responsibilities. I have been left in charge of a headquarters. I have access to all kind of secret documents. You would not guess the nature of some of them. What if she had been seen speaking to me? Have you ever heard of M.I.5? What if its agents had seen us conversing? There may well have been one of them among the crowd. Such meetings are quite rightly kept under supervision by the contre-espionage department.'

I could think of no answer. Although Widmerpool's view of himself as a man handling weighty state secrets was beyond belief in its absurdity, I felt at the same time that I had myself shown lack of feeling in treating so lightly his former love for Gypsy Jones. Love is at once always absurd and never absurd; the more grotesque its form, the more love itself confers a certain dignity on the circumstances of those it torments. No doubt Widmerpool had been through a searing experience with Gypsy Jones, an experience even now by no means forgotten. That could be the only explanation of such an outburst. I had rarely seen him so full of indignation. He had paused for breath. Now, his reproaches began again.

'You come and ask me for advice about getting into the army, Nicholas,' he said, 'and because I spare the time to

231

talk of such things—make time, when my duty lies by rights elsewhere—you think I have nothing more serious to occupy me than your own trivial problems. That is not the case. The General Staff of the Wehrmacht would be only too happy to possess even a tithe of the information I locked away before we quitted the Orderly Room.'

'I don't doubt it. I realise you are busy. It was kind of you to see me.'

Widmerpool was a little placated. Perhaps he also feared that, if he went too far in his reproofs, I might excuse myself from accompanying him to the Jeavonses'. He tapped me with his stick.

'Don't worry further about your remarks,' he said. 'The sight of that woman upset me, especially behaving as she was. Did you hear her language? Besides, I have been over-working as usual. You feel the strain at unexpected moments.'

He made no further comment. We found a bus, which transported us in due course to the neighbourhood of the Jeavons house in South Kensington. The bell was not answered for a long time. We waited outside the faintly Dutch edifice with its over ornamented dark red brick façade.

'I expect Mother has preceded us,' said Widmerpool.

He was better now, though still not wholly recovered from the sight of Gypsy Jones. The door was opened at last by Jeavons himself. His appearance took me by surprise. Instead of the usual ancient grey suit, he was wearing a blue one-piece overall and a beret. Some people—as General Conyers had remarked—considered Jeavons a bore. Such critics had a case, undeniably, when he was sunk in one of his impenetrable silences, or, worse still, was trying, in a momentary burst of energy, to make some money by selling one of those commodities generically described by Chips Lovell as 'an automatic boot-jack or infallible cure for the

232

common cold'. To find Jeavons in the latter state was rare, the former, fairly frequent. Even apart from his war wound, Jeavons was not at all fitted for commercial employments. He had hardly done a stroke of work since marrying Molly. His wife did not mind that. Indeed, she may have preferred Jeavons to be dependent on her. Whatever some of her relations may have thought at the time of her marriage, it had turned out a success—allowing for an occasional 'night out' on Jeavons's part, like the one when he had taken me to Dicky Umfraville's night-club.

'Come in,' he said. 'How's your war going? It's touch and go whether we're winning ours. Stanley's here, and a lady who has come to see about lodging Stanley's missus in the country. Then Molly met a fellow at Sanderson's who was trying to find a home for his cat, and she's gone and asked him to stay. The man, I mean, not the cat.'

'The lady who has come about moving your—is it sister-in-law?—is my mother,' said Widmerpool. 'I spoke to you on the telephone about it. I am Kenneth Widmerpool, you know. We have met in the past.'

'So you did,' said Jeavons, 'and so we have. It went out of my head like most other things. I thought Nick had just come to call and brought a friend. You can talk to Molly about it all when she comes downstairs, but I think your Mum has pretty well fixed everything up as it is.'

Jeavons's voice, hoarse and faint, sounded as usual as if he had a cold in his head or had been up too late the night before. He seemed restive, disorientated, but in good form.

'Who is Stanley?' I asked.

'Who's Stanley?' said Jeavons. 'My brother, of course. Who did you think he was?'

'Never knew you had a brother, Ted.'

'Course I've got a brother.'

'What does he do?'

'Accountant.'

'In London?'

'Nottingham. Given it up now, of course. Back to the army. Staff-Captain at the War House. Fancy your never having heard of Stanley. No reason why you should, I suppose. Still, it strikes me as funny. Rather a great man, Stanley, in his way. Gets things done.'

Among so much that was depressing, the news that Jeavons had a brother was for some reason cheering. It was certainly information to fascinate Isobel, when I next saw her, even to stagger Chips Lovell, who, regarding himself as an authority on his wife's relations, had certainly never heard of this outgrowth. Jeavons was known only to possess two or three vague connexions, sometimes to be found staying in the house, though never precisely placed in their kinship, in any case always hopelessly submerged in number by his wife's cousins, nephews and nieces. He had had, it was true, an old aunt, or great-aunt, to whom Molly was said to have been 'very good', who had lingered on in the house for months suffering from some illness, finally dying in one of the upstairs rooms. A Jeavons brother was quite another matter, a phenomenon of wartime circumstances. Jeavons, his dark, insistently curly hair now faintly speckled with grey, had himself taken on a subtly different personality since the onset of war. After all, war was the element which had, in a sense, made his career. Obviously he reacted strongly to its impacts. Until now his appearance had always suggested a temporary officer of the '14-'18 conflict, who had miraculously survived, without in the least ageing, into a much later epoch. The blue overall changed all that. Jeavons had also allowed his Charlie Chaplin moustache to grow outwards towards the corners of his mouth. With his own curious adaptability and sense of survival, he had effortlessly discarded what was in any case no more than a kind of disguise, now facing the world in the more contemporary role, equally artificial, of the man who had come to clean the windows or mend the boiler. We moved up the stairs.

'Met one of Isobel's uncles at the warden-post the other night,' said Jeavons. 'Alfred Tolland, the one Molly always teases.'

'How was he?'

'We had a talk about how difficult it is for people with daughters to bring 'em out properly in wartime,' Jeavons said.

He spoke without levity. Although he remained always utterly himself, Jeavons, after twenty years of marriage to Molly, had taken on much of his wife's way of looking at things. It would be more true to say the way the world into which she had been born looked at things, for Molly herself would probably have given little thought to how daughters were to be 'brought out' in wartime, even had she any daughters of her own. All the same, she would recognise that, to some people, the matter constituted a problem. Jeavons, who had never made the smallest effort to adopt that world's manner of talking, its way of dressing, its general behaviour, had at the same time, quite objectively, absorbed certain of its traditional opinions, whether his wife held them or not. Alfred Tolland, for example, had probably found in Jeavons an unusually sympathetic listener to his—no doubt antediluvian—views on how young ladies should conduct themselves or be conducted, certainly more sympathetic than he would ever have found in Molly herself. The fact that Jeavons had no daughters, had no children at all, would never have prevented him from holding strong views on the subject.

'Take my advice, don't give up your home-farm,' Chips Lovell had once heard Jeavons say to Lord Amesbury, admittedly a fairly formidable figure to counsel when it came to discussing the economics of estate management. 'Eddie Bridgnorth gave up his and never ceased to regret it.'

To have prefaced this recommendation with the avowal that he himself came from a walk of life where people did not own home-farms would have seemed to Jeavons otiose, wearisome, egotistical. Everything about him, he knew, proclaiming that fact, he would have regarded such personal emphasis as in the worst of taste, as well as being without interest. Marriage to Molly had given him opportunities to see how a lot of hitherto unfamiliar forms of life worked. He had developed certain opinions, was prepared to give evidence. Home-farms fell into that category. The notion that he might be trying to pass himself off as a fellow-owner of a home-farm would have seemed to Jeavons laughable. Whether or not Jeavons's advice tipped the scale was never known, but Chips Lovell reported that Lord Amesbury did not sell, so that. he may have been convinced by this objectivity of reasoning. Perhaps it was of such matters that Jeavons was thinking when he would stand for hours in the corner of the drawing-room at one of Molly's parties for young people (when the rugs would be turned back and they would dance to the gramophone), smiling to himself, gently clinking the money in his pocket.

'Do help with the drinks, Teddy, dear,' his wife would say on such occasions. 'Are you feeling all right or is it your inside again?'

Then Jeavons would move like a sleep-walker towards the bottles.

'What's it going to be?' he would mutter, almost beneath his breath. 'Rotten tunes they always play nowadays.'

However, although Widmerpool had shown signs of restiveness at our too long delay in the hall, Jeavons was far from one of those comatose, stagnant moods that evening. There could be no doubt that the war had livened him up. He felt at home within its icy grasp. The house was more untidy than ever, the hall, as usual, full of luggage. I noticed that the marquetry cabinet bequeathed by Lady

Warminster had reached no farther than the foot of the stairs. Some of the heavier pictures had been taken from their hooks and rested against the wall. Packing cases and trunks were everywhere.

'People keep on arriving for a night or two,' said Jeavons. 'Place might be a doss-house. Of course, Stanley is only here until he can fix himself up. Then Molly must bring this other fellow to stay. Seems a nice bloke. She had to go and see the vet. No avoiding that. Can't fight a war with quite the number of dogs and cats we normally have in the house. Got to find homes for them.'

'What happened to Maisky, your pet monkey?'

'Rather a sad story,' said Jeavons, but did not enlarge.

The conditions he described were less abnormal here than they would have been in most households. Indeed, war seemed to have accelerated, exaggerated, rather than changed, the Jeavons way of life. The place was always in a mess. Mess there was endemic. People were always coming for a night or two, sometimes for much longer periods. There were always suitcases in the hall, always debris, untidiness, confusion everywhere. That was the way Molly liked to live, possibly her method of recovering from the tedium of married life with John Sleaford. Jeavons, whether he liked it or not, was dragged along in her train. No doubt he liked it, too, otherwise he would have left her, for no one could have stood such an existence unless reasonably sympathetic to him at heart. The sight of Jeavons's brother sitting on the sofa beside Mrs Widmerpool brought home to one the innate eccentricity of Jeavons. This man in uniform, with a captain's pips and three 'First War' ribbons, was recognisable as a brother more from build than any great similarity of feature. He was far more anonymous than Jeavons: older, solider, greyer, quieter, in general more staid. When you saw Stanley Jeavons, you recognised the adventurer in Ted. I thought of Moreland's emendation, the distinction he drew between adventurers and those not wholly unadventurous, to both of which categories adventures happened—to the latter, perhaps, more than the former. Jeavons, although tending to play a passive role, could not be said to have led an entirely unadventurous life; perhaps one could go further, say without qualification that Jeavons was an adventurer. There was no time to think longer of such things at that moment, because Jeavons was making some kind of introduction.

'Stanley's a brass-hat now,' he said. 'God, how we used to hate the staff in our war, Stan, didn't we? Fancy your ending up one of that mob.'

As we came into the room, Mrs Widmerpool had at once bared her teeth in a smile to indicate that we had met before. I was about to speak to her, when she jumped to her feet and seized Widmerpool by the shoulders, unable to allow Jeavons the undivided honour of presenting him to his brother.

'My soldier son,' she said, nodding delightedly like a Japanese doll.

'Oh, don't be absurd, Mother,' said Widmerpool.

He grinned back happily at her through his spectacles, his composure, lately so shattered by Gypsy Jones, now completely restored. Mrs Widmerpool returned to the sofa, continuing to nurse on her knee a cardboard box, which at first I thought might be some sort of present she had brought Widmerpool, but recognised a second later as her gas-mask, carried with her into the drawing-room. She looked, as her son had described her a year earlier, 'younger than ever'. She was squarely built, her heavy, nearly classical nose set between cheeks shining and pink like an apple. She wore a thick tweed suit and a tweed hat with a peak. Stanley Jeavons, who seemed rather glad to be absolved from talking to her further for the time being, turned his attention to Widmerpool.

'What's your outfit?' he asked.

They began to speak of army matters. I was left with Mrs Widmerpool.

'*You* are one of Kenneth's literary friends, I remember,' she said, 'are you not?'

'Well, yes.'

'Kenneth used to be such a reader too,' she said. 'Now, alas, he has no time for books. Indeed, few of us have. But I suppose you continue in the same manner?'

'More or less.'

Before I could enlarge on my own activities, Molly Jeavons came into the room, making all the disturbance that naturally noisy people always bring in their train. Dark, large, still good-looking at fifty, there was something of the barmaid about her, something of the Charles II beauty, although Molly, they said, had never been exactly a 'beauty' when younger, more from lack of temperament to play the part, than want of physical equipment. These two sides she represented, merging in middle age, suited her tomboyish, all enveloping manner. This manner seemed designed by her to dispense with aristocratic frills unsuitable to the style in which the Jeavonses lived, but —caught by Time, as all idiosyncrasies of talk and behaviour can be—the final result was somewhat to emphasise the background she was at pains to understate. She was wearing various rather ill-assorted woollen garments. After greeting Widmerpool and saying something about his mother's cottage, she turned to me.

'We've been having the most awful time, Nick,' she said, 'trying to fix up the rows of animals that always infest the house. Sanderson, the vet, a great friend of mine, has been an angel. I talked to the sweetest man there who was trying to find a home for his cat. His wife had just left him and he'd just been turned out of the furnished flat he was living in because the owner wanted it back. He had nowhere to go and was absolutely at the end of his tether. He seemed so nice, I couldn't leave until we'd arranged the cat's future. The long and the short of it is he's going to stay for a night or two here. He had his bag with him and was going to some awful hotel, because he has very little money. He seems to know a lot of people we all know. You probably know him yourself, Nick.'

'What is he called?'

'I simply can't remember,' she said. 'I've had such a lot of things to do today that I am feeling quite dizzy and the name has completely gone out of my head. He'll be down in a moment. He is just unpacking his things—and now I must hear how the arrangements about the cottage are getting on.'

She joined the conversation taking place between Jeavons's brother, Widmerpool and Widmerpool's mother. Jeavons, who had been listening abstractedly to these negotiations, came and sat beside me.

'What's happening to all the Tollands, Nick?' he asked. 'I haven't heard anything of them, except that your wife, Isobel, is going to have a baby and is staying in the country with Frederica.'

'George has gone back to his regiment.'

'Ex-Guardsman, isn't he?' said Jeavons. 'He'll be for a holding battalion.'

'Then Hugo has become a Gunner.'

'In the ranks?'

'Yes.'

Hugo, regarded in general by his family as a fairly unsatisfactory figure, in spite of recent achievements in selling antique furniture, had taken the wind out of everyone's sails by his enlistment.

'One will be called up anyway,' Hugo had said. 'Why not have a start of everyone? Get in on the ground floor.'

Such a view from Hugo was unexpected.

'He looks a bit strange in uniform.'

'Must be like that song Billy Bennett used to sing,' said Jeavons:

> 'I'm a trooper, I'm a trooper,
> They call me Gladys Cooper.

Ages since I've been to a music-hall. Aren't what they used to be anyway. Still, it does Hugo credit.'

'Robert has some idea of joining the navy.'

'Plenty of water in the trenches, without going out of your way to look for it,' said Jeavons shuddering. 'Besides, I feel bilious most of the time, even when I'm not rolling about in a boat.'

'Chips Lovell, like me, is thinking things over. Roddy Cutts, being an MP, arranged something—a Yeomanry regiment, I think.'

While we were talking someone came into the room. I had not taken very seriously Molly Jeavons's surmise that I should probably know the man she had picked up at the vet's. She always imagined Isobel and I must know everyone roughly the same age as ourselves. Perhaps she liked to feel that, if necessary, she could draw on our reserves for her own purposes. I thought it most improbable that I should have met this casual acquaintance, certainly never guessed he would turn out to be Moreland. However, Moreland it was. He looked far from well, dazed and unhappy.

'Good God,' he said, catching sight of me.

Molly Jeavons detached herself from the talk about Mrs Widmerpool's lodger.

'So you do know him, Nick.'

'Of course we know each other.'

'I felt sure you would.'

'Why are you here?' said Moreland. 'Did you arrange this?'

'Will you be all right in that room?' Molly asked. 'For goodness sake don't touch the blackout, or the whole thing will come down. It's just fixed temporarily to last the night. Teddy will do something about it in the morning.'

'I really can't thank you enough,' said Moreland. 'Farinelli . . . one thing and another . . . then letting me come here. . . .'

He had probably been drinking earlier in the day, was still overwrought, though not exactly drunk, not far from tears. Molly Jeavons brushed his thanks aside.

'One thing I can't do,' she said, 'is to give either you or Nick dinner here tonight. Nor any of these other people either, except Stanley. We simply haven't got enough food in the house to offer you anything.'

'We'll dine together,' I said. 'Is there anywhere in the neighbourhood?'

'A place halfway up Gloucester Road on the right. It's called the Scarlet Pimpernel. The food is not as bad as it sounds. They'll send out for drinks.'

'Do you feel equal to the Scarlet Pimpernel, Hugh?'

Moreland, almost past speech, nodded.

'Give him your key, Teddy,' said Molly Jeavons. 'We can find him another in the morning.'

Jeavons fumbled in one of the pockets of his overall and handed a key to Moreland.

'I'll probably be pottering about when you come in,' he said, 'can't get to sleep if I turn in early. Come back with him, Nick. We might be able to find a glass of beer for you.'

I went across the room to take leave of Widmerpool and his mother. When I came up to her, Mrs Widmerpool turned her battery of teeth upon me, smiling fiercely, like the Wolf in Little Red Riding Hood, her shining, ruddy countenance advancing closer as she continued to hold my hand in hers.

'I expect you are still occupied with your literary pursuits,' she said, taking up our conversation at precisely the point at which it had been abandoned.

'Some journalism——'

'This is not a happy time for book-lovers.'

'No, indeed.'

'Still, you are fortunate.'

'Why?'

'With your bookish days, not, like Kenneth, in arms.'

'He seems a Happy Warrior.'

'It is not in his nature to remain in civil life at time of war,' she said.

'I will say good night, then.'

'Good luck to you,' she said, 'wherever you may find yourself in these troublous times.'

She gave me another smile of great malignance, returning immediately to her discussions about rent. Widmerpool half raised his hand in a gesture of farewell. Moreland and I left the house together.

'What the hell were you doing in that place?' he asked, as we walked up the street.

'Molly Jeavons is an aunt of Isobel's. It is a perfectly normal place for me to be. Far stranger that you yourself should turn up there.'

'You're right about that,' Moreland said. 'I can't quite make out how I did. Things have been moving rather quickly with me the last few months. Who was that terrifying woman you said good-bye to?'

'Mother of the man in spectacles called Widmerpool. You met him with me at a nursing home years ago.'

'No recollection,' said Moreland, 'though he seemed familiar. His mother began on Scriabin as soon as I arrived

243

in the house. Told me the *Poème de l'Extase* was her favourite musical work. I say, I'm feeling like hell. Far from *de l'extase*.'

'What's been happening? I didn't even know you'd left the country.'

'The country, as it were, left me,' said Moreland. 'At least Matilda did, which came to much the same thing.'

'How did all this come about?'

'I hardly know myself.'

'Has she gone off with somebody?'

'Gone back to Donners.'

The information was so grotesque that at first I could hardly take it seriously. Then I saw as a possibility that a row might have taken place and Matilda done this from pique. At certain seasons, Matilda, admittedly, had a fairly rough time living with Moreland. She might require a short spell of rich life to put her right, although (as Mrs Widmerpool could have said) wartime was hardly the moment to pursue rich life. Sir Magnus Donners, as a former lover, himself no longer young, would provide a comparatively innocuous vehicle for such a temporary interlude. The Moreland situation, regarded in these cold-blooded terms, might be undesirable certainly, at the same time not beyond hope.

'I'll tell the story when we get to the restaurant,' said Moreland. 'I haven't eaten anything since breakfast. Just had a few doubles.'

We found the Scarlet Pimpernel soon after this. The place was not full. We took a table in the corner at the back of the room. At this early stage of the war, it was still possible to order a bottle of wine without undue difficulty and expense. The food, as Molly Jeavons had said, turned out better than might have been expected from the mob-caps of the waitresses and general tone of the establishment. After some soup and a glass of wine Moreland began to recover himself.

'One always imagines things happen in hot blood,' he said. 'An ill-considered remark starts a row. Hard words follow, misunderstandings. Matters that can be put right in the end. Unfortunately life doesn't work out like that. First of all there is no row, secondly, nothing can be put right.'

'Barnby says he is always on his guard when things are going well with a woman.'

'Still, your wife,' said Moreland, 'it's bloody uncomfortable if things are not going well between yourself and your wife. I speak from experience. All the same, there may be something in Barnby's view. You remember, the business about me and—well—your sister-in-law, Priscilla?'

'You conveyed at the time that a situation existed—then ceased to exist, or was stifled in some way.'

I did not see why I should help Moreland out beyond a certain point. If he wanted to tell his story, he must supply the facts, not reveal one half and allow the other to be guessed. He had always been too fond of doing that when extracting sympathy for his emotional tangles. No one had ever known what had happened about himself and Priscilla, only that some close relationship had existed between them, which had caused a great deal of disturbance in his married life. Some explanation was required. The situation could not be pieced together merely from a series of generalisations about matrimony.

'Anything you like,' said Moreland. 'The point is that, during that rather tricky period, Matty could not have behaved better. She was absolutely marvellous—really marvellous. It was the one thing that made the whole awfulness of life possible when . . .'

He did not finish the sentence, but meant, I supposed, when the affair with Priscilla was at an end.

'Why on earth, if Matty was going to leave me, didn't she leave me then? I'll tell you. She enjoyed the emotional strain of it all. Women are like that, the lame girl in Dostoevsky who said she didn't want to be happy.'

'How did it start?'

'Matilda was in a show that opened in the provinces—Brighton or somewhere. She just wrote and said she was not returning home, would I send her things along, such as they were. She had already taken most of her clothes with her, so I presume she had already decided on leaving when she set out.'

'How long ago?'

'Two or three weeks.'

'Is it generally known?'

'Not yet, I think. Matilda is often away acting, so it is quite usual for her to be absent from home.'

'And you had no warning that all was not well?'

'I am the most modest man in the world when it is a question of trying to make a woman fall for me,' said Moreland. 'I never expect I shall bring it off. On the other hand, once she's fallen, I can never really believe she will prefer someone else. These things are just the way vanity happens to take you.'

'But where does Donners come in? She can't have fallen for him.'

'She has been going over to Stourwater fairly often. She made no secret of that. Why should she? There didn't seem any reason to object. What could I do, anyway? You remember we all dined there that rather grim evening when everyone dressed up as the Seven Deadly Sins. I recall now, that was where I saw your friend Widmerpool before. Does he always haunt my worst moments? Anyway, Matilda's visits to Stourwater were of that sort, nothing serious.'

'Is Matilda living at Stourwater at this moment?'

'No—staying in the flat of a girl she knows in London, another actress. The point is this: if I allow Matilda to divorce me, Donners will marry her.'

'No.'

Moreland laughed.

'Indeed, yes,' he said. 'I see I have surprised you.'

'You certainly have.'

'It now turns out that Donners asked her to marry him before—when she was mixed up with him years ago.'

'What are you going to do?'

'What can I do?'

'But will you let yourself be divorced?'

'I've tried every way of getting her back,' said Moreland. 'She is quite firm. I don't want to be just spiteful about it. If she is consumed with a desire to become Lady Donners, Lady Donners let her be.'

'But to want to be Lady Donners is so unlike Matilda—especially as she turned down the offer in the past.'

'You think it unlike her?'

'Don't you?'

'Not entirely. She can be tough, you know. One of the worst things about life is not how nasty the nasty people are. You know that already. It is how nasty the nice people can be.'

'Have you no idea what went wrong?'

'None—except, as I say, the Priscilla business. I thought that was all forgotten. Perhaps it was, and life with me was just too humdrum. Now I'll tell you something else that may surprise you. Nothing ever took place between Priscilla and myself. We never went to bed.'

'Why not?'

'I don't really know,' said Moreland slowly, 'perhaps because there did not seem anywhere to go. That's so often one of the problems. I've thought about the subject a lot. One might write a story about two lovers who have nowhere to go. They are at their wits' end. Then they pretend they are newly married and apply to a different estate-agent every week to inspect unfurnished houses and flats. As often as not they are given the key and manage to have an hour alone together. Inventive, don't you think? I was crazy about Priscilla. Then Maclintick committed suicide and everything was altered. I felt upset, couldn't think about girls and all that. That was when Priscilla herself decided things had better stop. I suppose the whole business shook the boat so far as my own marriage was concerned. It seemed to recover. I thought we were getting on all right. I was wrong.'

I was reminded of Duport telling me about Jean, although no one could have been less like Jean than Matilda, less like Moreland than Duport.

'The fact is,' said Moreland, 'Matilda lost interest in me. With women, that situation is like a vacuum. It must be filled. They begin to look round for someone else. She decided on Donners.'

'She was still pretty interested in you at the party Mrs Foxe gave for your symphony.'

'How do you know?'

'She talked to me about it.'

'While I was getting off with Priscilla?'

'More or less.'

Moreland made a grimace.

'Surely she'll come back in the end?' I said.

'You see, I'm not absolutely certain I want Matilda back,' he said. 'Sometimes I feel I can't live without her, other times, that I can't bear the thought of having her in the house. In real life, things are much worse than as represented in books. In books, you love somebody and want them, win them or lose them. In real life, so often, you love them and don't want them, or want them and don't love them.'

'You make it all sound difficult.'

'I sometimes think all I myself require is a quiet life,' said Moreland. 'For some unaccountable reason it is always imagined that people like oneself want to be rackety. Of course I want some fun occasionally, but so does everyone else.'

'What does Matilda want? A lot of money?'

'Not in the obvious way, diamonds and things. Matilda has wanted for a long time to spread her wings. She knows at last that she will never be any good as an actress. She wants power. Plenty of power. When we were first married she arranged all my life for me. Arranged rather too much. I'm not sure she liked it when I made a small name for myself—if one may be said to have made a small name for oneself.'

'She will have to play second fiddle to Sir Magnus, more even than to yourself.'

'Not second fiddle as an artist—as an actress, in her case. Being an artist—to use old fashioned terminology, but what other can one use?—partakes of certain feminine character-istics, is therefore peculiarly provoking for women to live with. In some way, the more "masculine" an artist is, the worse her predicament. If he is really homosexual, or hope-lessly incapable of dealing with everyday life, it is almost easier.'

'I can think of plenty of examples to the contrary.'

'Anyway, there will be compensations with Donners. Matilda will operate on a large scale. She will have her finger in all kind of pies.'

'Still, what pies.'

'Not very intellectual ones, certainly,' said Moreland, 'but then the minds of most women are unamusing, unoriginal, determinedly banal. Matilda is not one of the exceptions.

Is it surprising one is always cuckolded by middle-brows?'

'But you talk as if these matters were all concerned with the mind.'

Moreland laughed.

'I once asked Barnby if he did not find most women extraordinarily unsensual,' he said. 'Do you know what he answered?'

'What?'

'He said, "I've never noticed".'

I laughed too.

'I suppose,' said Moreland, 'had you asked Lloyd George, "Don't you think politics rather corrupt?", he might have made the same reply. Minor factors disappear when you are absorbed by any subject. You know, one of the things about being deserted is that it leaves you in a semi-castrated condition. You're incapable of fixing yourself up with an alternative girl. Deserting people, on the other hand, is positively stimulating. I don't mind betting that Matty is surrounded by admirers at this moment. Do you remember when we heard that crippled woman singing in Gerrard Street years ago:

Whom do you lead on Rapture's roadway, far,
Before you agonize them in farewell?

That's what it comes to. But look who has just arrived.'

Three people were sitting down at a table near the door of the restaurant. They were Mark Members, J. G. Quiggin and Anne Umfraville.

'I feel better after getting all that off my chest.' said Moreland.

'Shall we go back?'

'Do you think Lady Molly will have forgotten who I am?' said Moreland. 'It's terribly kind of her to put me up like this, but you know what bad memories warm hearted people have.'

I saw from that Moreland had perfectly grasped Molly Jeavons's character. Nothing was more probable than that she would have to be reminded of the whole incident of inviting him to the house when she saw him at breakfast the following morning. Like so many persons who live disordered lives, Moreland had peculiar powers of falling on his feet, an instinctive awareness of where to look for help. That was perhaps the legacy of early poverty. He and Molly Jeavons—although she made no claims whatever to know about the arts—would understand each other. If he overstayed his welcome—with Moreland not inconceivable —she would throw him out without the smallest ill-feeling on either side.

'We might have a word with the literary critics on the way out,' said Moreland.

'What happened to Anne Umfraville in the light of recent developments?'

'I don't know,' said Moreland. 'I thought she was interested in your friend Templer. I understand she was passing out of Donners's life in any case. She must have made some new friends.'

We paid the bill, pausing on the way out at the table by the door.

'Who told you of this restaurant?' said Quiggin. 'I thought it was only known to Anne and myself—you have met, of course?'

His air was somewhat proprietorial.

'Anne has a flat not far from here,' he said. 'Mark and I have been working late there.'

'What at?'

'Proofs,' said Quiggin.

He did not explain what kind of proofs. Neither Moreland nor I inquired.

'How is Matty, Hugh?' asked Members.

'On tour.'

'I do adore Matilda,' said Anne Umfraville. 'Have you been to Stourwater lately? I have rather quarrelled with Magnus. He can be so tiresome. So pompous, you know.'

'I don't live near there any longer,' said Moreland, 'so we haven't met for a month or two. Sir Magnus himself is no longer occupying the castle, of course. It has been taken over by the government, but I can't remember for what purpose. Just as a castle, I suppose.'

'What a ludicrous way this war is being run,' said Quiggin. 'I was talking to Howard Craggs about its inanities last night. Have you got a decent shelter where you live?'

'I'm just going back there,' said Moreland, 'never to emerge.'

'Give my love to Matty when you next see her,' said Members.

'And mine,' said Anne Umfraville.

We said good night.

'I think people know about Matilda,' said Moreland.

We passed through streets lit only by a cold autumnal moon.

'Have you the key?'

Moreland found it at last. We went upstairs to the drawing-room. Jeavons was wandering about restlessly. He had abandoned his beret, now wore a mackintosh over pyjamas. His brother was in an armchair, smoking his pipe and going through a pile of papers beside him on the floor. He would check each document, then place it on a stack the other side of his chair.

'We got rid of them at last,' said Jeavons. 'Molly's gone to bed. They struck a pretty hard bargain with Stanley. Still, the place seems to suit. That's what matters. I'd rather it was Lil than me. What was dinner like?'

'Not bad.'

'How was our blackout as you came up the street?'

'Not a chink of light.'

'Have some beer?'

'I think I'll go straight to bed, if you don't mind,' said Moreland. 'I feel a bit done in.'

I had never heard Moreland refuse a drink before. He must have been utterly exhausted. He had cheered up during dinner. Now he looked like death again.

'I'll come up with you to make sure the blackout won't fall down,' said Jeavons. 'Never do to be fined as a warden.'

'Good night, Nick.'

'Good night.'

They went upstairs. Stanley Jeavons threw down what was apparently the last of his papers. He took the pipe from his mouth and began to knock it out against his heel. He sighed deeply.

'I think I'll have a glass of beer too,' he said.

He helped himself and sat down again.

'It's extraordinary,' he said, 'how you get a hunch from a chap's handwriting if he's done three years for fraudulent conversion.'

'In business?'

'In business, too. I meant in what I'm doing now.'

'What are you doing?'

'Reservists.'

'For the army?'

'Sorting them out. Got a pile of their personal details here. Stacks more at the office. Brought a batch home to work on.'

'Then what happens?'

'Some of them get called up.'

'I'm on some form of the Reserve myself.'

'Which one?'

I told him.

'You'll probably come my way in due course—or one of my colleagues'.'

'Could it be speeded up?'

'What?'

'Finding my name.'

'Would you like that?'

'Yes.'

'Don't see why not.'

'You could?'

'M'm.'

'Fairly soon?'

'How old are you?'

I told him that too.

'Health A.1?'

'I think so.'

'School OTC?'

'Yes.'

'Get a Certificate A there?'

'Yes.'

'What arm is your choice?'

'Infantry.'

'Any particular regiment?'

I made a suggestion.

'You don't want one of the London regiments?'

'Not specially. Why?'

'Everyone seems to want a London regiment,' he said. 'Probably be able to fix you up with an out-of-the-way regiment like that.'

'It would be kind.'

'And you'd like to get cracking?'

'Yes.'

'I'll see what we can do.'

'That's very good of you.'

'Might take a week or two.'

'That's all right.'

'Just let me write your name in my little book.'

Jeavons returned to the room.

'That friend of yours is absolutely cooked,' he said. 'He'd have been happy to sleep on the floor. His blackout is all correct now, if he doesn't interfere with it. Well, Stan, I don't know how much Lil is going to enjoy living in a cottage with Mrs W.'

'Lil will be all right,' said Stanley Jeavons. 'She can get on with all sorts.'

'More than I can,' said Jeavons.

Stanley Jeavons shook his head without smiling. He evidently found his brother's life inexplicable, had no desire whatever to share its extravagances. Jeavons moved towards the table where the beer bottles stood. Suddenly he began to sing in that full, deep, unexpectedly attractive voice, so different from the croaking tones in which he ordinarily conversed:

> 'There's a long, long trail a-winding
> Into the land of . . . my dreams,
> Where the night . . . ingale is singing
> And the white moon beams.
> There's a long, long night of waiting,
> Until my dreams all . . . come true . . .'

He broke off as suddenly as he had begun. Stanley Jeavons began tapping out his pipe again, perhaps to put a stop to this refrain.

'Used to sing that while we were blanco-ing,' said Jeavons. 'God, how fed up I got cleaning that bloody equipment.'

'I shall have to go home, Ted.'

'Don't hurry away.'

'I must.'

'Have some more beer.'

'No.'

'Come and see us soon,' said Jeavons, 'before we all get blown up. I'm still not satisfied with the fold of that curtain. Got the blackout on the brain. You haven't a safety-pin about you, have you, Stan?'

Outside the moon had gone behind a bank of cloud. I went home through the gloom, exhilarated, at the same time rather afraid. Ahead lay the region beyond the white-currant bushes, where the wild country began, where armies for ever campaigned, where the Rules and Discipline of War prevailed. Another stage of life was passed, just as finally, just as irrevocably, as on that day when childhood had come so abruptly to an end at Stonehurst.